YA Paranormal

Deep down, Summer knows missing. Something her head can't ...., ... won't let her forget.

Alex must find her before his *people* do.

With no-one at his side, and a black-eyed enemy from the past hunting them, can he put all feelings aside and fight for the girl he loves once again?

Their fate is already written.

The prophecy is already set.

Is love between them impossible?

Summer's Lost © 2019 by Kristy Brown

MuseItUp Publishing

https://museituppublishing.com

Cover Art © 2019 by Eerilyfair Design

Layout and Book Production by Lea Schizas

eBook ISBN: 978-1-77392-046-7

First eBook Edition *December 2019

For Darrell, my rock. Thanks for always listening and telling me the truth.
And to my ever-supportive Mum and Dad, who always believe in me, even when I don't.
And Karen, the kindest sister with the biggest heart.

Acknowledgements

Thanks to Lea, a very patient editor and publisher. With her help, I've come a long way over our years together.

Summer's Lost

The Summer Solstice: Book Two

Kristy Brown

MuseItYA, division of

MuseItUp Publishing

www.museituppublishing.com

Alex

I've chosen a side. Finally, I know what I want. Finding *her* is everything.

Summer

I'm on a writing course at a top university, with a handful of great friends. I should be happy. So why aren't I?

1: Alex

"It's been over a month since we found you collapsed in that cave…yet still you seem…"

"Seem what?" I snap.

"Short tempered…distant."

"My usual charming self then?"

"Well yes." Kit frowns. "And no."

"Well, which is it? Am I me, or not? You're the expert, right?" Huffing, I carry on with my task.

"You are you…I guess. You're just—"

"Just what?" I glance up from my new carving, which soon I hope will resemble a deer.

"It's just…you never want to hang out anymore. You never have time to talk these days." Fiddling with her dreads, looking as uncomfortable as I feel.

"We're talking now, aren't we?" I raise a brow, turning my attention back to the piece of bark.

"Not really." Moving in front of me, blocking the light. "You don't even look at me anymore."

"Don't be stupid, Kit." I roll my eyes in her general direction. But she's right, I don't. Feelings I'm not ready to deal with rise like bile in my throat. The sister I thought was mine is lost to me, and no amount of wishing it to be different can change that.

"Look at me then." She crosses her arms. I glance up. "Was that so hard?"

"You're weird."

"And you're…"

Lennox appears. Gripping the knife tighter, my palm sweats.

"There you both are."

I stop carving and stand up. For two reasons: one, I don't like being talked down to, and two, he's still as scary as hell.

"How are you today, Alex?" His black, tiny eyes meet mine.

"Okay, I guess." Even with his human face on, all I picture is the demon talking.

"Are you feeling fully recovered yet? Back to our old Alex? After what that 'thing' did to you…it may take some time. We were all so worried." He smiles, a lying smile.

Bet you were, you lying piece of shit, and I'm not 'your' Alex. "I'm fine. I did a hundred press ups before breakfast, and tonight I'm planning a ten-mile run."

"Good, Alex, that's good." He nods. "Soon you'll be ready to track her again. This time you'll be strong enough to finish the job."

"Of course, he will," Kit adds, like I need her endorsement. "No little girl is going to stump him twice, right, brother?"

"Right." My insides cringe at her casual use of the word 'brother.' "I'll finish it this time, believe me. Nobody plays me." Keeping my eyes on Lennox, he gives me a wide, yellow grin. My palm starts to ache from gripping the knife, preparing for any sudden change in events. I could be outed at any moment; it would only take a second for him to snap my neck. Any slight slip on my part and he'd see right through this pretence. He'd know. I can't risk them wiping my mind again or something much worse…

"That's excellent news, Alex." He nods to us before leaving. Mentally, I'm sticking my middle finger up in his direction. Sitting back on the tree stump, I carve, turning my back on Kit. If I can't see or hear her, then I'm less disgusted at what she's done, how she feels…

"You need help with anything?" She speaks, breaking our beyond-awkward silence.

"Like what? You offering to kill the girl, so I can get some much-needed fishing done?" I smirk, still avoiding that penetrating gaze.

"Well don't say I didn't ask. Can't we just go back to the way we were?"

"Stuff changes, people change," I grunt, carving deeper into the wood. "Ouch, bloody hell!"

"What?"

"Nothing, I cut my finger." My lips curl around the cut, sucking the blood from it.

"Let's see." Grabbing for my hand, I pull away.

"I'm a big boy. I can put my own plaster on, thanks."

"It may need a stitch. I'll magic it for you in no time."

"No thanks, besides, I'm done with all the magic crap."

"And with me?" Her voice is a throaty whisper.

"Actually," I say, changing the subject, "there is something you can do for me."

"What?"

"Tell me how the ritual can still take place when 'she' turned your precious moonstone rock thing to dust? I mean, don't you kinda need that?"

"Well," she whispers, "there's talk of others just like us…Krons. They too believe in chasing 'The Light.' Guess it's just a matter of time before '*it's*' found. Also, Lennox has a new, better plan. He says he doesn't even need the moonstone."

"Really?" *Crap!*

"Between you and me…" She steps closer. "…I overheard him talking about other 'Lights.' Which would make complete sense because the Earth's a big place, you'd need one huge doorway to Heaven, or lots of little ones…well, that's my theory anyway." Seeming far too pleased with herself but has a point. For now, I can't think about the big picture, I have to think about 'The Light' in my picture. The girl I must save in order to save the world, and myself. If there are others like Summer, well I'll deal with that when the time comes.

"So, the game begins again." Was this the plan all along to take out one Light then another? I'd never be free, never be rid of my burden. Or is there more like me, stolen children made to kill?

"Yes, Alex, the game begins again. You have to be ready to play it."

"I'm getting there."

"And this time we'll win. We'll save the world."

Lies! Just lies! I'd respect her more if she'd admit to being evil's pawn and liking it.

"Well if you say we'll win, that's good enough for me." I can't even be bothered to hide my sarcasm.

"Always the tease!" She slaps my arm. Flinching, I don't like her touching me, knowing the thrill she's getting out of it. I shudder slightly, hoping it's not noticed. Her eyes widen, like she sees through my charade.

"You hit like a girl," I say, trying to throw her off the scent.

"I am a girl! Thanks for noticing…" *God, is she flirting with me?*

"Haven't you got stuff to do?"

"Maybe…" Turning to leave, before looking back. "You know we'll win, right? You have to believe it. Say it."

"Say what?" The cut in my finger's throbbing.

"Say this time we'll win."

"God, if it'll make you go away, this time *I'll* win." *And I will.*

"See, that wasn't hard now, was it?" Smiling, seeming satisfied, ambling away through the trees.

My finger stops hurting. It's now clean and healed completely. Kit put her magic crap on me anyway; just goes to show the lack of respect for my wishes. Packing up my stuff, I walk the short distance through the woods back to camp. You're wondering why I haven't made a run for it yet, right? Believe me, if I wasn't watched every minute, I may have, ten times over. Although, I'm not back to my full strength, so I'll take their food and lies until the time is right. The plan is to gain their complete trust, so when I go, I'll be far, far away before they realise. Also, I'm waiting for one of Kit's visions to locate Summer. That angel gave me the gift of choice and even though I'm playing a role right now, the pretence will end soon.

Back inside my little tent, which I'm guessing looks like nothing to you, but it's all I have. That's one of the things I love about Summer—she looks beyond what I have, or don't have. Always sees me—the real me, and in her eyes, I'm worthy.

This tent's been my home for such a long time. Now it's just somewhere to stash my few belongings. I don't really sleep anymore. How could I rest knowing the place is crawling with demons? To sleep, I go to one of my many hiding places, behind a bush, in a ditch…hoping they remain a secret. Guess I'm watched everywhere unless I'm out running. No one here could hope to keep up with my pace, but then there's always Kit's visions. Cringing, hoping she stays away from my bathing in the stream, the long showers in the waterfall…

The real crapper is that I can't talk to anyone, trust anyone. Everyone here is either a demon or led by one. The entire camp must be in on it, like a sleeping army ready to strike. And it constantly feels I have a target painted on my back.

Rummaging under the camper bed, I pull out the carving of her face. Sad eyes follow me around the tent, offering the smallest piece of hope that I'll see her again. This, my memories that I play over on loop, and a gold and amber heart necklace, is all I have to hold on to. The chain lives in my pocket; it's like carrying a piece of her everywhere I go—my little bit of Summer. Changing into running clothes, I pull a baseball cap low over my forehead, keeping the messy hair from my eyes. Need to get out of camp for a while, away from the liars and priers. Trusting no one except my own gut, which is fine, I'm used to being alone. I'm not sad; don't be upset for me. I'll find her, I always find her. Running out into the open arms of night, it's exhilarating.

"Hey!" Kit's voice hovers behind me. "Where you off to?"

That voice is like a punch in the gut. I refuse to look behind me. Pushing on harder, my trainers grind against the muddy track. Carrying on and out through the woods, crossing countless roads until I'm standing at the gates to Summer's old college. She's long gone by now, God, she'd better be; yet I'm drawn here night after night. This time I walk through the large iron gates, through the grounds and into the main building. It's late, so there aren't many students about, apart from the ones pulling 'all-nighters.' Heading for the library, just wanting to be near her, and sitting in her old favourite spot is the best way to do that. A security guard clocks me as he talks to the librarian at the counter. I nod, keeping my cap low, and move past. Paranoid that he could be one of them, a Kron—anyone could be. Walking down an aisle toward the history section I come to a halt. Someone is sitting at her table. The girl looks up meeting my gaze. *Andie!*

It's Andie! Summer's bestie...this is great! She can help. I'm not alone after all.

"Hey." I smile, scurrying toward her.

"Hey?" Her voice wavers, whilst scanning the place for the security guard.

"I'm not gonna hurt you." I stop a few inches away.

"Good to know."

"It's me." I remove my cap. "Alex."

"Alex?"

"You changed your hair," I say, looking at the shocking pink ponytail sitting on her head. "The blue was better." Moving to sit down opposite, she stands, the panic in her eyes is easy to read.

"Err, yes… sorry," she flusters, "Who are you?"

2: *Summer*

These last few weeks have been great. It's a slow process, but I'm starting to put the whole 'fire trauma' behind me, well a little to the side at least. I'll never be one hundred percent over it—it killed my parents, wiped out a lot of memories and left me feeling hollow inside. I'm working hard on forgiving people for staring at my scar; guess it's a natural reaction when you first meet someone. I don't try to cover it so much, it's part of me, the girl I used to be, and if I can deal, then so can everyone else.

University is thrilling. Getting to read all the greats, compare the classics and find my own writing style. Who knows, maybe someday people will read my stuff and call them classics? It's the one true love in my life and it, along with my friends, is what keeps me going. Today is Saturday, a chill with your mates' day, a get up late day. Not for me though. Today is a road trip to the beach day.

We're almost there, after an hour's drive, which is going to be so worth it. There's a big festival here this weekend with rides, stalls and music. Later, loads of us are heading to a beach party.

"We're here." Persia chirps up after being almost mute the entire journey. She looks stunning (as always). Wearing a brilliant white halter-top and short shorts combo, which contrasts beautifully against her rich chocolate skin. Looking down at my denim shorts and black t-shirt, wishing I'd made more effort.

"Awesome," Luke adds, tying his shaggy blond hair back. Looking pleased to be back to his natural habitat, the coast. Luke's a good friend, which is crazy considering we only met recently. It was one of those times when you meet someone and just know in your gut that you're going to get on. We met in the library; both of us a little lost between the art and poetry sections. I know what you're thinking—he's hot, right? Guess he is with the surfer dude thing he's got going on. Do I fancy him? Maybe, but I'm here to learn and party, besides, what if it went wrong? That would be the end of our friendship. Plus, of course, he may not even like me that way. Yes, I've caught him peeking my way the odd time, but ignore it. I'm just finding myself again and can do without any complications. There's another big issue too called Olivia, but we'll get to that. Anyway, what we have is fun, easy…comfortable. Sometimes we just sit together reading. He never questions my past or pushes me to try and remember it.

"God, I so need the toilet." Liv (Olivia) jumps out of the car. "You'd think there'd be a sign."

Pleased to get out, I clamber over the front seat and out of the driver door. It's a three-door, battered, brown hatchback; we're just students, after all. Stretching my legs to shake off the journey. Being squashed between Luke and Liv was a squeeze to say the least, with the chatty brunette being on the more curvaceous side, well compared to me that is, the pale human stick insect.

Luke introduced me to Liv at fresher's week. They went through school together. It sometimes feels like they should be a couple, but they insist they know each other too well for that. There's an awful lot of protesting on her side, makes me wonder…

So anyway, I couldn't sit up front with Persia because her old school mate, Elle, filled that seat. Looking at them both, it was probably a school for the young and beautiful. Like Persia, Elle is at least six feet tall and the next Miss

World, if she weren't so quiet. She's sort of pixie-ish, with that pageboy style platinum blonde hair and striking silver-grey eyes, which I'm guessing must be contacts, like Persia's purple ones. I avoid standing next to them at all costs, as it just makes me look and feel very average. Guess my eyes are my best feature, they're an autumnal golden colour, and my long blonde hair's great to hide behind.

"Let's do this," Luke says, untying his surfboard from the car rack.

"I'm off to find a loo." Liv hurries away.

"Okay, meet us back here!" I yell.

"Right I'm off to hit those beautiful waves. See you guys at the bonfire later?" Luke beams.

"You're not coming to the fair?" I ask, disappointed.

"Nah, not a fan of rides."

"Not even candy floss?"

"Nah, I'm sweet enough."

Rolling my eyes at his blatant flirting, before waving him away.

"What shall we do first?" Elle asks, which is an event in itself as the girl rarely speaks.

"Rides!" I say, not open for any debate. Excited; this will be my first funfair that I can remember.

"Okay, let's take a slow walk. Liv can catch up." Persia smirks at me and locks her car.

"I'm back!" Liv strides across the parking lot. "And FYI, don't use those loos, so disgusting. I need a shower now."

We laugh, walking in the direction of the booming pop music. Turning the corner, there it is in all its corny multi-coloured glory, the funfair. I let out a squeal that's accompanied with a little clap.

"Okay, chill girl," Persia chuckles. "Best get you in there before you erupt."

Before heading to any rides, I just want to lap up the cheesy ambience and smells. *Oh, those smells!* Liv and I buy hot dogs smothered in onions and ketchup. Then we get candyfloss that we ravish like toddlers. But it's so good, so sweet and sticky.

"Wanna try the rides yet?" Liv asks.

"Maybe." I'm bloated. "Maybe I'll give my stomach a few minutes to recover."

"How about it, Persia? Elle?" Liv pleads.

"Think we'll stay with Summer," Elle says.

"Guys, I'll be fine, seriously what could happen? Maybe I'll fall in the popcorn machine or get knocked over by the ghost train." Sighing, they're both great but sometimes they act like minders, not friends.

"Funny," Elle says, without a hint of a smile.

"Okay, let's go in the hall of mirrors for a bit," Liv suggests. We follow, and my poor stomach is glad of a rest.

Every mirror makes me look ridiculous. I'm told that's the point. Laughing at each other as we become squat then wobbly, we stay here for a while. One reflection makes my eyes look owl huge, like two golden suns in the distorted glass.

"Look at my eyes, Persia, they look like they're on fire."

"It's just the mirror messing with you."

"But yours look purple, like always."

"It's just the lighting." She walks away before I can question it.

"Hey!" Liv leaves her abnormally long reflection behind. "You guys up for the waltzers yet?"

"Sure." My stomach feels more normal again. I'm nervous and excited for my first ever ride. The early rotations are quite pleasant as we wave at Elle and Persia. But in a matter of seconds, our little waltzer car spins so fast that I can no longer see, the thrill becomes an instant regret. "I feel sick." Groaning, staggering from the ride toward the smirking faces of my friends.

"You're such a wimp." Liv laughs from behind. "That was brilliant. Let's do it again."

"No," I say, hoping that my legs will stop shaking soon.

"Boring!" Liv turns and points to a little white tent that has a sign outside, 'Gypsy Rose Lee.'

"Ooh let's do this." She's almost bouncing, still on a sugar high, I presume.

"You don't seriously believe in all that nonsense?" Persia frowns.

"It's just a bit of fun, who knows, maybe she'll tell me my future husband. Come on, Sum, feel the fun!" She pulls on my arm. Unease snakes up my spine. "What's wrong? You've gone so pale."

"I…I don't know…something you said, someone's said that to me before…weird." I try shaking off the creepy feeling of déjà vu, wondering why it's bothered me so much.

Persia's eyes widen.

"What's wrong?"

"Who's said that to you before?" Grabbing my shoulder.

"No idea, why?"

"You know with your patchy memory, just wondered if you'd remembered something else." Persia takes her hand off me, giving Elle an unreadable glance, but before I know it, I'm dragged inside the tent. It's dimly lit with a candle flickering on a round table.

A face appears from the shadows.

"Hello, girls. Do come in." Gypsy Rose croaks. Her face is withered, and her lavender velvet robes could use a dry clean.

"Hi." We giggle.

"You both want a reading, yes?"

"Yes." Liv takes a place at the table and pays the woman. Gypsy Rose waves her hands around in a dramatic fashion, claiming to be purifying the energy and whatnot. Telling Liv everything she wants to hear. Her husband will be good looking and rich, blah, blah…Liv seems happy with her vague reading and the old woman beckons me to the chair.

"No, really, I'm fine." Not wanting to waste time and money on such a fake.

"Come, for you…free."

"Go on, Sum, what you got to lose?" Liv nudges me forward. Glancing back to Persia waiting in the doorway, shaking her head, eyes full of worry, but it's too late to back out now. Liv pushes me down on the chair. The candle's flame burns higher, waving back and forth as though in a rage. I gulp. Close against the flame the woman seems so much older, one wrinkle for every year perhaps?

"Well now, Summer…"

"She knows your name." Liv gasps.

"Yes, because you just called me it," I huff. She's so gullible. The candle flickers out, and I want to leave. The material walls feel like they're closing in around me. The old woman leans over the table, grabbing my hand. My breathing is shallow and my heart's racing. We lock eyes, I gasp at the wild look in hers. Trying to pull my hand free, but the woman only grips tighter. Her eyes widen, then she gasps too, dropping my hand like it's hot metal.

"What is it?" My voice catches in my throat.

"He's coming for you. Beware, he's almost here."

3: Alex

Shit! "You don't recognise me?"

"Err, should I?"

"Not even a little bit?"

"Nope, sorry."

Shit, shit and shit! What the hell do I do?

"Okay, this is gonna sound really out there..." Raking a hand through my hair.

"I can do *out there*." Andie crosses her arms across her chest.

"God...where do I start?"

"At the beginning, that usually works."

"It's complicated." Pacing back and forth, checking for the guard who, luckily, seems to have moved on. "There's so much even I can't get straight."

"Okay..." She draws out the word. "You realise I can call for help at any moment, right?"

"Please don't. Just wait. I'm not great at the whole talking thing." I stop pacing. Andie stares at me with slight amusement or maybe fear? It's hard to tell.

"Look, this is all interesting and all...the library's gonna close soon and I don't know you from Adam. I mean, you could just be baiting me for when you attack me later. No offence."

"None taken." *Hurry up, Alex. You're losing her!* "Okay, this is crazy, but please just hear me out. If you don't believe me by the end, I'll leave you alone. Promise."

"I'm still here, aren't I? Go ahead, I'm all ears." She looks over her glasses and pushes them up her nose.

Here goes nothing. "You've had your memories wiped clean by an angel and—"

"What? What the f…you're nuts!" Stepping back, almost falling into the shelves behind.

"Please, just hear me out."

"Fine. Go ahead." Glancing beyond me for the security guard who could turn up any minute.

"There was…is, this girl, Summer." Warmth arises in me just saying her name. "You were close friends." She looks bewildered but hasn't made a run for it yet. "Summer is 'The Light,' a key to heaven's gateway that leads souls to her, so they can enter the afterlife." Pacing again. By the look on her face, she's not buying it. I must get her to remember, or at least want to. "There's these people, The Krons, who are…were, sort of my people until I found out they were demons who have lied to me my entire life. They stole me at birth, trained me to hunt and kill The Light."

"This Summer girl," Andie adds.

"Yes, so they could control the gateway, and eventually control all souls as well. This would make them all-powerful. A person would do anything to save their soul…" A dark crease has appeared down the centre of her forehead. "Anyway, Summer and I are soul mates…" Andie's sudden outburst of laughter confuses me.

"Sorry," she splutters. "Go on."

"You didn't laugh at the demon part, but you do at that? Oh, of course you don't do the whole love thing, do you?"

"How…how do you know that?" She's not laughing now.

"Like I said, your mind's been wiped of the last few months, as if Summer, the angels…me, never even existed."

"Okay, I'm playing so far." Her eyes narrow.

"This is where you two would come every day to study and gossip. This was your place. There's so much to tell you—"

"What's she like, this Summer person?"

"Beautiful, funny, caring, kind, selfless…You'd…you like her."

"She sounds awesome. Sure you haven't made her up?"

"No!" *God, I thought we were actually getting somewhere.* "She was, *is*, awesome and I know she felt the same way about you."

"Sounds too good to be true." Sighing. "I need more…"

"More what?"

"Evidence that you know me. I mean, I'm open to anything, within reason…but I'm no pushover. You're asking me to believe all this…demons and crazy stuff…for all I know you could be high."

"Okay…give me a minute…" Scratching at my stubble, I try to think of something to convince her. "Okay, you have tattoos on each wrist, Chinese symbols for some vague bollocks like 'be unique' and 'change the world?'"

"Close. But anyone can see my wrists." She waves them about. "You could've followed me, researched Chinese symbols on the net." Leaning over grabbing a book from the table like she's ready to hit me with it and escape.

"Follow you? Please don't flatter yourself." She looks pissed at me. Apologising, I begin to pace in a small square, trying to remember everything I recall Summer ever telling me about Andie. "Got it!" Stopping, feeling smug. "Your dad's a drunk and your mother left when you were little." Feeling a massive grin on my face, which I remove upon seeing the hurt in her eyes.

"Hmm…guess I don't tell many people that."

"See?"

"This is all very…elaborate. How come you didn't get your mind wiped?"

"They usually wipe everybody, but this time it's different. This time the angel, Persia, gave me the gift of choice. You see it's a cycle. I keep finding her in order to kill her, but instead we end up falling for each other…over and over. So this time I could either forget everything, and repeat it all again, or remember and try to change it. Of course, I'll always choose her."

"So, you're a murderer?" Her eyes widen, and she takes a step as though about to rush out.

"No. Please." Putting both hands up, giving her ample room to a free path. "Please, just give me a chance. I've never killed anyone, and don't ever intend to. If you feel at all threatened by me, ask me to leave and I will. But I know you, Andie, you won't stop wondering if I'm telling the truth…You must feel it? That hole, like there's something important missing from your life?"

"I always feel like that…would you buy it if you were me? I mean, what a story. Demons, angels…you just expect me to buy all this?"

"Guess not." I'm running out of options. My phone beeps in my back pocket. Ignoring it, it's most likely Kit checking up on me.

"Aren't you gonna answer that? Might be important. Could be an angel or something." Andie's brows raise.

"Holy crap!"

"What?" Taking another step back, until she's almost sitting on the bookshelf.

"My phone! Why didn't I think of it before? I took pictures of her…"

"Stalker much?"

"They were all deleted when they wiped everyone's mind, but they left me one, and now I know why."

"Why?"

"Persia *wanted* me to find you." Pulling out the cell and swiping through old pictures. "Here!" I hold the phone up with a picture of her and Summer sitting on a park bench, talking. Admittedly, it's a little fuzzy and far away, but you can see that it's them. "Look!" Andie steps forward, snatching the phone. Studying it for ages, removes her glasses, then puts them back on a few times before speaking.

"I don't understand…I've sat at that bench hundreds of times but…but I've always been alone. How is this possible? I have no recollection of ever seeing this girl before." She stares at the image. "This can't be real." Her hand is shaking as she gives the phone back.

"So that's it? You're just dismissing all of it? What is it with people and trust?" Sighing, about to turn in defeat.

"Thought you knew me."

"A bit."

"So, then you know I'm up for a challenge, unless you really are a weirdo here to kill me?"

Relief overwhelms me. "God, I was hoping you'd say that, not the weirdo part." We stare at each other for a while. I wait to see which way she's going to go.

"So…you believe me?" My brows raise, anxious for the reply.

"Let's just say the jury's still out. But that's me in that photo…You have my attention."

"Thank you." Exhaling deeply.

"So, you're not keen on the pink?" Pointing to her hair.

"It's okay, but the blue was more you."

"Say I believe you…what do I get out of it?"

"Your best friend."

"Guess I've nothing to lose."

"So, you'll help me?"

"Will you cut me up if I don't?"

"Maybe," I joke. "Look, if I wanted to kill you, trust me, you'd be dead already. I don't kill humans, think you come under that category."

"Funny. Well then, where do we start?"

I tell her what Lennox had told me. How he stole me from my mother at birth. And that he thinks something went wrong with me, the spell.

"They took you, almost killed you," I tell her.

"Did they? They sound like real tossers. I'm trying not to have a little mental freak out."

"You'll be okay." I smile. "It will take time to process. So, what do you think? Will you help me?"

"We should start by finding out who you are…were."

"Does it matter?"

"Doesn't it? Maybe if we knew your background, we could know more about you. Like perhaps it could make you stronger or less angry. Maybe there'll be clues to what you are…why you're different? You must be curious? And it will help your case if there's more evidence for me to see, right? When there's a mystery, don't 'The Scooby Gang' always start at the beginning?"

"Who? And I'm not angry." I sneer.

"You think?" Rolling her eyes, and something about that reminds me of Kit and I feel sad, and sort of angry.

"Okay." I agree. "Let's go back in time."

"You're kidding, right?"

"No, I can't time travel, that really would be ridiculous."

"As much as angels and gateways…Anyway, we can't do it now, the library's about to close. You'll have to come back tomorrow."

"Will do. So, you believe me?"

"Not a hundred percent, but studying is dull, and this seems not so dull, and you haven't made any moves to hurt me…yet. Plus, I can't un-see that photo now."

"I'll take anything." Sticking my cap back on. "Andie?"

"Yes?"

"Thanks for trusting me."

"I didn't say I did."

* * * *

The next night can't come soon enough. I've tried to keep busy and off the Kron's radar all day. Any wood needed gathering and I'd go chop it. Any errands needed running; I'd be on my bike ready. In the quiet moments before excessive training, I'd sit and carve. It's starting to look like a deer now.

Evening is upon me at last and the sky sags with rain. I begin stretching, ready for my usual evening run. Nervous at the thought of digging up the past, maybe finding out who my parents were. Are they alive? Are they still looking for me? *Of course not, Alex, get over yourself, it's been over nineteen years…*

"And where are you off now?" Kit sits cross-legged outside the tent.

Shit, does she know? Bet she does…why hasn't she told the others? No, this is just me being paranoid, right?

"For a run, as usual." Gesturing to my shorts and trainers. "Not really a clubbing outfit." I force a smile, which she probably sees straight through.

"Okay." She shrugs and gets up. "Just don't be long."

"And why not?" Clenching my fists. This witch has ordered me around for too long.

"Looks like a storm's coming."

"So? I don't care."

"Well, how long you gonna be?"

"Long as it takes." Holding in the urge to swear, my jaw clenches.

"Have you told Lennox?"

"No, but I'm sure you will." Turning away to hide the annoyance I'm feeling.

"See you then," she snaps.

Not if I see you first, traitor. "See ya."

She was right. The storm comes before I even make it out of the woods. But it's refreshing, maybe it could wash away my sins and regrets, although I may need a tidal wave for that. By the time I make it to the library, I'm a dripping mess. Andie looks up from her book and smirks.

"What?"

"If you were my type, which you're not, you'd be a hot wet mess right now…"

"Err…"

"Ha! Your face! Like I said, you're not my type."

"Funny." Pulling a towel from my backpack, I start drying off.

"So, two visits to a library in two days…must be new and exciting for you?"

"Piss off. Talk about judging. I spend a lot of time in these joints, well when my 'people' think I'm training that is. I may look like this, but you need more than looks to get by in life." Huffing. It never bothered me before what people thought; just Summer…guess this girl hit a nerve.

"Alright, 'touchy,' my bad. Come on."

"Where we going?"

"The computer section. We should start by accessing the old newspaper archives from the year you were born."

"Good idea." I pick up my bag and follow her. There's no one in this area except one girl in the corner, who seems oblivious to us. I grin at her bag. The design reads, 'I'm up and dressed. I'm a student. What more do you want?' We sit at a computer in the far corner near a radiator.

"Warm your trainers and socks on it for a bit." Andie starts typing.

"Aww, didn't know you cared."

"Whatever. Do what you want." I take her advice and stick the soggy socks and shoes on the radiator. Pulling my t-shirt off, sticking that on it too.

"Really?"

"What? Thought I'm not your type?" Her eyes drop to my chest, she flusters and looks away. Maybe she saw the scars? Wounds of a tough childhood and a demonic father…

Andie asks me lots of questions about the town I was born in, which I don't know. My birth date, which is October 18th…unless that's just another lie…

"Okay, so let's narrow the search to missing persons for that year."

Two articles come up, one about a missing woman and the other about a missing baby.

"Crap!"

The girl in the corner looks over.

"Crap indeed." Andie gasps. We read in silence. My heart thuds heavier with each sentence. 'Baby Boy Snatched from Hospital.' It goes on to interview the mother, *my* mother. It says how she only left him, me, for a moment and how guilty she feels. An eyewitness describes seeing a thin man in a dark coat and hunting hat, walking nearby with a baby in his arms. Blah, blah and blah. So that would be my 'father' Lennox. I feel sick at the thought of him. It. That thing, with a human face and demon heart. I take a huge breath as the article goes on to say that the woman gave birth to identical twins that day and that the other boy, although a little sickly, is safe and sound.

"You never knew you had a twin?"

"No, I bloody didn't." My head's a jumble of anger and confusion. *What the hell?* There's another part of me out there…walking around with this face? Living what should have been my life. Something else Lennox has taken from me. I could've been normal, happy with a real family, a twin brother who should have been a best friend. My face heats up, my palms are wet. Rage bubbles to the surface and I'm desperately trying to hold it in.

"I've gotta go." Need to get out of here before I rip the place apart. Stumbling out of the chair like a drunk, I grab the warm soggy stuff from the radiator. I'm almost tripping pulling on the damp trainers.

"Don't go." Andie grabs my wrist, then pulls away noticing my 'get the hell off me' expression. "We may find out more."

"No!" Taking a step back from her. "I'm ready to tear this place up… Don't wanna hurt you." She nods, and I escape, hitting out at everything I pass. Not even stopping upon hearing the glass smash from punching a window. Blood drips from my knuckles.

* * * *

Andie is at the gates waiting for me the next night.

"How come you're here?"

"You were seen by a security guard and maybe caught on camera. You made a real mess last night."

"Oh that." Shrugging, feeling foolish. "Are you scared of me…are you going to stop helping me?"

"I never said that. You didn't hurt me so—"

"I wouldn't hurt you! I'm not a monster, not anymore."

"It's cool, okay?" She smiles to my great relief. "Anyway, I think I've found something you'll want to see."

"What?"

She hands me a note. "Here."

"What is it?"

"The woman's last known address. You could find your mum…"

My heart flips and the paper trembles in my hand. "You do believe me then?"

"Well, let's just say that all this can't be a big coincidence…it's got me intrigued."

"Thank you." Going to squeeze her arm but change my mind.

"It's all good and as long as you promise not to kill me, I'll help all I can."

"I don't know about that."

"I'm not scared of you."

"No?"

"No. What's scarier is your story, if all that stuff is true about demons…" She shudders. "Are you going to track her down? Your mum, I mean."

"Guess I have to now. If anyone can fill me in, it's her. I need to know if she's normal, human. If she's in on any of it…and my brother…"

"You don't believe that poor woman let that thing take her baby, do you?"

"Don't know what to believe anymore. Maybe Lennox lied about all of it. Maybe my mum was, *is* a witch or a demon. Why me? Why am I so special?"

"Random thought. If your kidnapping story was in all the papers…why is it that your evil tribe doesn't know about your twin? It doesn't add up."

"Dunno…guess they took me and scarpered. Plus, my 'tribe' don't do technology, we, no, *they* are very basic. I had to beg to even get a phone and that's only so they can track me."

"So, you don't think they know? Really?"

"I'd bet my bike on it."

"So, you find this woman, then what?"

"Then I'll go back to camp, play a role and hopefully be told where to find Summer."

"Good luck. My number is on there too." Taking out my phone, I punch the numbers in then text her my digits. She smiles as her phone lights up. "Let me know if you need anything this end. And of course, I wanna know how this thing plays out. 'Cos, if you fail, which I'm sure you won't, give me a heads up if demons are gonna start running things."

"I'll try to keep you posted." I smile as she walks away. "Hey, Andie."

"Yeah?" She turns.

"Like the blue hair again."

"Thanks." She strokes her newly dyed hair. "You were right, if it ain't broke, don't fix it."

I head back to camp to grab my wheels, my Shelly. It's time to take a ride. It's time to face the past.

4: *Summer*

"Penny for 'em?"

"Huh?" I jump, resurfacing from my thoughts.

"Sorry, didn't mean to startle you."

"You didn't," I lie, making eye contact with the extremely cute guy. "I was miles away."

"Bonfires can do that to you…if you look at them for too long, bit like rivers." He smiles, and I smile back. This guy seems nice, I feel almost relaxed with him, unthreatened. He has no idea of who I am, what I've been through. There's no pity in his smile. Maybe it's the calm of the sea swishing in the background or maybe the heat of the fire against my skin…or could it be I'm becoming more comfortable with myself? Was I saved from that fire for a reason? Maybe this is the time to start living a little.

"I'm Chris, by the way." He sticks out his hand and I shake it.

"Summer."

"Suits you. You here all alone, Summer?" He takes a swig from his beer can.

"No, my friends are here, they've gone to get more drinks." A wave of unease crosses my mind. Should I be so open with someone I've only just met? And yet the ease of his chat and charm of his face, I'm not doing anything dangerous…I'm just being a normal girl.

"Want a drink?" he asks. "Your friends seem to have forgotten you."

"She's got one, thanks," Luke steps between us and hands me a bottle.

"Luke, this is Chris," I say, trying to undo the weird testosterone-fuelled tension. "Chris—Luke." Nodding to Luke, but he ignores Chris's outstretched hand.

"Maybe we'll see you around, Chris." Luke crosses his arms, and I want to slap his idiotic face. Even he looks small in comparison to this Chris but doesn't seem at all bothered that my new friend could kick the crap out of him. He might even deserve it for being such a jerk.

"Hey, man, I meant no harm. We were just talking, okay? Didn't know you two were…together." Chris shrugs.

"Well we are." Luke puts his arm around my shoulders.

"Luke?" Glaring at him, but he doesn't budge. "God, Chris, I'm so sorry about this…"

"Hey, no worries, Summer. I was just being friendly." Chris winks at me. "Maybe I'll see you around." He walks over to a crowd of beer-guzzling guys and that's it, my normal girl at a party moment has been stamped on. Pulling out of Luke's hold, my face and hands feel too hot.

"What the hell was that?" Shouting, trying to release the heat from my body.

"Err, sorry, Summer." He pushes the straggly blond hair from his eyes. "I…I just didn't like that guy all over you."

"He was hardly all over me!" My hands shoot to my hips and a few people stop talking to watch. Lowering my voice. "Well?"

"Guess I'm just being protective. Guys like that are only after one thing."

"And you know that just by looking at him?" Huffing.

"I know the type, a gym monkey with no brains under all that muscle."

"You're not my dad or my boyfriend." Taking a deep breath to try and cool down.

"Summer, you're bright red, maybe you should move away from the fire."

"Don't tell me what to do, okay?"

"Look, I'm sorry. I'd be the same if it were Liv…"

Would he? "I'm not stupid okay and I don't need saving."

"Got it." He grins, and annoyingly, I can't help but smile. "Forgive me?"

"Suppose so. Life's too short, right?" Unclenching, my skin cools down within seconds to a normal temperature.

"Right," he steps in, giving me a quick hug. "Where do you think the others have got to?" *Points for changing the subject.* "Stay here and I'll go find them…you'll be okay?"

Rolling my eyes, he gets the message and scurries off, putting distance between him, the awkwardness, and me.

Staring back into the flames, stepping closer until the fire warms me like a thick coat. The gypsy's words from this afternoon keep repeating on me. 'Beware, he is coming for you.'

"Hey."

"Bloody hell! Wish people would stop sneaking up on me."

"Gotcha." Liv nudges my side; I hate being nudged so I do it back harder, making her stumble on the sand. "OI!"

"Serves you right." I laugh.

"Shall we move away from the fire?"

"I like it here, makes me feel safe."

"You feel safe near open flames? You're such a weirdo sometimes." Liv shakes her head, pulling me away.

"Is Luke okay? We had a few *words*…"

"He never said." She frowns. "What about?"

"Nothing really. Think he's just looking out for me. Is he stupidly over-protective with you too?"

"Err, yeah, sometimes." Her voice trails off and I can't help but wonder if I've upset her.

"You two enjoying yourselves?" Persia turns up, followed by Elle. Both look as though they've just stepped out of the pretty shower, whereas my face must look as tired as I feel.

"Of course, the whole day has been awesome." Liv swigs a last mouthful of beer.

"We should start heading back soon. Where's Luke?" Persia scans the revellers.

"He was here two minutes ago. He can't be far," I tell her. Eventually we spot him checking out some guy's surfboard, before lifting a keg of beer over his head, to show the other cavemen, and perhaps me, his strength. *Figures.*

Why is it that the journey home always feels so much longer than the way there? Almost the entire ride is filled with a loud, uncomfortable silence. Even Liv has nothing to say to fill the empty void. I'm no mind reader, but I'm guessing she's over-analysing the whole Luke pretending to be my boyfriend incident. And no, I never told her, I'm not that callous. Guessing he did though, not to be cruel, but because I don't think he sees Liv as girlfriend material, so he wouldn't see any of this as an issue. Liv, however, would never admit to having feelings for him, not even to herself. Reckon she's always been into him; I'd bet my entire book collection on that. So yeah, there's tension in the car. I keep thinking of something to say to break it, but anything I say now will sound pathetically lame.

"That fortune teller was weird." There, I've spoken.

"Totally off her rocker," Liv agrees, keeping her gaze trained out of the window.

"Well it creeped me out," I say, catching Persia staring at me via the rearview mirror, eyes cold, unreadable.

"You shouldn't listen to such tripe," Elle huffs.

"So, you two don't have to believe," Liv says, turning her attention forward. "It was just a bit of fun."

"Summer didn't seem to enjoy it." Persia speaks over her shoulder not taking her eyes off the road. We turn the corner and enter campus grounds.

"I mean what's with all the serious stuff? 'Beware he is coming for you.'" Liv chuckles. "What a load of bull."

Luke joins in the sniggering.

"But you didn't think that when she told you about your amazing future husband," I snap. And there's that awkward atmosphere again. *Great*. For the last few minutes, nobody speaks. I'm aware that I'm the barrier keeping Liv physically, hopefully not mentally, from Luke.

"Home sweet home." Persia smiles, turning off the ignition. We scramble out. Doors are slammed harder than necessary. I can't put my finger on it, but today has had a strange effect on us all somehow.

"I'll walk you all to your rooms," Luke offers.

"It's okay." Persia nods. "We've got this. You take Liv across to her dorm and we'll see you tomorrow." Persia and Elle escort me to our building. Glancing behind I catch Luke doing the same. Against the moonlight, his eyes look full of sadness, longing…God, I hope he isn't feeling what I think he's feeling. As much as I love his company, I love Liv's too. It can't be me that comes between them and splits up our little group. I can't, won't lose these amazing friends, having lost so much already. These people are a shot at normalcy, a chance at a new start. God, I should really get over myself. Of course, he doesn't like me that way. Not when there are hundreds of girls on campus. I'm nothing special…damaged goods almost…

We arrive at my room, which is sandwiched between Elle's and Persia's.

"You don't think…" I look up to Persia.

"What?" She frowns.

"That someone is coming after me, do you?" Feeling stupid on hearing how crazy that sounds.

"Do you?" Elle asks.

"I…her words were so menacing. Even *she* looked freaked out." Turning the key to open the door.

"Summer." Persia grabs my shoulder.

"Yeah?" I look back at her, knots forming in my belly.

"She was just a good actor, a fraud."

"Yeah, of course. You're right." Shrugging and trembling in unison.

"Night then." They head to their rooms.

"Night." Locking the door behind me, leaning against it, suddenly very aware of my own breath and that I'm alone.

Lights flash around me. Music churns against my temples, as the cheap organ grinds out from a rusty carousel. The fairground is full of laughter that seems to mock my despair. Children whinge for ice creams, gangs of spotty teens leer at passing girls. Feeling claustrophobic while weaving in and out of the throng. Feeling small under the cacophony of heavy beats and booming voices. Floating along like a feather, unnoticed, pushed through the crowds. Dizzily drifting, not knowing where this next wind will take me. Falling to the ground, I'm no longer light, now heavy, and solid, like leaded weights bind my ankles and wrists. Dragging me down, I'm too exhausted to fight. I hit the ground wondering when the pain will come, but it doesn't. Opening my eyes, I'm still at the fairground but now it's empty and soulless. A light passes overhead. It's coming from a little white tent that stands alone. Without moving, I'm in the doorway.

"Hello? Is anyone here?" Peering into the tent. Little fat wrinkly hands reach through, pulling me inside. Sitting on a chair that I don't remember being there, I gulp.

"Look into the crystal ball, Summer, right into its very heart." The ball seems to bulge and grow until it's the size of the table beneath and all I see is glass. "Look harder," the voice commands. "Deeper."

Wanting to yell at it to leave me alone, that I don't belong here or understand. But when my mouth opens, I am mute.

"Look, girl!" At first, there are random faces, which flicker and change before me. Thousands of human faces crying out in pain. Focusing harder on the ball, a small crack appears at its centre. It grows larger like an inkblot spreading over tissue. But this is not ink; this is fire burning its way through from the core of the glass ball towards my face. As it reaches the surface, the ball explodes into thousands of tiny red-hot shards. Covering my eyes, finding my voice. Screams erupt. Tiny cuts puncture my arms.

"Look at it, dear," the old woman demands.

Peering out from behind bleeding hands. She's laughing at me and I don't understand the joke. She laughs harder. The skin over her face bubbles and slides right off her skull. The howling laughter carries around the tent.

"Stop it!" I beg. Pain rips at my body as skin peels away from my hands and arms. Screaming until my throat burns away. I'm too hot, melting. The laughter stops. The woman's skinless skull comes to within inches of my smouldering face.

"Beware," it creaks. "He comes for you."

I wake up screaming. The light switch snaps on. Persia and Elle are running at me.

"Summer?" Persia's at my side like a human guard dog. "What? What is it?"

"Too hot, I'm too hot," I cry. "Get it off me."

Elle grabs my arms and holds me. "Calm down," she whispers. "You're safe. It was just a bad dream."

"Big breaths…that's it." Persia takes breaths with me, which could be taken as a little patronising, but right now I don't care. Looking over my arms, relieved that they're still covered in skin. As the world shifts from crazy to normal, I feel pretty silly.

"God, I'm so sorry to wake you."

"Hey, it's fine." Persia smiles. "You may have to apologise to the entire dorm in the morning though."

"What on Earth were you dreaming about?" Elle lets go of me.

"I…I honestly can't remember." I lie, knowing that they're not buying any of the gypsy stuff.

"Okay, get some rest and we'll see you for breakfast." Persia ruffles my hair as they go to leave.

"I don't think I'll be leaving this room ever after this." I slump back down onto the bed.

"Don't be so melodramatic," Elle scolds, making me feel like a silly child.

"We'll see you in a few hours," Persia says.

"Hey, how did you guys get in here?"

"Oh, you must have left your door unlocked." Elle shrugs. Did I? Don't think so…

"Go to sleep. We'll laugh about this tomorrow, trust me." Persia waves as the door clips behind her. Jumping from the bed, I bolt the door, which I'm almost certain I did before.

5: Alex

After sneaking back into camp and packing a few essentials, food, a change of clothes and a handy knife, I leave, hopefully unnoticed. Quietly pushing my bike to the edge of the woods not to wake anyone. Leaving a note earlier on the bed, just in case my so-called stalker 'sister' wanders in, saying that I've gone off to the mountains to train for a few days and that I'll be back soon ready to fight. That should please them all. I bet waiting around for their 'weapon' to be ready is frustrating the hell out of them.

Driving through the night, it's eerily quiet with just the ever-dependable Shelly and my thoughts for company. There are so many questions; where to even start? Finally, I'll be face to face with my real mother. I'm beyond nervous and there's a little bit of sick sitting in the back of my throat. The closer I get to the town, the more an inner voice nags me to turn back…back to what though? Back to a bunch of crazed, power-hungry, murderous demons? Yet, I must see them again, play the game, at least until I know where my girl is. Will this woman even recognise me? Accept me? Will my brother be there? Is he a better version of me? Are they happy without me? It's not like I need them, or anyone…except for Summer. But I've got to see for myself before I can move on in life. You'd want to know too, right?

Arriving at the corner of Kent Avenue, the address from Andie's note, I turn the engine off. The street where this birth mother should be, but a part of me is sort of hoping that she's not. Glancing at my watch, it's just after three a.m. Moving my bike behind a bush, telling her I'll be back soon. The street is too quiet with its unified little brick houses, white picket fences, and over-filled hanging baskets. So, this is what life would have been…everything I never had. It's fine, by the way; I refuse to be a victim, so don't make me one. Yeah, admittedly, there's a tiny teeny part deep down that aches to know how life could have been…but there's no magic to turn back time, and if there was would I have crossed paths with Summer?

Upon reaching number thirteen, I feel like an intruder. *What the hell am I thinking coming here?* This can't be healthy for my mother or for me. Mother? The word feels alien. Nerves dictate to leave but my feet remain rooted— why aren't they moving? There's a bench across the road, partially hidden by a large oak tree, so I head for it. Sitting down, there's a few hours until sun up, a few hours to decide.

My eyes open when a young girl whizzes by me on a pink bike, laughing. *Shit. Guess I fell asleep. Stealthy, Alex, real stealthy.* Checking the time, annoyed at myself that it's eight thirty. Number thirteen is still in darkness. Did I miss her? Does she work? The little girl comes back and circles me a few times.

"You're gonna make me dizzy if you keep doing that." My voice comes out sort of threatening, which is unintended.

"Okay." She smiles, braking in front of me.

"Aren't you scared?"

"Of what?" the girl asks, cocking her head to one side.

"Of me."

"Should I be?"

"I'm a stranger. Don't you know kids should never talk to strangers?"

"You're no stranger than last time. In fact, you're much nicer today. Are you in a better mood? My daddy says I'm not to talk to you anymore."

"To me?" Now I'm confused.

"Yes, you shouted at me last time, but then you went away, and didn't come back. You look different, I don't like the stubble, and you look all dirty. Have you been fighting?"

"What makes you say that?" I smile, this girl reminds me a little of Kit, when we were young with none of this crap over our heads.

"You have a scar under your eye and your clothes look messy…you always looked clean before."

"Oh." Realising she thinks I'm my brother. This twin thing is gonna take forever to get used to. "Well, I'm sorry for shouting at you."

"Okay." She shrugs and rides away.

God, what am I thinking? This is stupid. What, is she just gonna let me in and offer me a coffee? This could ruin the life she has now. What if me turning up is a total nightmare for her? I get up to leave. *This is insane.! I shouldn't have come here. Yet, there's always been a part of me that's felt empty…*A door slams, I freeze. Footsteps patter across the road, and I know she's standing right behind me.

"Liam?" Her voice is hoarse, like it's tainted with thick tears. *Liam?* I can't turn around, nineteen years of not having her, nineteen years of a huge draughty hole in my chest where she should have been.

"Liam…is it really you?" Do I make a run for it or face her? Stepping away; ready to leave, like a bloody coward. "Liam, wait… please?" I must turn around, not just for her but for me too. "Please don't run away again…please, whatever it is we can get through it together. I forgive everything." A warm hand touches my shoulder, making me shudder. Slowly, I turn, and we finally face one another. Her eyes widen, and her mouth forms an O shape. My pulse races, and I gasp almost forgetting to breathe. We stand in silence, staring at each other.

"Ethan?" Her face pales. She sways, and I catch her before she hits the ground. She's in my arms. After a few long seconds, her eyes flutter open and she smiles up at me.

"Hey, is she okay, Liam?" A sturdy man comes out from a house close by.

"I'm okay, George." She nods. "Just had a funny turn." The man eyes me with contempt.

"Hope you're here to stay and look after your mother this time? Don't want to call the police on you again." George gives me a laughable, threatening glare.

Police, eh? He thinks I'm my other half—we must really be identical. He hovers about before going back inside.

"Can you stand?" I ask, helping her up.

"Thank you...Ethan."

"Huh?"

"Ethan...is it really you?" Her trembling hand reaches for my cheek.

"I..." I have no idea what to say.

"Oh God, Ethan. You've come home after all this time. You've found me." Before I know it, she's holding me, like really holding me, with so much warmth, so much love. It's painful and amazing all at once. I reach out and return the embrace. We stand this way for quite some time, on the side of the road, not caring who passes us by.

"Ethan..." She pulls back. "...let me look at you."

"My name is Alex now," I tell her, trying not to upset her more. Emerald eyes that are exactly like mine, water. Sprinkles of grey peek through her raven hair, and her chin is square like mine, without the dimple. You can tell that she was pretty when she was younger, before life came and brutally punched her full on in the face.

"You are my son, whatever you call yourself. I would know you anywhere. Come in the house. We can talk." Takes my hand to follow her.

The living room's neat; everything has a place but me it seems.

"Please sit." I do. "Do you want a drink?" she asks, wiping tears away.

"No thanks." Beyond dazed, not knowing how to feel, how to act, who to be… Not wanting to disappoint after all this time.

"God, Ethan, I can't believe you're really here." Moving toward me, sinking to her knees, placing both palms gently against my cheeks. "I searched for so long. The police stopped after a few years, but I never gave up hope. Look at you…so grown up and handsome." Trembling fingertips graze my scar, and I flinch. "What's happened to you? What kind of life have you had? I will always be sorry for not protecting you. Can you ever forgive me, Ethan?" Clearly, she's an innocent in this mess. Knowing nothing about my reality and was never involved. So at least half of me is human. Half of me is good.

My chest tightens. "There is nothing to forgive. You couldn't have known. Life has been hard, but nothing I couldn't handle." My voice is a low whisper as the back of my throat stings with pent-up emotions. I won't cry, it will only make her feel guiltier and I'm not here for that. The guilty will be punished, I swear it. Guess I'm here because I'm human. It's taken me a long time to realise it. I will fight to be a complete human. I'll overcome my father's blood and beat this.

"Ethan…"

"Please, I go by Alex now." Placing one hand firmly on her shoulder.

"Alex it is then." She attempts a smile but fails miserably. "If I hadn't left you alone at the hospital…not a second goes by without regretting it. If only I could take it all back."

"No." Standing, pulling her to her feet. "No, don't ever think like that. It is what it is. Of course, I wish things were different, but they're not." I sigh. "The 'people' that took me would've come sooner or later. Maybe it's best they took me sooner."

"Who took you? What did they need you for? Did they…did they hurt you?" Closing her eyes.

"No," I lie, sparing her the nasty details of being whipped, beaten and desperately unhappy for most of my childhood. "No, I'm okay."

"And you're here now, so we can make up for lost time." She snivels.

"Maybe one day. But there are things I must do before I can come back."

"You're leaving?" Her eyes widen.

"For a while, but I promise to return. I just needed to see you, to know you're alright."

"I am now." She smiles. "You promise you'll come back?"

"I don't lie." Well apart from the whopping great lie with the Krons, pretending to be evil and all. "This Liam, my twin, is he here? I'd like to meet him before I go."

"No, it seems I'm rather good at losing the people I love."

"What do you mean?"

"Well my husband, your father, left me when all the trouble started fifteen years ago."

"What trouble?" I sit back down.

"Liam, he…he was never an easy child. He'd tell lies at first and have tantrums. As he got older, he became sly, I hate to say this of my own son…I do love him."

"Of course."

"Well, he got into trouble in class. He'd start fights, which led to exclusion from three different schools that led to stealing and drugs. He landed himself in the wrong sort of crowd when he reached fifteen. He was always a sickly child growing up. Think he just wanted to prove himself. He became mean, hateful…"

"Sounds tough." Sighing, disappointed that this guy isn't the awesome twin I'd imagined.

"It was…is. I saw you and thought you were him, come home to be forgiven, loved."

"So, you have no idea where he is?"

"I wish I did. He left one night a few months ago. Packed a few things, stole my savings and the little jewellery that I had, and that was that."

"I'm sorry," I say, feeling guilty. She must be so lonely; she doesn't deserve any of this…what Lennox did is unforgivable…he *will* pay.

We talk for about four more hours. I can't bring myself to leave. She fills me in on life events, more about my so-called twin, who gets more and more unlikeable by the minute. Yet, a large part of me is gutted that he's not here. Maybe if I'd been here, maybe he would've been a good kid. She gets upset when I try to leave. I promise over and over to return as soon as possible. She goes upstairs telling me she has something for me, returns and places a photo in my hand. It's her, a younger version, looking happily exhausted, holding a baby in each arm. We must have only been a few minutes old. Tears threaten to spill, I squeeze my eyes tight.

There's a knock at the front door, releasing me from my moment of weakness.

"Must be the window cleaner." She scurries off, purse in hand. After a few mumbled noises, I hear coins dropping to the floor.

"Everything alright?" I ask, entering the hallway.

"Everything's fine, Alex. Dandy in fact." Lennox steps into the doorway. I curse under my breath seeing two of his 'people' holding my mother.

"Alex? What's happening? Who are these people?" she pleads.

"Let her go. What the hell is wrong with you?" Turning to Lennox, I want to rip his pea-sized head right off his scrawny neck. "Why are you here?"

He waits a few moments and then says, "More to the point, why are you?"

Crap, how do I get out of this? Think, Alex!

"Let's all take a seat, shall we?" Lennox removes his hat and walks into the living room. His stooges push my mother forward.

"Hey, don't be so rough with her, alright?" My hands curl into fists. I'm outnumbered, but if they push her again, I'll not just stand here and watch. Kit enters the room. *Fab, the gang's all here.* The goons yank my mother's arms, forcing her down on a stool in the corner.

"Hey! That's enough!" I rush forward. "Unless you want to try it with me," snarling, hand itching to reach for the knife hidden down the side of my boot.

"Calm down, little brother." Kit steps in front of me before my mother can witness what a monster I can be. "No one's here to hurt anyone, okay?" She smiles. This is the longest eye contact we've had since finding out who she really is and those very wrong feelings she's harbouring.

"It's okay, boys. Let go of the lady," Lennox orders. They do, but stand over her like she is daft enough, or brave enough, to make a run for it. "So," Lennox addresses me, "seems that since you're here, you must know everything…and that you've been deceiving us." He raises a brow.

"I…" *Shit, he knows!* I've twisted Summer's chain inside my pocket so tightly, that my fingers are numb. "How did you even find me?"

"Kit sensed something was off, which was confirmed when she received a vision of you and this woman together. And I knew from her description it was your mother, and that she never moved." Lennox moves in close enough that spit hits my chin. "Plus, your phone was off, so you obviously didn't want to be found."

"You never trusted me, did you?"

"Once I did, but not anymore. Anything you want to confess?" His eyes narrow on mine, toying with me because he already knows. Shaking my head, needing to think fast, or he may hurt my mother. I did this; I led more trouble to her door.

"It's a mistake. I found out where she lived, and curiosity brought me here. That's all." keeping my eyes down. My mother's quietly sobbing, and I'm scared for her. I'll kill every last one of them if they hurt her, I swear.

"Alex, please…who are these people? What do they want with us?" she asks.

"Shut her up," Kit hisses at the thugs as one clamps his dirty fat hand over her mouth.

"There's no need to involve the woman. She's nothing to me." Cringing at my own words, a muffled cry comes from the corner.

"Really?" Lennox inches in so close, our noses are almost touching. Wanting to take a step back but my will screams at me to stay put. "So, she's not your birth mother, then?"

"She's just some woman who happened to give birth to me…"

"That she is. But tell me, son, how did you know she existed? We told you your mother had died." There are no words. He's got me there. *Point to him.* "You know. You remember, don't you? That angel didn't wipe your memories. You've been playing us the whole time. Bravo, boy, maybe when this is all over you can have a career on the stage."

"But this will never be over, will it," I state. "There will always be a 'Light' that you want me to put out, a light you want me to become."

"Well, you are clever." Lennox sighs. "Snap her neck."

My mother's eyes widen as she screams against the gag.

"No! Wait! Don't!" Looking to Lennox for an ounce of humanity that I know isn't there.

"Wait!" Lennox orders as the goons make a move to obey.

"I'll do anything you want. Please, just leave her alone." Desperately, raking both hands through my hair. "I'll come back and never see this woman again."

"That's good, Alex." He grins his creepy yellow grin. "You're smart and deep down, you've always known your place in all this."

"Alex? What does he mean?" my mother asks.

"It's okay, I've got this." Nodding to her, hoping she backs down for her own safety. I turn back to Lennox. "What do you want me to do?" Yeah, so they have the upper hand for now, but Lennox is right about one thing, I am clever and somehow, I'll get out of this.

"You will go to your little girlfriend. You will bring her to us and sacrifice her on the next full moon."

"No! I won't!"

"Yes, you will, or mummy dearest gets it. Simple choice. Which will it be?" Lennox raises his brows in anticipation.

"Well, we don't know where she is…so good luck with that." Crossing my arms. *Ha! In your face.*

"We do," Kit says. "I had a vision a few weeks ago."

"And you never told me? Figures."

A wounded look passes over her face. "We were waiting for you to heal. It would seem you have." Her eyes wander over me, like she's sizing up a piece of meat. *She wishes!* "So, you were just acting? All this time you were just waiting for the right moment to escape. Didn't know you had it in you…you sure fooled me."

"I learnt from the best." Narrowing my eyes on hers. "If there was an academy award for acting like you cared for the last nineteen years…you'd be writing your speech." *She looks hurt. Good.*

"So, what is your decision?" Lennox sticks his hat back on.

"I'll find her." *I'll concede for now.*

"Thought so. And all for a woman you don't even know, how incredibly human of you. Sometimes it's hard to believe that you are my son."

"What?" My mother gasps. "What's he talking about, Ethan?" Rising from the stool but is pushed back down. "What do you mean? You're not his father!" Lennox laughs. I want to punch his face through to the back of his skull.

"Didn't you ever think it odd; a man matching your husband's description took the baby from the hospital? How could he have when he was with you the entire time? I discarded his face as soon as it was safe to…it made me feel cheap."

"What are you talking about?" she asks.

"We'll take mummy with us as our 'guest' until you bring the girl to us."

"What? No, you don't need to do that—"

"Insurance, son. You do your part, and all will be well."

"What's that?" Kit snatches the photo from my hand and passes it to her boss. Lennox's eyes widen, as does his smile.

"Well, well, two babies? That would explain a lot! Where is the other boy?" he demands, bending down to my mother. "Well?"

"Leave him alone!" she sobs. "You'll never find him."

"Oh, we will, you see, I always get my way." He turns to me and winks. "It's just a matter of time."

6: Summer

A week's gone by since the whole freaky gypsy saga. Nothing of relevance has happened apart from the recurring nightmares involving said gypsy, a shadow of a faceless stranger, thousands of people hurting, running toward me, reaching for me, and flames…lots of flames.

Here I am, dragged on yet another night out at our student union bar. I say dragged, but I'm not putting up much of a fight. I'm studying hard and partying even harder, wanting to fit in. Wanting to experience student life with no regrets. I don't have many memories but intend on making plenty.

"Hi, guys!" Liv heads over to our little booth which, let's face it, may as well have our names carved into it. "This is Pippa." The new girl smiles widely. Pippa's about my height and very blonde, almost too blonde. Our similarities end there, with curves and boobs so big, makes me wonder if her back aches.

"Hi, Pippa, nice to meet you." Returning a smile.

"Pip." She nods.

"Pip," I say, offering a hand across the table. The girl looks at it like she's checking for an STD before shaking it. She doesn't gawp at my burn though, so I want to like her.

"So, Pip…" Persia leans across the table between our various empty bottles and glasses. "…where did you meet our Liv?"

"Oh…," Liv steps forward. "…she has the dorm room next to mine. We just bumped into each other one morning."

"And what are you studying?" Persia leans in more knocking a bottle over just as Luke snatches it up."

"Great reflexes." Pip smiles at him.

"Yeah, thanks." *Is he blushing, really?* Getting up, he offers the new girl a space on our bench. A frown passes over Liv's face and before Pip's even got comfortable, it's gone. She scoots over to him, so close their arms are touching.

"I'm studying psychology," Pip says.

"Pretty deep." Luke being Luke chats away easily with her, like he does with everyone. I can't help but feel a pang of jealousy, which yes, makes no sense at all since we're just friends…I'm almost certain of that.

"So, where did you say you're from?" Elle pipes up from the corner.

"I didn't…have you got all night?" Pip laughs. "Sorry, didn't catch your name."

"I didn't give it." Elle stiffens.

"Sorry about miss grouchy pants over there. Elle's really not that badass once you get to know her," Liv says, and I'm cringing through a smile.

"I'm Elle." Nodding once. "Good to meet you." *Could have fooled me.*

Pip nods back turning all attention back on Luke.

"Anyone want another drink?" Persia shoots up, like she's had a wasp sting to the backside.

"You paying?" I ask.

"My round." She shrugs.

"Want me to come help carry?"

"No," Persia snaps, and everyone stops talking. "Err, no it's fine. If I need help, I'll yell."

"Okay." Dragging out the word letting her know she's walking a little too close to the 'loony line.' We give our orders and Persia strides over to the bar.

"Hey," Pip says, after almost ten minutes of chitchat, still without our drinks. "Let's have a game of truth or dare." *God, really?*

"I'm so in!" Liv shrieks. Maybe this next drink should be her last.

"Err, don't think…" I don't think this is a good idea. I can't remember any factual stuff about my past and have a feeling I'm gonna get a lot of dares. "Where's Persia got to?" I'm going to need another top up if we're about to do this. Looking over to the dimly lit bar, she's been gone ages.

"Whoa." Pip gasps. "Who is the hot hottie?"

Persia seems very close to some random, ridiculously hot guy. They're standing close together. I catch myself in a gasp, unsure if it's seeing my aloof friend with a guy or the guy himself. Something about him, his clothes, and his stance doesn't seem to quite fit in around here. That's something we already have in common…wait, what on Earth am I thinking? A guy like that would never be interested in me. Bet he's already worked his way around half the girls on campus. The very thought makes my skin tingle. He looks older, maybe just a year or two? Dressed in a leather biker jacket and ripped jeans with boots that could cause some real damage. God, I'm still staring…. *Shit. He's looking over.* Looking away, feeling my whole face flush.

"Well, that boy needs to be shown a seriously good time and I'm just the girl for the job." Pip eyes the guy like a rump steak.

"What?" Almost spitting my drink out.

"I call dibs, I did see him first." Pippa shrugs. Something about her expression is predatory. I don't argue because what would be the point? He'd never see me in 'little Miss Texas, huge boobs' shadow. And anyway, what chance does anyone have when he seems so interested in Persia? Against her, no one has a hope in hell.

"Drinks." Persia rocks up to our table holding a loaded tray. Staring past her, and to my strange delight the mystery guy is still there. Forgetting to breathe for a moment because it looks like he's staring straight at me, but it must be the dim lighting or one too many tequilas on my part. We grab our drinks and Persia takes a place next to me, blocking any view of the mysterious guy.

"So?" Liv's eyes widen. "Who's the hottie?"

"Oh, he's just an old family friend. It was odd seeing him again." Persia shoots Elle a pointed glance. There's definitely more to this story…

"Let's toast to Uni life, shall we?" Elle raises a glass and we all chink ours against it.

"So, there are no like, feelings between you two?" Pip asks Persia.

"Nope, none. That has never been an issue and can safely say will ever be." Persia swigs her drink. Now I'm even more intrigued by the hot, broody guy.

"What…is he like racist or something?" Pip folds her arms.

"What? Don't be daft!" Persia chokes a little on the drink, slamming the glass down on the table.

"Gay then?"

"Would it matter?" Persia's nostrils flare.

"No, I like a challenge…if he doesn't fancy you, maybe he'd like a little white sugar…" Pip licks her lips.

"Now who's being racist?" I mutter. If looks could kill, I'd be twelve feet under.

"What were we talking about before?" Liv says, and I'm thankful for the change in subject. The atmosphere was getting a little too intense for a casual Saturday evening. "Oh yeah, truth or dare. Persia, you in?" Liv ties her curly brown hair into a ponytail, like she's about to go into battle.

"Definitely not." Persia's nostrils are doing that flaring thing again, over what though, a game…a guy? I can't help but steal a cheeky glance now and again. There's something about him that makes me curious…

"Count me out." Elle announces. She's too serious sometimes, I want to just shake her.

"I'm in," Liv laughs. *Shocker!*

"Me too," Luke says. "Haven't played this game in years." *Funny that.*

"Awesome. Summer?" Pip smirks, daring me to chicken out. Like she knows anything about me.

"Sure, why not." Not wanting to look boring in front of the gang. Like I've said before, fitting in is on top of my 'to do' list. But what truths can I tell? I've only known myself a few months. Resigning myself to the fact that I'll be doing a lot of silly dares.

"Right, I'll start," Pip says. I wonder if she's a real blonde. Something in this girl's manner is false, but I'm not going to be the bitch and point it out. For someone new to our little group, this Pip sure has no inhibitions. Sort of envy her for that. "Okay, Luke, truth or dare?" She somehow manages to get even closer to him.

"Truth." He shrugs.

"At what age did you lose it?" Pip raises a teasing brow. I feel very uncomfortable for Luke and for myself right now, what if I get that question?

"Err..." He shoots me an awkward look. "…about fifteen."

"Fifteen?" Liv gasps.

"In my defence, that's quite late for a guy. Give me some credit, Miss Judgy."

"Okay, Liv, your turn." Luke grins widely; totally enjoying watching her squirm. "Who was your first snog?"

Liv smiles in relief and hopefully I'll get a nice question too. Saying that, I don't remember a first kiss or a first anything. This night is beginning to suck big time. At least that hot guy hasn't left yet. Maybe I'll dig a little deeper on that one.

"Richard Green, behind the science lab." Liv blushes. "I was twelve, he was fourteen."

"What a rebel." Luke laughs, and Liv smacks his arm.

"Summer, truth or dare?" Liv asks.

"And don't make it lame like Luke's 'snog' question." Pip sighs.

"Hey! I was trying to be a gentleman." He chuckles. "I was gonna ask if those were real?" He points at Pip's chest. "But thought I'd get slapped."

"You still might." Pip grins.

"Truth?" Muscles I'd forgotten about clench.

"Who was your first kiss?" Liv shrugs when everyone groans. "What? I wanna know."

"Lame." Pip rolls her heavily made up eyes and for a second, I feel like scratching them out.

"I honestly don't remember," I say, inspecting each bitten down nail.

"Wow, you must have kissed a lot of guys." Again, my nails want to go to work on Pip's smug little face when she chuckles.

"Summer has amnesia," Persia informs her. "And can't remember anything up until a few months ago."

"Shit, really?" Pip does sort of sound sincere. "God, that's awful. I'm so sorry."

"Why? It's not your fault...but thanks."

"Okay," Luke says, coming to the rescue like he so often does, whether it's needed or not. "Pip's turn. Have you ever been in love?"

"Girly or what!" Liv laughs.

"Yes." Pip's smug expression disappears. I may not remember my hometown or parents, but know a broken heart when I see one.

"And you, Liv, same question." *Awkward! Yeah, she has with you, you idiot!* Luke can be such a dumbass sometimes. Liv's face turns a bright shade of tomato before excusing herself to the bathroom. This game is getting less fun by the second.

"Truth or dare, Luke." Pip continues, "Is there anyone here that you have romantic feelings for?"

"I don't remember picking truth." Luke downs another drink.

"Maybe we should stop playing now," Elle suggests, and I almost forgot she was here.

"Boring! You weren't even playing." Pippa turns her attention back to Luke. "So? Who is it?"

"Like I'm just gonna tell you, newbie."

"Ha, so there is someone. I knew it!"

I'm just about to get up and check on Liv when she returns.

"Hey, what did I miss?" she asks, sitting down as if fleeing the scene didn't just happen.

"I was trying to find out from 'Captain Surf' here which one of you ladies he wants to get all sweaty with." Pip's brows wiggle. Liv's mouth hangs open.

"Now I need the loo. Excuse me ladies." He pushes by Pip, who checks out his butt. A part of me wonders who he might have said. If it's me, then I'm glad he kept that quiet.

I'm not being big-headed— Just get a romantic vibe off him sometimes...

"Okay, Pip." Liv rubs both hands together like an evil mastermind. "Truth or dare?"

"I'll take a dare. I'm no chicken."

"Right. Err…oh, I know, dare you to take your top off." Liv laughs.

"No problem." In one fluid motion, Pip has the top over her head, throwing it at Liv. I try not to stare at the crimson red bra and protruding cleavage. Looking around the bar, she's getting plenty of attention and at a guess, lapping it up.

Luke's eyes comically widen on returning. Pip's mighty boobs flop over the table.

"What did I miss?" Scratching his head trying not to stare. To the boy's credit, his tongue isn't hanging out.

"Okay, Summer, your turn." Liv smiles.

"Dare." I shrug and everyone 'oohs' in drunken excitement. "Well I can't do truth unless it's based on the past few months and nothing particularly interesting has happened."

"Hmm, fair enough…" Liv squints whilst searching the bar area. "Got it! The guy at the bar…"

"Which one?" Following her gaze, there must be at least twelve guys over there.

"The gothic hottie at the end, Persia's *friend*." Pip air-quotes and Persia rolls her eyes. "Go give him a big smacker on the lips."

"W-what?" I gulp.

"I don't think that's a good idea," Persia adds.

"Me neither." Pip frowns. "I called first dibs."

"I…can I have a different dare?"

"Nope." Liv crosses her arms. "Take the dare or do three shots."

"Three?" No way I could manage even one more. Feeling queasy. Maybe it's from the alcohol or maybe it's the thought of going up to a complete stranger and kissing him. I mean, what if he laughs in my face? Rising slowly from the chair; a look of shock passes from Persia to Elle to Luke and back again. "Okay, but just a peck. The guy could be a complete psycho, no offence, Persia."

"None taken." Grabbing my arm. "I advise against this." She's almost pleading. Does Persia have feelings for this mystery guy? Now I really am intrigued.

"I'll do the shots for her," Elle offers.

"Nope, you're not even playing. She has to take the dare or do the shots," Liv says.

"Thanks though, Elle. It'll be quick, promise. It's just a bit of fun." I smile at Persia and go. She's so serious all the time, even with alcohol; she always stays weirdly sober, like Elle.

I'm walking in the guy's direction. *Am I really going to do this?* There's this nagging feeling I'm about to make a total fool of myself. My heart is pounding, no, hammering against my chest. My legs feel strangely light. His back is to me. All eyes are upon me. Reaching out to touch his shoulder but can't bring myself to do it. I turn away. Liv's nodding like one of those nodding dog car ornaments, goading me on. The rest don't look so sure. Pip, from what I can make out, is giving me the mother of all evils. Maybe she peed on this guy earlier to mark her territory. *What am I doing? It's just a kiss…*

Turning as he does, we catch feet and I stumble. Surprisingly, I don't find myself in an epic face plant. He's caught my elbow to steady me. His hand is warm, sending tiny ripples of heat around my body. My skin is practically humming. He steadies me back to standing. Close-up, smelling like chopped wood, musky and intoxicating.

"Sorry," I whisper in a barely audible voice. He's silent, looking down at me with the most amazing emerald green eyes. Feeling giddy and small. I can't look away and don't want to. We stand in this awkward position for far too long. His jaw tightens, and the hand leaves my elbow. An odd look crosses his expression, before he stiffens, turning back to the bar.

"Sorry." Clearing my throat. "I'm such a klutz."

"No worries," he says over his shoulder. I notice what looks like a burn trickling down his neck, which he quickly covers with his hand.

"Err…" Tapping his shoulder. *What's come over me?* I want to keep talking to him and for my skin to hum again like it did when we touched.

He turns. "Yes?"

"This is gonna sound really pathetic. Me and some friends are playing truth or dare…"

"And what did they dare you?" he snaps. Perhaps getting annoyed with me, silly little drunk girl throwing herself at him...bet this happens to him every day of the week.

"They…they dared me to kiss you," I blurt. *Oh God, ground, swallow me up!*

"Did they now?" His voice is a mixture of amusement and disbelief. Those intense green eyes are haunting me, and my stomach flips over in a triple somersault. He leans down, head slightly tilted. *Crap, is he going to kiss me?* Holding a huge breath; I may actually be turning blue. Gasping, as his stubble brushes my ear, he whispers, "Walk away," before straightening up.

"W-what?"

"Trust me, walk away." He turns away and picks up his pint.

Barging through the doors, holding the tears in from the public humiliation. Am I that unattractive? Did this scar repulse him? Why do I even care what a stranger thinks? '*Walk away,*' God, he must think I'm some stupid little girl, a joke. I hope to never ever lay eyes on him again. The guy's a total creep…so why am I crying?

7: Alex

Every inch of my being awakens, sensing her. The anticipation of seeing Summer again screams from within. Things are well beyond screwed up. The plan is to deliver The Light to Lennox or he'll kill my mother. I hardly know the woman, but I can't stand by and let them kill an innocent. Besides, maybe one day I'd like to know her better. Do I have some amazing life saving plan? Nope. I'm just going with the flow, hoping one will jump out somewhere down the line. I'm Alex Doones, raised for this kinda shit. I'll save them both or die trying, 'cos there's no other options. Right now, Summer's somewhere on the other side of this door, and I just have to walk through it. The thought of holding her again, kissing those sweet lips, pushes me forward. I stand in the busy, dimly lit bar. We could be this, normal together, doing normal in love things. Love…a word I never found the courage to say to her…this time will be different. I'll destroy them all for her, kill every last demon on the planet if I have to.

Scanning the crowd, it's hard to figure out if she's at a table hidden away in a little alcove at the back. After driving for days, I'm so close. There's a sharp intake of air, mine, on catching her beautiful profile at a table over by the far end of the room. I'm moving, not quick enough…

"So, you came?" Persia, the angel who saved me in the cave, steps out of nowhere.

"You knew I would." Trying to sidestep around her, she matches my footwork.

"So, I'm not actually allowed to be with her?" I growl. Powerful or not, this chick is pissing me off. I'm tired of missing her, wanting to hold her, my Summer, my everything.

"I never said that." Crossing her arms, holding eye contact.

"So, what then? What's the point of giving me the choice to remember? This is bullshit." My fingers rake through my hair. "Just let me by, would ya?" Pushing past, Persia grips my arm, and shit, she's strong.

"Don't make a scene, please." Smiling, eyeing me with a cold stare.

"I'm not a fucking kid!"

"Then don't act like one. Let's get you a drink and talk a little more. You've waited this long, what's ten more minutes?" She's not asking. *A lifetime!* I want to shout but I'll humour her, for now. Leading me to the bar, the angel orders a drink and releases my arm. "What's happened since I left you?"

"Thanks for that by the way, leaving me to those arseholes." Grabbing the pint, I take a huge swig.

"I had to get Summer away, she's the priority."

"And mine," I snap.

"Your feelings are not in question." She smiles, and I relax a bit.

"Good, because I haven't put my life or my mother's in danger for a fling."

"What are you talking about?" The smile disappears.

"I found my birth mother. Lennox told me some stuff before he, you know, brainwashed me again. But you gave me a choice and I remembered all of it. I have a twin; did you know that?" I'm pointing in her face and immediately stop. We look over to Summer's table. She's laughing with some new friends. She looks happy, glowing even. My chest aches with want. "Who's the dude?"

"What?"

"The guy? He hasn't taken his greedy eyes off her." *MINE mate, all mine!* "The surf wannabe…are they…together?" *That would totally piss all over my parade.* The inside of my cheek is bleeding from all the hard chewing.

"And if they are?" Persia asks. "Don't you want her to be happy?"

"And my happiness doesn't matter? You let me choose just to end up alone? What's the soddin' point of that?"

"Do you want her to be happy?" she asks again and starts to get on my very short nerves.

"Yes. With *me*." Slamming the pint down on the bar. "Is she happy? Are they together?"

"As happy as she can be. And no, Luke is just a friend."

"Good." Relieved beyond words, picking the drink back up. We stand in a silent stare-off for a few seconds. "Can I see her now?"

"No."

"Is this a joke? Hasn't the universe had its fun with me yet?"

"Don't be so dramatic. What were you saying about your mother and a twin?"

"Yeah, so Lennox couldn't fathom out why I was such a failure. His 'witchy woo' crap didn't work on me as an embryo and all that. Turns out there's another me walking around all handsome somewhere, and from what I can gather from my birth mum, he's a real charmer. So, I'm guessing—"

"That the spell went into him and not you. He's the baby Lennox should have taken."

"You got it."

"They're going to use him as the new Light…but the ritual stone was destroyed…"

"Yeah, Kit said something about them having something even better, but she wouldn't go into detail."

"No." Persia gasps. "No, she wouldn't dare…"

"What? Who wouldn't dare what?" An icy chill runs down my spine seeing the angel looking so frightened.

"Coral knows of the old rituals…she wouldn't ever tell them…would she?"

"You gonna tell me?" I ask.

"No human can know our secrets."

"You look worried."

"I am." She glances back at Summer and I feel nauseous. She's keeping something huge from me, in order to find out, I have to play by the rules. I need their help, but I'm guessing they need me on their side too.

"So, now my mother's a hostage until I deliver Summer to them."

"But you know I can't let that happen." Grabbing my wrist.

"People are staring." Lowering my voice, nodding toward her friends. "Do you really think I'd sacrifice the girl I love? Really?" Pulling my arm out of her grip. Students standing at the bar stare at us. "Nothing to see here, the lady is fine, go about your pointless lives." I turn back to Persia who is looking at me with strange amusement. "We'll have to just work together on this one. Even though I prefer to work alone. You angels won't let my innocent old mum die, right?"

"We'll come up with something."

"Glad to hear it. Also, Lennox is hunting down my twin as we speak. Him being the new shiny toy 'n all."

"You think this twin of yours will come here?"

"Eventually. Kit'll probably track him down, now they are aware of his existence."

"We never knew of him either. He must be under a pretty powerful protection spell…" Persia waves at the bartender, who bypasses everyone else and gets her order. I wait in silence until he leaves.

"Protection spell? By who? You guys don't know about him, and I'm pretty sure Lennox doesn't…"

"You make a good point…unless…" She gasps, My skin ices over when her face transforms into a frightened mask.

"Unless?"

"Unless he has no soul. That would explain why we cannot see or feel this boy's existence. After all, he is just a product of dark magic."

"What does this mean to us?"

"He has no soul, no emotions, or feelings of guilt."

"That's not good." My frown deepens.

"Well at least we know what we're dealing with. We'll have to be even more vigilant in our protection now. We can't sense him at all, so unfortunately for Summer, we must be close by at all times." Persia exhales a deep breath.

"Agreed. So, are you gonna be a nice little angel and let me go over there?" Summer turns, my stomach tenses when her eyes find mine. It's a big room and her face is slightly in shadow, but I know she's looking at me.

"No." Persia whips me from my trance.

"No? She should have the choice too right, to know or not to? This way she's not really living."

"It will be your choice in the end." Persia's lilac eyes water, making me wonder if angels ever cry, because crying would be to feel human emotion, cause if they don't, I'm screwed. I need this one on my side. Do they see everything in black and white, right or wrong? Do they ever wander into grey?

"My choice? The kiss you mean. I just have to kiss her?"

"If that's what you decide. If it's really what you want." The barman plonks a tray of drinks down and Persia fishes around in her purse for payment. Waiting to speak until he's stopped drooling over something he could never have, and he is gone.

"You know what I want, or what's the point of any of this? I could get any girl here, pretty much, I'm never short of offers…"

"Sounds awful." Persia smirks.

"But they're not her…not Summer."

"So, you'll let her remember everything: the loss, the pain, the truth of what she is?"

"There's more to her than that and you know it. There's more to us than pain. God, she looks so at ease…" My eyes wander back to the girl sitting behind an imaginary barrier. "She looks like she belongs…I never really could."

"And why is that, Alex?"

"They made me a monster. I'll always be cursed by the life they forced on me."

"You are not a monster. You fought it and won. She could be happy without you. Have you considered that?"

"Yes, of course," I admit. "But what if she could be happier with me when her feelings are raw, real? God, why did you give me this choice? Why let me remember and not be with her?"

"I thought it was right. If you are meant to be, then you will find each other. Fate will bring you together. Are you going to trust in fate and walk away?"

"I never said that."

"You're torn."

"No shit!" Finishing the drink. "This is all new; normally I take what I want."

"So, what's stopping you?"

"You and all your head-messing…and I don't want Summer to resent me, for not letting her be normal."

"And your feelings don't matter?"

"No, not if she doesn't know me. You've confused everything."

"I was just trying to help by showing both sides."

"Well you're not helping." Looking back at the table, Summer is only a few steps… years away. "I want to go see her at least. Will you let me?"

"What for?"

"Just because." I shrug.

"No."

"No? What harm can it do? She won't know me. Let me see she's okay." Truth is, I just want to be close to her, this is torture. My fists clench in frustration. "Why the hell not?"

"If what you say is true, it's best for now to keep Summer in the dark. She can go about a normal human life and if this twin does show up, wouldn't it be better for everyone to be thinking straight?"

"You're serious?" Squeezing my eyes shut, she's right. Protecting Summer should be the priority. Opening my eyes, I'm stumped.

"You know it's the right thing to do."

"Yeah."

"So, you agree to stay in the shadows and protect our girl?"

"For now." Catching the barman's attention, needing another drink. "And if I run into her?" *Accidentally on purpose…*

"Don't," she snaps.

"But if I do?"

"Be cruel, make her dislike you. You of all people can pull that off."

"So, you want me to be an arsehole again?"

"Shouldn't require much acting on your part."

"Cheeky cow."

"Then you'll do this? Work with us whilst we figure out our next move?"

"Yes." I sigh. "But promise you'll find a way to save Summer and my birth mother."

"Promise." She pulls the tray of drinks from the bar counter. "You should leave before she sees you."

"I'll finish my drink first."

"Drink quickly. Keep me informed and…stay away."

"Bloody said I would, didn't I?" She narrows her eyes. I'm pushing my luck, but the power is mine; I could just blow everything up with one kiss and God, I so want to right now.

"I mean it, Alex."

"Yeah, yeah, I get it." *I'll leave when I'm good and ready.* Returning to the table, sitting with my girl, trying her hardest to block my view. The plan was just to find her and plant one on that beautiful mouth, never thought past that. Never dreamed I'd be resented for it, for waking her up…guess deep down I'm still a selfish dick.

I should be leaving. My head's still reeling from the conversation with Persia; reeling from the fact that the girl I'm destined to be with is only a stone's throw away. The angel makes sense, I suppose. Patience, though, has never really been something I've been good at. Can't go against Heaven's wishes, right? I can wait a little longer, take lots of cold showers in the process and try my hardest not to stalk her. I need to leave. Standing here just staring at their table, watching them have fun is painful. Turning back to the bar, willing myself to go… but my pint is not quite empty yet.

Goosebumps erupt across my arms and neck, sensing her near. I grip the bar counter for support. *Don't turn around. Don't turn around!* But I so fucking want to. Turning anyway, since when did I listen to reason? Needing to look just once. Screw Persia and the stupid rules. Our feet collide as a mass of blonde hair whizzes past my vision. Catching an elbow, pulling her to stand, she apologises. God, just hearing that voice again is the cruellest torture. Still touching her, my skin's buzzing, I force myself to let go. Turning away, feeling tortured eyes boring into my neck, I automatically hide my scar, the burn that connects us. But shouldn't I want her to connect the dots?

"I'm such a klutz." Her voice is small, pleading with me to turn around. I do. Those memorable eyes are so full of beauty; I can see the fire behind them, that secret glow that's just for me. My focus falls on those lips; they're saying something, but I don't hear. Remembering how her mouth tastes on mine. God, I should've left. She's saying something about truth or dare and I order myself out of these warm, fuzzy thoughts.

"And what did they dare you?" I ask.

"They dared me to kiss you." Her cheeks flush in that cute way they do, and I want to make her flush all over.

"Did they now?" Rubbing my stubble trying to bide time. *What the hell do I do now?* She's begging me to kiss her. Only, it wouldn't be a simple kiss. It would be the end of the easy life she knows, the beginning of what she really is…*and I made a promise.* Leaning in, not knowing fully which way I'll go until my face is a hair away from hers, chickening out when our faces touch for a moment. Bending to whisper in her ear. The familiar smell of lavender and fresh water hits my senses. Memories rise of our hot 'nearly' moments at our secret farmhouse. "Walk away." The words escape and I can't believe they're mine. I'm the biggest tool in the universe. But I've put Summer first, because I love her that much. Shouldn't I get a frigging medal? Stepping back, her eyes are wide.

"What?"

"Trust me. Walk away." Putting on a low villain voice. If only she knew how much this is killing me. Her eyes pool with water and I turn away. I've managed to hurt the girl I love with a few harsh words. Imagine the pain I'd cause by simply kissing her? She'd remember all of it. The evil in the world, how important she is to everything, to every being on the planet…the immense pressure she felt at being 'The Light.' Yes, we'd be together at last. Would she end up hating me for it? Can I really put that burden on her again just because I'm crazy about her? I need to become a shadow; I can protect my girl better by staying back. Playing a bastard will hurt both of us. I look across to Persia, nod and do what I should have already done, I leave.

8: Summer

Since the embarrassing incident at the bar, a whole week's gone by. Thankfully, no one's brought it up for a few days. Apart from Pip, that is, who thinks I'm being oversensitive about the whole thing, which she kindly told me to my face—and anyone else who would listen. *Squirm.* Guess she's going to take some getting used to, being a 'speak before thinking' kind of girl. She's also very loud, with that sexy Texan drawl.

It's been a normal week really. Classes have been good. We're comparing great classics like *The Taming of the Shrew* against *Romeo and Juliet*. In the evenings, when I'm not studying, we've checked out the local pubs in town, as I didn't want to go back to our Uni pub yet in case, *he* turned up to humiliate me some more. Persia assures me that her mystery 'friend' was just passing through, but still, I've relived that moment over and over in my head. *'Walk away'* it was so harsh, demoralising. And I can't stop thinking about the guy. Still remembering how he smelt; it was so familiar somehow…Persia says I'm being silly; bet she's never had a guy turn her down.

Nothing Creepy or gypsy-ish to report, although I could've sworn there was a little old lady standing in Persia's doorway yesterday. Guess this crazy imagination is running on overtime. I blinked, and the lady vanished. Persia thinks it's probably old memories flashing up from the trauma, the fire. Even the nightmares have eased up. Although all week I've been getting a sharp, cold chill down my neck, like when someone's watching you. When I turn around, there's nobody there. Liv thinks I'm being ultra paranoid. Luke offered to accompany me to all classes and back to the dorm every day—the look on Liv's face was priceless. Thanking him, I told him to stop indulging in this ridiculous paranoia of mine.

So here we are, another Saturday night. Pip suggested we see a movie instead of our usual haunt, which I was thankful for. Luke wanted to see a horror, but Liv and Pip wanted to see the new rom-com. Persia and Elle were too busy studying, so I sided with the girls; horror films give me the shivers.

"Sorry, Luke," I say, offering him some popcorn.

"It's fine, but next time I'm totally choosing."

Leaning in so he can hear me above the adverts, I say, "I hate scary films, they always make me jump."

"That's okay..." he says, lips almost brushing my ear, "...you can hold onto me." I laugh awkwardly and pass the popcorn over to Liv then Pip, who's sitting on the end. After about forty minutes of watching some pretty boy chasing some stupidly beautiful woman and then realising, he's in love with the ordinary looking best friend, I duck out to the toilet, scrabbling over Luke and Liv, stepping on Pip's foot as I pass.

"Sorry, I'm such a klutz," I tell her. For a moment I could've sworn Pip called me an idiot, but when I look back, she's smiling.

Walking through the foyer, all the films must be playing since there's just a few workers wiping down the counters and filling the drinks fridges. A cold chill kisses along the back of my neck. I spin around, but again there's nobody near. Scanning the foyer for any possible stalkers or ghosties, unable to shake off this creepy feeling. Quickly, I move into the ladies' room and lean against the back of the door. Anxiety spikes and my breathing becomes heavy. Both feet stumble forward as someone pushes from the other side. I'm blocking the door. Moving to open it, but there's no one there. The door pushed me...didn't it? Creeped out, I use the toilet and get out of there fast. My phone rings like a sonic boom inside the quiet foyer. Persia's name lights up, I step outside into the night air to answer.

"Hey, what's up?"

"Why aren't you watching the movie?" She sounds annoyed.

"I needed the loo. Why you even ringing if you thought I wouldn't answer?"

After a very long pause she says, "Do you need a lift?"

"Think we'll be just fine, thanks, Mum." Persia's pretty overprotective sometimes. "We'll catch the last bus, okay? And the others are here; in case the bogey man happens to be riding it."

"If you're sure?"

"Yes." I sigh.

"Where are you?"

"Outside the cinema. Why?"

"Are you alone?"

"Yes, you called me so it's your fault. I like to take calls in private."

"Well get back in there or you'll miss the end."

"It's a bit crap actually." I hear a noise to my left and freeze.

"Summer? Are you still there?"

"Yes," I say after a few seconds of scanning the car lot trying to pinpoint the sound. "Yes, sorry…thought I heard…"

"What? What did you hear?"

"Nothing, I guess. I'm off back inside. See you later." I end the call and walk to the entrance; my hand is on the door when I hear it.

"Summer, oh, Summer…"

"Luke?" He's trying to scare me knowing I hate horror films. *That little git!* There's no sign of him. Tiptoeing around the side of the building, fleeing around the back, it's pretty spooky out here, so I move fast. Striding around the other side until I'm standing about a metre behind him. His back is to me and his hood is up. Luke's so immature sometimes. I'm ready to scare the shit out of him, so he'll never try this again.

"Boo!" Springing forward, my voice echoes all about us.

"Boo." He turns. "Got ya."

Oh crap! It's not Luke! Trying to calm myself by pretending that this is just a normal, sane guy who's stepped out for a smoke. My heart is galloping telling me that it's not. His eyes are shadowed by the hood, but the wide grin is easy to see. He's a lot bigger than me, probably faster too. I need to talk my way out of this…

"Sorry…thought you were someone else." Trying hard to sound unruffled.

"I've been waiting for you…you're not quite what I expected." I gulp, his voice is so sinister. *Okay, crazy freak it is. Shit, shit, shit!* Beginning to back up, then realising it's a bad idea. Back there is even more isolated. This maniac could hide my body in the dumpster without even breaking a sweat. Maybe I can bluff my way out of this, you know, make him feel like I'm his friend…

"You were waiting for me? Sorry, do we know each other? You must be mistaking me for someone else." Stepping casually to the right, he mirrors me. "Well I'd best be getting back. My friends will be missing me." The shake in my voice gives me away.

He steps in and could easily reach out and grab me. I step back—he steps forward.

"Look, we're almost dancing." He laughs but there's no warmth in it.

"Like I said, I've really got to go."

He grabs my arm and I can't move. My pulse pumps with a heat that may burn me from the inside. Retracting the hand, he winces in pain.

"You little bitch, see what you did?" Holding the palm up. In the darkness it sort of looks like a burn mark.

"I-I didn't do anything." Seeing a chance while he's distracted, I turn to run but there's a hand on my back and my body hits the ground. My chin's sliding hard into the gravel. Managing to flip over, my entire left side screams out in pain. Think something's broken…He walks up my body and stands over me just above the hips. "Please, I don't know why you're doing this but it's not too late to stop…I never saw your face." Begging and sobbing, which makes me even more of a target. *I bet he loves the power.*

Pulling down his hood, I gasp as the moonlight catches his features; it's him, the guy from the bar!

"Please…" Covering my face with shaky hands, the guy leans down and rips them away. He's sitting on my stomach. I'm frozen in place, too scared to move. Eyes blurry from tears, body shaking with intense heat. Our faces are inches apart. His eyes aren't at all like I remembered. Something inside them has died. "Please…why me?"

"Well now you've seen my face…Light." Spit hits my cheek. *Light?* "Let's dim that light, shall we?"

"Please, you're not making any sense…"

"Oh, Summer, you are so naïve. If I cared at all, it may even pain me."

"How do you know my—"

"Get the hell away from her!" A male voice rings out into the night, and I breathe a tiny bit easier. *Thank God, someone's found me.* Tilting my head, a dark figure runs toward us.

"Please help," I whimper, and the guy is up and off me, running at my mysterious knight in shining armour.

Rolling onto my side, pain explodes., I think I've broken an arm, possibly a hip. The two dark figures throw each other over car hoods. There's lots of crashing and shouting. Whispering a silent thank you to whoever risked his life for me, I pray that he's okay.

"Summer! Oh my God!" Luke scoops me off the ground, holding me like a child in his arms. He carries me back inside and lays me on the floor as an audience gathers around us. "What the hell happened?"

"Somebody attacked me." I try to stop the ugly sobbing. The crowd gasps. Liv and Pip push their way through.

"Someone call the police and an ambulance!" Liv hollers.

"I'm okay, think I've cracked a few bones. Trying to smile, I catch Pip's eye, but she looks away.

"Everybody move!" Crowds part and Persia is by my side, checking me over like a human x-ray machine. *She got here fast...*

"Summer, what happened?" Elle kneels next to Persia.

"That guy...he…" And I'm crying again.

"He what? I'm gonna bloody kill him!" Luke marches out of the cinema. Persia gives Elle a look and Elle runs after Luke. I mean, Elle is great and everything, but as far as back up goes…well…

"He's gone." I look to Persia. "They won't find him. Some guy saved me."

"What guy?"

"I didn't see, but I hope he's okay."

"The ambulance and police will be here soon," a cinema attendant tells us.

"Everyone can go now, thank you." Persia waves everyone away. People move to the sides but continue to stare. Liv and Pip whisper close by.

"How come you're here?" I ask her.

"Your phone call worried us."

"Oh…" I have this flashback of that guy calling me a light. What the hell did that mean? "Persia, he said some really weird stuff…he knew my name."

"What else? Did you get a good look at him?"

"Persia, it was your friend."

"What friend?"

"The guy from the bar." Her hand brushes over my scraped chin I flinch in pain. I wait for her to say something, anything…

"We'll talk about this when you're all fixed up." She smiles but it never reaches her eyes. Instead, I see fear.

9: Alex

This past week's been utter torment. Can't help but feel shitty about telling the girl I love to 'walk away.' I should leave and give her a chance at normality, but that would be the biggest lie ever. Don't I owe it to us both to stay? Don't I love her enough to go? As you can see, I'm no further along with any answers. And whilst Summer's a target for the Krons and my not-so-pleasant twin, there's no choice but to hang around. The angels can protect her, but no one can do that better than me—fact.

I think she senses me sometimes—even if I'm wrong, I want to believe that's true. Sitting at the back of the lecture hall, or standing outside her window at night, I see her looking for me. I *feel* it. We have this invisible string holding us together that I cannot bear to cut. After all, if I let go now, what has been the point of any of this? We're thrown together over and over, so there must be an end game, a happily ever after? This pessimistic head of mine says I'm dreaming but I must believe the day will come when we can be together, like really together. I won't give up unless Summer does and then maybe I'll still try. I will always find her, protect her…want her.

Parking Shelly, I watch Summer and some friends disappear inside the cinema. That Luke guy is with them again, making me so bloody jealous. You could argue that it's not his fault that I can't be the guy that takes her out, the guy that laughs with her. Punching out in frustration, knuckles colliding with Shelly's rusting body. Biting down hard to keep the pain in, I'm bleeding. *Great.* Don't know my own strength sometimes…

"I'll be back." Patting the bike as a silent apology, I head into the cinema. Wandering through the almost empty foyer, damaged hand hidden in my pocket. Keeping my head down, aiming for the men's room. Catching the refection in the mirror, I look as beaten as my hand. Don't remember the last good sleep I had, and I'd kill for a shave and a hot shower. For now, though, I'll have a quick wash in the sink and hope no one walks in and calls security. Just in case, I grab a random chair from the corner and wedge it under the door handle.

The only choice is the cucumber scented hand foam, so I scrub my face with it. Whipping my top off, and going to work on two slightly festering armpits, before running some hot water through my hair and sticking my head under the hand drier. Checking back in the mirror, I'm looking more like my old self. Guess it's not our secret waterfall, but it's not too shabby for me. Placing the chair back, the door swings open and an attendant walks through. I walk out into the corridor just as a familiar blonde disappears into the ladies' room. I freeze, almost forgetting the promise. The urge to connect takes over and before I realise, my palm is against the door. All I have to do is push…my skin tingles with anticipation, sensing she's close. Pushing the door, there's resistance. *Shit, she's on the other side!* All that stands between us is a piece of wood. All fight or flight responses go into meltdown. My heart wants to stay and fight for her, my head and feet however agree as I run out of the exit, not stopping until reaching Shelly. *What the hell was I thinking? What was my ingenious plan if we had seen each other? Bloody idiot, Alex!* Right now, wishing I smoked, but I gave that up years ago. Unfortunately, Lennox caught me, making me smoke twenty in succession. God, I puked. Didn't think it was humanly possible to puke that much. At the time convincing myself it was because he loved me, in his own twisted way he cared.

'Don't you know how important you are?' he yelled. Now, years later, I realise that he never said, 'To me,' how important you are 'to me.'

A dark figure catches my attention lurking around the cinema entrance. It disappears around the side of the building. Glancing back to the doorway, a small blonde girl, my girl, exits alone. Who's protecting her? She's taking a call; I walk across the car park, drawn in by those soft mumbles. Trying not to make a sound, edging my way across the tarmac with stealth. She's shouldn't be out here alone…or maybe this is my chance to...*to what, Alex? Ruin her life?* I should leave, get on Shelly and go, but not until Summer's safe. Will I even go then? *Now what's happening?* She disappears around the side of the building. *This can't be good.* Heart thudding against my chest now she's no longer visible. Long, silent moments pass whilst I argue with myself, which is getting to be a 'thing' now. To follow or to wait? Is that dark figure still back there?

Sounds of a scuffle and something heavy falling to the ground. I'm already running. Turning the corner, the figure stands over a whimpering girl on the floor. *My effing girl*! Rage erupts. *I'm gonna tear this bastard apart!* My 'fight' button is firmly on.

"Get the hell away from her!" I rush at them. Coming at me fast, his fists connect with my gut. I'm down, winded. *Crap, this guy is strong.* I flip up to my feet. *Bet you're not as quick as me!* My fist strikes his face and I'm punching out and kicking. Each returning blow hurts. Pushing him away, his body flies across the ground. Running, standing over him, bending to give the final blow, but get distracted by Summer.

Someone's found her…that Luke guy, come to take his hero moment I bet. Need to focus…

"Ouch!" I yell, holding my nose and stumbling off the guy. He's laughing hard. Blood spurts out and I wipe it away with my jacket sleeve.

"You shouldn't have done that. Come on, let's finish this, if you dare." Beckoning him forward before taking off across the car park. Luckily, he follows, which was the plan. I'm no coward; just needed to lead him away from her. He's right behind me. I turn, grab his throat and throw him onto a car. Heading for the trees, he comes after me for more. I wait for him to catch up. We size each other up. This guy just about matches me physically; we're about the same build and height. This doesn't bother me; I've fought worse and won, being trained for this kind of shit. My fists are clenched ready. He runs at me, both of us growling like animals. We collide as I head butt his chin and we stumble back a step. A low rumble of laughter fills the surrounding trees.

"What's so funny, freak?" I spit, believing he may have loosened a tooth.

"This." Pulling his hood down. I gasp, looking upon his features—*my features!*

"Surprise." He smiles.

"You? You?"

"Me, me." Narrowing his eyes, which in the moonlight don't look at all like mine. His are dark, empty, and lifeless. His nose is slightly narrower, but apart from that this dick could be me, on a bad day, of course. Studying each other; he grins as if to say he's the superior twin. There's always a twin that's better looking, which would be me, and I'm no monster…not anymore.

"So, you're my brother…you must be Ethan," he says with distain. "He told me you'd be here."

"He?"

"Lennox—daddy dearest." He folds his arms, mirroring me.

"So, he found you. And I suppose you've come to take 'The Light?'"

"Always knew I was different." His eyes lock on mine and I see Lennox looking back at me for a creepy moment. "Special in fact, destined for greatness. They know you won't do it, so I'm here to help." He shrugs, and I almost laugh. "You're not the true vessel of 'The Light's' power, I am."

"And I've never felt so free." Glaring, wanting to kill him where he stands. But I'm not that person anymore…am I?

"I won't hurt your girl. I'll make her death quick as a favour to you, brother." And my God, I think he's being sincere, he actually believes that he's putting himself out for me. "But I will take her essence; and be the next gateway."

"You can bloody try," I snarl, fingers twitching to tear his face off.

"I like a challenge."

"Well now you've got one." Staring him down, whole body itching to rip this arsehole apart if he dares lays one finger on Summer.

"I'll do it slowly then; make you watch as she screams your name. You love her, you love that 'thing' don't you?"

"Don't talk about her. Ever!" I step forward.

"Oh, I'll do much more than that. Don't worry, I won't take her innocence; she needs that intact for the transformation to work. There are so many other things I will do to her, to that body…" My fist connects with his jaw, he staggers to keep upright. Now we're even for my nose. "Hit a nerve, did I? Maybe you should have done her when you had the chance. Ironic really that it would have probably saved her. Take the purity, no more spell… Possibly no more 'Light' but I would've risked it. Seems us sharing the same face may be of use after all since she seems to like it so much. Trust me, this bitch will be begging for death by the time I'm through." He laughs.

"Well aren't you a treat." Feeling in my back pocket for my knife, realising it was lost in the fight. *Crap!* That's fine, I'll just have to squeeze the life out of him, my hands ache to do it. The thought scares me momentarily. *Do I want to be a killer? Lose myself and never really deserve her? Could I kill my own brother? Hurt my real mother?* "You're lucky, you can walk away now, but never *ever* return. If I see you again, I'll have no choice but to take you down."

"Lennox never told me about your amazing sense of humour," he goads.

"And our mother never fully touched on what a sadistic prick you are."

"She didn't? Well I'm surprised. She never usually has anything nice to say." He leans casually against a tree.

"She loves you and you've thrown that back in her face your entire life." I turn to leave, so done with this dick.

"Yeah, she loved me so much that all she was bothered about was you, Ethan. What would you be like? Where could you be? Who took you? Were you still alive?"

I stop, looking back at him. "My name is Alex."

"Well, Alex, seems you're no better than me."

"You're soulless."

"And?" He shrugs.

"You'd let our mother die for power. I'm better than you'll ever be."

"Will you let her die for your girl? Maybe you and I aren't so different."

Unable to answer, glad when the sirens ring out in the distance. "I want to take 'The Light' and so do you, brother, our methods are just slightly different!" he shouts. *Unlike you, I won't lose.* "Goodbye for now, brother! May the best twin win!"

Speeding toward Shelly, full of anger, and a new quiet fear. *Oh, I will win, of that there is no doubt. I'm just not sure what I'm prepared to lose…*

10: *Summer*

Crying out in pain, I'm placed onto a stretcher. Persia and Elle insist they ride in the ambulance, which I'm grateful for, not wanting to be alone right now. In fact, I can't imagine wanting to be alone for the foreseeable future. Talk about knocking the wind out of my sails…I feel violated. Guess I was never an extrovert like Pip, but the part of me that's survived everything, the brave me is whimpering in a corner somewhere. Persia holds my hand as the tears spill over my cheeks.

"It's okay," she whispers, "let it all out."

There are no words. Half an hour ago some guy, Persia's 'friend', tried to…God, I think he may have…killed me. I don't understand.

"We're here, okay? We're not leaving you." Elle's smile doesn't match the concern in her eyes. She leans over, lightly skimming both palms over my damaged side.

"What are you doing?" I sniff.

"Ssshh." Her hands feel magically warm and comforting.

"Persia?"

"Elle fancies herself as a bit of a doctor." She winks.

The rest of the journey I'm strangely calm. My body is no longer screaming in pain, it's just sort of numb, like my brain.

Standing over me, his hands grip my throat. My head's shoved into the concrete repeatedly. Cold blood trickles down my forehead.

"You are The Light? You? Really? Well, you're not so special, now, are you?" He laughs and whips his hood down. That face seems familiar. Frightened and confused by this

person, yet I reach out to touch him, needing to know he's real. Stroking the side of his face as his eyes flicker between deep emerald and an empty blackness.

"Do you love me, Summer? Do you like my different faces? Do you love all the sides of me?" Hundreds of black serpents erupt out of his mouth and eye sockets...I try to scream, but there's no sound. Squeezing my eyes shut, as the snakes turn to ash before hitting my face.

"He is coming for you." A woman's voice replaces his; the old gypsy woman from the fair. "I told you. You didn't listen. Now you will burn!" She squeals, face bubbling like pink liquid soap, and I'm left alone panting wildly.

"Here, take my hand." A new voice enters. I wrench myself up to sit. There stands a girl with bright blue hair and the most genuine smile I've ever seen. I take her hand...

I don't recall falling asleep, or even feeling tired. Guess they must've given me something to calm me down. Opening my eyes, wincing at the whiteness of the room.

"There you are, sleepy head." Persia sits in the chair at my side.

"There was a girl...with blue hair...did you see?"

"Sum, you're not making any sense." She frowns.

"I'm in a hospital?" Looking around at the clean room. It's pretty sparse apart from a picture on the opposite wall of Monet's Water Lilies, which I'd love to escape into. Yeah, I can remember great works of art...but last month? Not so much.

"Yep, you sure are."

"What time is it?" I ask.

"A little after noon."

"Where's Elle?"

"Gone for coffee." Persia leans over and places a hand over mine. Looking at her slightly dishevelled hair, I'm guessing she stayed with me all night. Wriggling up the pillow, surprised that there's no pain, just a little soreness. Taking a peek under the sheets, I'm sporting a rather unflattering lemon hospital gown. My left thigh and leg are pretty banged up, covered in a pattern of black and purple blots.

"I haven't broken anything?"

"They said you were really lucky, just lots of bruising. It looks nastier than it actually is."

"Funny, I don't feel lucky."

"Summer...look, I didn't..." Persia instantly shuts up as a plump nurse walks into the room. *What—didn't know your friend was a complete psychopath? Didn't think to at least warn me? Nothing? Not even a 'Hey, Sum, my friend is totally hot, but has a tendency for a bit of murder, but only on a Tuesday...*

"And how are we feeling, Summer?" The nurse asks, taking the chart from the end of the bed.

"Fine...I guess," I lie.

"There's a policewoman outside...wants to ask you a few questions."

"No." Persia gets up.

"It's okay," I tell her. "After all, it's my call, right?"

"I'll send her in then." The nurse frowns at Persia and leaves.

Within seconds, a female officer enters. "Hello. Summer isn't it? I'm Officer Simpson, but you can call me Penny." The woman's not much older than me, probably early twenties. She has a kind face, putting me at ease. "May we speak in private?"

"It's okay," I tell her before Persia does. "She's like my sister, the closest thing I have to family. We can talk freely." I catch Persia's little smile.

"Okay." The officer nods. "Can you walk me through everything that happened last night? Take it back to the moment you arrived at the cinema. Don't leave anything out, no matter how small. Do you think you can do that?"

"Don't you think it's a little early for the third degree?" Persia states, nostrils flaring.

"Summer? I could come back later?"

"No," I say, "I'd rather do it now." Persia flops down, annoyed, but haven't a clue why. I go over everything I remember about the attack. When I'm done, Persia and the policewoman look at me with pity, making me feel like even more of a victim.

"And did you see his face?"

"Well I…" Glancing across at Persia who gives a small head shake. *What the hell is she playing at?* We both know it was her mysterious mate from the bar. *What does the guy have over her? Why would she even protect him? Would she put a psychopath before me? I have to trust she has her reasons, so I'll keep quiet…for now.* "He was hooded…it was dark, so I didn't get a proper look. Sorry."

"Oh." The officer seems disappointed, me too.

"Dark clothing, black hair…muscled. It all happened so fast. Like I said, not much."

"Okay, I'll let you get some rest. Don't hesitate to contact us should you remember anything else." Penny smiles.

"Of course."

"We wouldn't want him hurting anyone else."

"He won't," I blurt. "The guy knew my name…I think he was after me specifically."

"Really?"

"Yes, he said something about a light…it's all a bit fuzzy." And it really is. Saying it out loud sounds like some crazy, far-fetched drama. It feels like one big nightmare, but the bruises prove otherwise.

"As you can see, Officer Simpson, Summer's still a little dopey from the morphine. Maybe you should come back another time?" Persia folds her arms.

"Yes, of course. Do you really think he knew your name?" Officer Penny asks.

"To be honest, I don't know much of anything right now." Smiling over another lie. "I just want to sleep."

"Well you know where I'll be, the station on the high street." She nods.

"I'll walk you out." Persia exits with the officer. A few minutes pass, I wonder what they could be talking about. Persia enters saying something about getting me a better view.

Now feeling like I could trust Penny, but then I felt that about Persia. Convinced she's keeping something from me, something big, and I want to know what and now. I give her a hard glare.

"What?" she asks.

"You're kidding, right?"

"Can we get into this later, after you get some sleep?" She straightens out the sheets.

"Look at me!" Those lilac eyes slowly find mine; she's hiding something all right. I know guilt when I see it. It's the same look I have staring at my reflection, desperately willing myself to cry for the parents that I've lost but can't remember. I'm like a robot, an emotionless bloody robot. "Well?"

"Calm down, you'll have the nurses rushing in here." Scolding me like a child, which just fuels my anger.

"I don't care! You're keeping secrets. I know it and so do you!"

"Please, Summer, not here," she pleads, which is new.

"Then where? When? Does Elle know? Bet she'll tell me."

"I heard my name." Elle walks in looking from me to Persia, with white-blonde eyebrows raised.

"You're both lying!"

"Let's all take a breath, shall we?" Elle puts the coffee tray on the side table. Her patronising tone makes me want to just smack them both, bet they wouldn't look so pretty with a red hand mark across their faces.

"No, I won't calm down! You're protecting that guy— that monster, and I want to know why! He attacked me, knew my name…you said he was an old friend, Persia…well I'm your friend too, right? Is he your boyfriend? Does he have something over you? What? What could he possibly mean to you for you to protect him? Why me? What if he isn't stopped…what if he finishes the job next time?"

"Sum, you're overreacting…" Persia presses her lips together.

"You're joking, right?"

"I didn't mean it like that…it came out wrong." She goes to touch my hand and I pull away.

"Please, just give us a few days to sort this out." Elle looks unnaturally perplexed.

"And how are you gonna do that, eh? What are you? FBI or secret ninjas?" Sweating with anger. "What could you two possibly do that the police can't?"

"We'll get to the bottom of this…I promise." Persia grabs my shoulder, giving it a quick squeeze.

"But he knew my name…called me a Light? What's that supposed to mean…a Light?"

"Maybe he was asking if you had a light." Elle shrugs.

"And attacked me for being a non-smoker?" Laughing at that absurdity.

"You need to rest." Elle walks closer to the bed.

"Don't you tell me what I need. You weren't there…I know what happened!" She reaches out and places her palm across my forehead. "Now what are you doing?" After a few seconds her touch is soothing and welcome.

"Rest." I hear the soft voice and want to obey it. Without fighting, I close my eyes.

* * * *

Sunlight streams across my face. There's a little girl sitting on the end of the bed, wearing a white, Victorian type bonnet. She smiles.

"Hi," I say, "Are you lost?"

"Morning." My friends both chime as they enter. Elle flings open the curtains, I shield my eyes.

"Who were you talking to?" Persia asks.

"The little girl…" Pointing at the empty bed. "I swear she was just…never mind."

"I guess those drugs are still working their way out of your system." Elle sighs.

"Drugs? Where am I?" Sitting up, head pounding like a major hangover, all limbs are heavy and weak.

"You're in the hospital," Persia answers. "Don't you remember anything?"

"No…what the hell happened?"

"You had a run in with a bike." Elle sits on the end of the bed.

"I did?"

"Yep, you ran to catch the bus home after the cinema and wham!"

"God...is the cyclist okay?"

"A few cuts and bruises...he'll live." Persia smiles.

"I should apologise. How awful."

"We didn't get his name. Anyway, he's been discharged. An officer came by, do you remember?"

"Vaguely. Seems odd for a bike accident?" I say.

"Just routine, I'm sure. You're not in any trouble." Persia chuckles.

"Her name was Penny, right? Don't remember much, just that she seemed nice."

Elle shoots up and walks over to the window. "Nice view you've got of the car lot."

"Pity I can't apologise to the poor man." Disappointed, but guess there's not much I can do. "Couldn't we ask the hospital for his address?"

"They won't give out personal details," Persia says.

"Of course. How long do I have to stay in here?"

"Maybe a day or two." Elle stares out into space. "The doc says you have a bad concussion, which is probably why you can't remember the accident. They just want to keep an eye on you."

"So, I have short term memory loss on top of my long-term loss? Well aren't I thorough!" I laugh, which just holds back the tears a little longer. "Have the others been to visit, Luke and Liv?"

"Yes, and Pip. They're outside, shall I call them in?" Persia goes to open the door.

I run my fingers through my tangled hair. *Do I want Luke to see me like this? God, what am I thinking? We're just friends...Like this is crucial right now? I can be such a weirdo sometimes.*

Persia steps back into the room followed by the others and Pip, who looks sort of blank, but I'm surprised she's here at all, after all, we seem to have little in common apart from our similar taste in cool people. Even still, it's kinda nice that she came.

"Hey you." Luke swoops down for a hug.

"Careful." Wincing as he brushes against my side.

"Sorry." He steps back.

"It's fine, just that side's a bit tender." No one speaks for a few moments, which is strange. Liv clears her throat.

"So, what's the food like?" She grins. We laugh which thankfully breaks the ice.

"Did you see what happened, Luke?" I ask.

"It was so fast. Err...you were running behind us to catch the bus. When I turned around, you were on the floor entangled with some poor guy and a bike." He shrugs. "Maybe that's what that crazy gypsy meant, 'He's coming for you,' he certainly did that!"

Wish I believed that. "Liv? Pippa? Did you guys see it?"

"Same as Luke, really." Liv looks anywhere but me.

"Same," Pip agrees.

Odd...Why are they acting so weird? There's a massive elephant in this tiny room. What's going on?

"What aren't you all telling me?"

"Don't be silly," Persia says. "What could we be keeping from you?"

"You may as well tell her, she's onto us anyway..." Elle adds.

"Really?" Persia frowns.

"Yes, you got us. We're planning on taking you out on the town when you're well enough, of course." Elle smiles widely, and I'm not sure if I believe her. But then again, what else could it be?

"Oh, okay…that sounds great."

"Let's not get a bus though," Luke beams. "A taxi may be safer." Everyone sniggers, and I can't help but feel I'm not in on the joke.

11: Alex

Two weeks have gone by since the attack on my girl. Two weeks of protecting her from the shadows. Standing back means fighting every natural urge within me to just go to her. I'm fighting so many battles right now, but the most frustrating, thought-consuming battle is the one with myself. Watching her getting back into everyday life after what that *shit* did, without being able to help her…ask her how she is…is tougher than I'd ever expected. Especially when that Luke guy seems permanently attached to her side like a human crutch…at least she's not in any pain now. He doesn't need to help her move around anymore, and yet he still is. She looks comfortable on his arm. Just picturing them together laughing, whispering, being totally free…makes me want to knock the guy into the nearest brick wall. I keep reminding myself that it's not his fault, I fell for her, so why wouldn't he? He's got good taste; I'll give him that. It's not his fault that he and Summer don't have the baggage that goes with Summer and me. I know deep down; she could be happy with him if I left her alone. She could live a half-decent life, but they could never know passion like we did, and never know deep, mind-blowing love like ours. No. I can't do it. I owe it to her, to us both, to stay and see how this plays out. I'm a fighter. And when it comes to her, I'll always fight. In the meantime, if he dares to make a single move on her, his pretty face will be eating wall.

My phone vibrates against my thigh. Glancing up at her dorm room window, the one I sit beneath every night, I pull my phone from my pocket. Andie's name flashes across the screen and I smile, which lately is a rare occurrence. Who would've thought that the one person I trust most in the world right now would be her?

"Hey."

"Hey," she replies.

"What's up?"

"Nothing, why?"

"Well, it's pretty late." I squint at my watch. "It's after two a.m. Why you calling so late…or so early? Can't sleep? Want my dulcet tones to soothe you?"

"Always the charmer."

"I can hear you rolling your eyes."

"You really *do* have special powers." She sighs.

"So?"

"So, what's going on? You haven't called, like at all."

"Didn't take you for the clingy type."

"Shut up." She yawns. "You know what I mean."

"Yeah, you miss me…" The light going on above in Summer's room distracts me.

"You still there?"

"Yeah," I whisper, standing back against the building.

"So, you turn up and tell me all this crazy stuff then ride off. Did you find your mum at least? Come on, you gotta give me something!"

"You're mad with me." Stepping away from the wall to stare at Summer's silhouette against the window, I freeze. My urges are going nuts…I could easily step out and let her see me…God, I want her to see me.

"Alex!" Andie's annoyance reaches down the phone, slapping me across the face. I fall back against the wall.

"Yeah, I'm still here. And yeah, I found my birth mum."

"What's she like? How did she react? Does she look like you?"

"Pretty cool. She sort of fainted. And yeah, my amazing looks come from her side."

"So modest. What else? Are you seeing her again?"

"It's a long story."

"No fair. Where are you?"

"Just stalking the girl I love; you know, usual stuff. I'm kinky that way."

"Just tell me where you are."

"No point. Nothing to report."

"No news on that then? On Summer?"

"Things are pretty tense. Remember that long lost twin of mine?"

"Yeah?"

"Well it just so happens he's not so lost after all. No, he's actually lurking around here somewhere."

"Really? What's he like?"

"Well he's great looking…obviously."

"Oh please!" She laughs, and I envision those eyes rolling again.

"But since he attacked Summer, I'm not too sure that we're gonna bond."

"Shit, Alex, is she okay?"

"I'm fine too, thanks." I laugh. "No, she's a bit battered, but I got there before any real damage was done. Thanks to the angels who fixed her broken bones."

"It makes no sense. Why hurt her if they need her for some ritual?"

"Think he was just trying to provoke me out of hiding. It worked."

"So, you and the angels are working together?"

"Kinda have to. It was Persia's idea to lay low, guess she's right. I can protect Summer properly if she's not wrapped up in me all the time."

"You're so full of yourself. You know that?"

"Sure do, Blue."

"And how's she coping? Is she a jabbering wreck?"

"The angels wiped her memory of the attack. She's okay, for now anyway. They also wiped her friends' minds and the police woman's. Luckily, my brain's still intact, for now at least."

"Maybe they realise that having you around is a good thing?"

"Maybe. But I still don't trust them, especially Elle…I know she doesn't like me."

"You'll win her over, you won me over and I don't like anyone. That poor girl though…they should really stop messing with her head."

"Hey, I'm just going along with them until it suits me." I sigh. She's right; this entire situation is getting out of hand.

"So, you've had no interaction with her?"

"Well we did have a 'thing' a few weeks back."

"A thing? Do tell." She chuckles.

"Now who's being dirty? No, it was pretty grim. There was no choice but to be an utter shit to her. We're like magnets; always pulling toward each other. So, to put her off I was a total jerk. I'm not proud of it."

"I'm sorry, must be hard on you. So what's next?"

"Next, you get some sleep," I tell her.

"I will when *I* want to. Shouldn't you?"

"I'm doing the night watch. One of the angels will take over in a few hours."

"Okay then."

"I'll be seeing you, Blue."

"Alex?"

"Yeah?"

"Promise to call me more often. I'm going mental back here."

"I'm not promising, but I'll try. Good enough?"

"I guess…shall I?"

"Shall you what, Andie?"

"Shall I come down there…wherever you are?"

"For what?" I tense up. Guess the thought of having to watch her back too doesn't sit right with me. After all, she's the closest thing I've got to a friend right now.

"I don't know…maybe I could be of some use? Maybe if she saw me…"

"She'd remember?"

"Well, yes…"

"It doesn't work that way, remember? It has to be me that breaks the spell, me and my irresistible lips…unless you wanna kiss her and see?"

"Don't be stupid."

"Joke! Anyway, the point of staying back is to protect her from *my* people and my twin..."

"Of course, there's so many things to get my head around. It's such a mess."

"I know, tell me about it."

"Bye then."

"Go to bed," I order, ending the call.

Movement in the corner of my eye makes me stiffen. Amongst the trees there's a small figure. I can't see its eyes, but I feel them on me.

"Who's there? Show yourself or I'll bloody drag you out! I'm not bluffing."

"Maybe I'd like that."

"Kit?"

"The one and only!" She steps out from her hideout, playing with her dreads, a tell-tale sign that she's nervous.

"What're you doing here? Oh, let me guess, stalking me, right?" Folding my arms to block any sudden contact she may attempt.

"Maybe we're not so different after all?" She walks closer, I hold my hand up to stop her.

"That's far enough."

"Alex, why are you treating me like this?" She does a top job of sounding hurt.

"Whatever. What do you want, Kit? I haven't got time for your games."

"You know what I want." She looks at me with such *want*. I quickly look away.

"Why you here? To piss me off? To build up my trust and break me…again?"

"I…" She looks sad, but she's an actress and a bloody good one. "I just want to help you, little brother."

"Don't call me that…ever." I snarl. "How could you possibly help me? Aren't we on opposite sides?"

"No, I don't want to help you protect The Light." She says it like it stings her. "I want to help you do the right thing; help you take her to Lennox."

"Sorry, what?" Stepping in, closing the gap between us. *Is she for real?* "Why the hell would I ever, *ever* do that? You're deranged, you're really something else."

"Please, just listen. If I ever meant anything to you, please listen…"

"Whatever feelings I had or didn't have for you have long gone, trust me on that."

"Why do you refuse to see what's standing right in front of you?" She's moves into my personal space. I cross my arms tighter, to stop myself from hurting her.

"I see you alright. A lying, manipulative, evil…sly…"

"Okay, there's no need to go on." Her eyes pool with tears.

"Isn't there?"

"We could be together, if only you'd stop being so pigheaded!"

"If only I didn't love someone else?"

"You'd get over her. You could never really have a full life together…I'll wait. I could wipe your mind again…you could try to love me…"

"You just try it! God, you're pathetic. Have some respect for yourself. The girl I remember was always strong, independent…"

"That's the nicest thing you've said to me since…"

"Since I woke up from your spells, your lies?" I spit. My hands clench and I hold them tightly against myself.

"I'm sorry," she whispers.

"For?"

"For everything."

"If that were true, you wouldn't be a part of this anymore."

"I have no choice."

"You always have a choice, Kit. What could Lennox possibly have over you to make you do this? I mean, we're not just talking about what you've done to me. We're talking world domination!"

"I can't walk away, ever. He will kill you if I do. I couldn't bear it." Tears fall over her cheeks and for a second, I want to give her a hug and tell her that it's all going to be okay, like I used to. But I don't and it's not.

"I can take care of myself," I tell her, looking at the floor. "If you have any good left in you…leave The Krons."

"I'll never walk away from you. You and I are tied together and…and I love you." She sobs into her palms.

"Love me? Oh please, if you loved me at all you'd want me to be happy." *Isn't this what I should be telling myself over Summer? Am I wrong, selfish to want her happiness to be with me only?* She looks up, wiping her face.

"Please, Alex, just—"

"Just what? Give up on the person I love most in this crappy world so that you lot can drain the life from her? And then you and the demons can rule over every soul on the planet? Do you know how bloody ridiculous that sounds?" I'm right in her face, so I take a huge, obvious step back. Wanting to hurt her, like she has me, repeatedly. But I won't touch her…I couldn't do that.

"Just listen, will you?" she shrieks.

"No need to shout."

"Don't be childish, Alex."

"Don't bloody tell me what to do! You're not my sister or my anything to me anymore." *That should really sting. Point to me.* We stand in a silent stalemate.

"If you give her up, I'll make sure that you're spared." She finally speaks, a lot more composed now.

"Really?" I'll play along.

"Yes." She smiles. "Yes, Liam won't have to kill you…you and me…"

"God, have you heard anything I've said? There is no 'you and me,' there never will be. And Liam? My lovely twin? You really think he could take me out?" I laugh.

"Can't we just be brother and sister again? I miss you." She steps forward, and I move away.

"We never were though, were we? The thought of you makes me sick. Do you hear me now?" She nods and looks away. "So, take your shitty offer and leave me the hell alone!"

"But, Alex—"

"Did you really think I'd give her up? Give her up and choose you?"

"I hoped…"

"If you knew real love, you'd know what you're asking of me is impossible."

"I do know real love."

"I've just puked in my mouth."

"Please, Alex. That's why I'm here. For you, it's always been you. But you won't see it. You refuse to see anything but her. She'll be the death of you both."

"Are you threatening us?"

"No, just stating a fact. Liam will hurt you…kill you if he has to."

"I'm not afraid of him."

"You should be."

"He may match me in strength, but I'll always have the upper hand, I'm fighting for something I believe in. He's just fighting."

"No, Alex, he's not like you, he has a dark power within him. He's barely even human. All the spells…evil poured into him before he was even born. He has no conscience, no remorse or fear."

"And when it comes to killing him, neither will I." I shrug, trying to take in what she's saying. *Perhaps I should be a little more guarded. I'll train harder, fight tougher, and not stop until he's gone.*

"I wish we could stop all of this." Kit sighs. "I wish we were never—"

"Never what we are? That you weren't helping demons to murder the world?" I glare at her and turn to leave.

"Where are you going?"

"You made your choices, Kit, and I've made mine." I walk away.

"And I'll always choose you!" Her desperation rings loudly in my ears. *But you didn't, you didn't choose me...*

Without looking back, I silently tell her goodbye.

12: *Summer*

The dreams don't stop coming. Persia's theory is that I have underlying anxieties from everything I've been through, leaking out through my subconsciousness. The themes are almost always the same, but with changing characters. I see 'him' a lot. The broody, mean guy from the bar that night. Maybe the humiliation is running deeper than I thought. Then there's the old gypsy from the fair, whose face always ends up bubbling or melting off in some horrific way. I always wake up sweating with that image. Often there are serpents, shadows, demonic creatures with black soul-less eyes, reaching out for me. Lately, a new character's been added, a faceless girl, but I know she's a friend. She wants me to take her hand, but I can never quite reach it. And then there's the faces, thousands of people that I've never met, reaching out, calling my name, some crying out in pain…some just asking for peace.

I woke up in the early hours and couldn't get back to sleep. Most of the time was spent staring out of my window into the darkness…lately it feels like the darkness is staring right back. It's the oddest sensation and yet every night I go back to the window…they're just dreams and not supposed to make any sense. When I discussed this within our little group, everyone chipped in with their own crazy dreams, which sort of helped a little. Trying to pretend what I'm seeing is normal, that I'm normal like they are. Pippa, however, being the ever tactful one, says to watch out for any other signs that indicate I'm actually going a bit mental. *Cheers for that.* I laugh it off, fearing it may be true.

Annoyingly, I still can't recall the whole 'bike' incident. The others don't seem to want to indulge me by going over it again. Luke keeps telling me I was lucky and to leave it and move on. Let's just say I'm a lot more cautious when crossing the road now.

It's Friday, lunchtime, and I'm gazing at my untouched food.

"So, what's everyone doing tomorrow?" Pip asks. "We could use some fun around here."

"What sort of fun?" Liv asks.

"I'm in," Luke says, pushing my plate closer to me, which should annoy me, but he means well. "Eat," he mouths. Saluting him, I pick up my burger. Liv glares at me, then at Luke and her face reddens instantly when our glances meet.

"We need fun…something different, daring even," Pip tells us. "Persia? Elle? You girls are in, right?"

"Depends." Elle stares like a robot out of the window.

"What about bungee jumping?" Liv says.

"Done it." Luke shrugs. "But if you guys want to, I'll join."

I almost choke on the burger. "I'm not doing that."

"Oh, Summer, they'll be no cyclists to knock you off." Pip gives me a black look. *She won't intimidate me. No, I won't be bullied.*

"You guys go but I'm not doing that," I say, not glancing at Pip throughout the rest of lunch.

"Mountain biking?" Liv suggests.

"Really, Liv?" I can't help but laugh at her awkward expression.

"Oh God, Summer, sorry I wasn't thinking." She grimaces.

"No worries, but yeah, if I never see a bike again it'll be too soon."

"Maybe Summer should not be doing anything too physical after her injuries," Persia says.

"I'm okay now, really." Why am I digging myself into this hole when I had a clear 'get out' clause? Maybe I don't want to be left out or be the fragile one all the time. Maybe I want to start making memories…

"Rock climbing?" Luke suggests. "A friend of a friend of mine runs a club, I could ring, see if he can fit us in?"

"Hmm, I don't know." I sigh, inwardly cursing myself for once again not grabbing that 'get out' clause.

"It's safe, promise. You'll be harnessed, and I'll be your partner." Luke stares at me until it gets to the uncomfortable zone. *God, I feel hot…I hope for Liv's sake I'm not blushing.* Grabbing my water, I take a big swig. Pip mutters something under her breath, which I don't quite catch.

"We'll come." Persia speaks for both of them, which they do a lot, like they have some sort of freaky telepathic vibe thing going on. Elle nods in agreement. "But we'll just be spectators."

"You guys wouldn't want to break a nail now, would you?" Liv chuckles, and they both smile, a fake smile at that.

"Okay, so, Luke, you'll sort it?" Pip asks, and he agrees.

My forehead scrunches. Luke leans across and pats my hand, promising to take good care of me.

"Okay then." Finally giving in, my half-eaten burger remains put. I now officially have no appetite.

* * * *

My phone startles me awake. Reaching out, I knock it from the bedside table onto the carpet. An unknown number flashes on the screen.

"Hello?" I have croaky morning voice.

"Hi, Summer."

"Who is this?"

"It's me, Pip."

"Oh, hey, Pip. How did you get my number?" I suddenly feel mean for never offering it to her.

"From Liv. You don't mind, do you?" *Like she cares what I mind.*

"Too late now." I yawn. "What's up?"

"Nothing. Just making sure you're up and raring to go?"

"Go?"

"Rock climbing? Luke got us in. Cool, right?"

"Cool…" *Oh God.* Levering myself up the pillow, one palm drags over my face. "What time is it?"

"After nine, we leave at ten. So be ready." She hangs up. *Rude!*

Dazed, I aim for the bathroom. Do I really want to do this? It's not like I can get a sick note from my mum…I don't have one…how clumsy of me to forget, although forgetting seems to be my thing. Okay, now I sound bitter and sorry for myself. Persia tells me never to go down the bitter/angry path, as it'll chew me up. So, I'm dealing, that's what I tell them anyway.

After a shower and a coffee, there's a knock at my door.

"Hi." Persia looks like she's about to model a runway.

"Hey." I smile back. "Where's Elle?"

"Present." She salutes over Persia's shoulder.

"You ready for this?" Persia frowns.

"Nope…Can't I watch with you two?"

"Well you could…" Elle shrugs, "but I think the others would be disappointed. It's all booked now anyway. It's your call though."

"Is it?" I sigh.

Laughing, Persia rubs my arm. "You'll love it once you get going."

"Let's get it over with."

* * * *

"Are you going dressed like that?" Pip looks me up and down.

"Yes?" I gaze down at my baggy t-shirt and long shorts combo. "Thought we were climbing rocks?"

"Just kidding." She nudges me while inwardly I seethe. "You look great." Great if she were off clubbing maybe. She's wearing the shortest shorts that she must have cut herself, and a very low vest top. I mean, she'll be up a rock; people will be able to see a lot more of her in those very short shorts. Now I'm sounding bitchy, jealous even. I'll try to enjoy myself.

"Now then, ladies and gent." The bulky tanned instructor greets us. "My name's Rick, and my partner here is John. We are here to make sure you are safe, and everyone achieves their goals."

We stare up at the rock wall; it looks higher than I'd imagined. My neck tingles slightly, like someone is watching me again. Checking back, Persia and Elle give me their best encouraging smiles. Wishing now I'd had the balls to say no. So here I am being either very brave or very stupid.

Rick and John harness us all up tightly. I'm a little embarrassed by their closeness and the harnesses are uncomfortable in my lady areas. Wanting to moan but won't give Pip the satisfaction. Maybe I'm being too hard on her, maybe, like me, she's just trying desperately to fit in…

"Right, who's first?" Rick asks.

"Me! Me!" Pip bounces up and down like a dog in heat.

"Okay then. Who's going with this young lady?"

"Luke? Will you partner me?"

Totally flirting! Why am I letting it bother me?

"I promised Summer I'd partner her," he apologises. *Ha.* I catch the daggers Liv's throwing us and know I'm blushing uncontrollably under my safety helmet. *Awkward!*

"Liv?" Pip pouts.

"Sure…I…" Liv glances at Luke.

"I'll be right behind you," he assures her.

Instructor Rick climbs slowly at their side, leaving John to go up with Luke and me. I'm taking big breaths, preparing myself. Looking up to see their progress and yes, I was right about seeing parts of Pip that I'd rather not. *Is that a thong?* Luke looks up and quickly looks back at me with red cheeks. Yep, he saw it too.

"Okay," John beckons us forward when the others are about half way up the rock face, "next two."

I'm getting hot. My throat is suddenly bone dry.

"You alright?" Luke touches my arm.

"Yes." I tremble. "Let's get on with it."

We climb slowly upward. I'm sandwiched between instructor John and 'done it before' Luke. They've slowed down to my pace; I hope they're not annoyed. I stop to catch my breath.

"We can go back down if you want. Just let go, your harness will hold you. The ground's not far at all," Luke offers. Something inside me wants to do this. I need to live again. This is so frightening and incredibly freeing at the same time. I want to wake up from my nothingness and experience life again.

"I'm good." Grinning widely to cover my lie, pulling myself up by grabbing the jagged rock. He laughs, moving closer to my side. He and John easily talk over me like they're out for a morning stroll, whilst I'm trying to control my ugly panting. The sun streams across my back and I'm sweating in some unsightly places.

"Come on slow coaches!" Pip shouts down. Her and Liv whip up the wall like complete naturals.

"You go ahead," I tell Luke. "John will make sure I'm safe. It must be killing you; you could easily overtake them."

"No. I said I'm staying with you and I am," he huffs. I'm secretly thankful for him right now.

"We're about twenty metres up," John tells us. "Don't look down."

So, what do I do? Yep, look down. Nausea ripples across my stomach, I grab shakily to the rock.

"Told you." John laughs. "You okay to go on?"

I nod, looking up to estimate how much longer I have to endure this 'fun' experience. Shouts of encouragement come from Persia and Elle below. *I'm doing this...I'm really doing this!* I grin.

"What is it?" Luke asks.

"What?"

"You look happy. Like you're almost enjoying it?"

"In a weird way...I am." Liv and Pip scramble over the top. A rush of debris cascades toward us as Pip fights to keep her footing, kicking hard before levering herself over the edge. My eyes stream as the dust surrounds me. Grit momentarily blinds me, and I panic. Losing my grip, my feet follow. Frantically kicking out into the air like a dangling puppet.

"Summer!" Luke shouts. His strong arms are around me, pinning me back to the rock. "Stop wriggling, you're safe. I won't let you fall."

I try to stop moving, to calm myself down.

"Find a place to hold and steady yourself!" John commands. I do. Luke's heavily breathing at my side.

"Sorry."

"You okay?" the instructor asks.

I nod.

"You want to stop?" Luke whispers.

"No, I have to do this." *I need to do this to feel alive again.*

"I'll never let you fall. You know that, right?" Luke's thumb brushes my cheek.

"Yes." I'm blushing between shaking and I hope he doesn't see.

Within seconds, Luke expertly swings back to his position next to me. *He has so done this a lot more times than he lets on.*

"Just a few more feet and we'll be at the top," John shouts.

"I can do this." I follow the others and drag myself up. My arms are so heavy, and I'm exhausted but I'm no quitter. We climb, it's stupidly hard and not fun at all but as my fingertips reach the top, it's exhilarating. Luke grabs my arm, pushing me over. Thank God for him. Rolling on my back, lying breathless staring at the pale blue sky. I'm ridiculously pleased with myself, happily exhausted.

"Well that was all very dramatic." Pip stands over me with her hands on her hips.

"What happened?" Liv asks. She looks pale and I'm not sure if it's with worry for me or she didn't enjoy the 'fun' as much as she thought she would.

"Pip accidentally kicked some debris in my face, and I panicked." Coughing, sitting up as John hands me a bottle of water from his rucksack. "Thanks." I gulp it down.

"Are you insinuating that I did that on purpose?" Pip gasps.

"No, of course not." Luke helps me to my feet. "Hence the word *accidentally*," I mutter.

"Right, have a five-minute rest," John tells us.

"What, we're not done?" Liv sighs.

"We have to get down again. Unless you want to spend the night?" Rick jokes. I look over the edge. Only a tiny Persia waves up at me. *Where's Elle?*

"Getting down is so much easier than getting up," Luke whispers in my ear, making me jump a little. "I got you, okay?"

"Okay." I have a feeling he's talking about more than rock climbing. Looking back down, Elle's returned to Persia's side. I wonder where she's been?

13: Alex

Even dressed in oversized, baggy scruffs, my girl looks beautiful. I'm not happy about her soon to be hanging from a giant cliff face though. It's not something the old Summer would be up for. It's like she's trying to prove something…I mean, she never showed the slightest interest in sports, adventure and stuff, stuff I love. We did jump from a waterfall once…but she was a gibbering wreck after it. A smile forms at the memory of that day. That little bikini…how close we came to real passion…I miss her, us. Summer doesn't miss me though, and that hurts like hell.

I'm out of sight, hidden at the side of the instructor's cabin. At a guess, this is where they keep all their ropes and gadgets. I don't need to be here. This is the angel's watch. They think I'm sleeping somewhere, which is rare these days, as sleeping sort of goes with relaxing. I'm anything but relaxed. So why am I here? Simple. There's no chance of my girl putting herself in danger without me being around to protect her. Besides, I get to watch, almost be a part of her life. Without sounding like a total creep, I'll take any pathetic chance there is.

"What are you doing here?" Persia appears. I jump. Guess I'm losing my stalker edge, but then who can hide from a friggin' angel?

"Same as you."

"You shouldn't have come. We have this covered."

"Like you did at the cinema? You know me well enough to know that I ain't budging." Folding my arms, I lean against the cabin wall.

"Persia?" Elle rounds the corner, looking displeased to see me.

"Oh," she raises a thin brow, "you're here."

"Hi to you too, frosty pants." Grinning, hoping to piss them off a little bit more. Yes, I should behave; Elle's a bloody angel that, if she chooses to, could wipe my mind…again. I can't lose these memories, not now. Would we ever find each other again? I promised that I'd always find her, so I'll play by their rules…until I decide to make a move and what that move shall be. For now, I'll just have to be content with the fact I can get under their skin and that they're letting me stick around.

"I've got this, Elle," Persia snaps.

"Okay then. Get rid of him." Elle tries to stare me down before walking away.

"She's a real treat."

"Elle's just doing her job," Persia says.

"Which is what? An emotionless robot?" I pace, catching a glimpse of Summer being harnessed up. *That instructor better keep his grubby paws to himself.* My skin starts to heat…I'm sweating with frustration.

"Do you want her to see you, Alex? Is that it?" Persia guides me back to the wall.

"No…yes." Raking my fingers through my hair. "I don't know anymore."

"Please, Alex, just be invisible a little while longer."

"Are you asking or telling me?" I grunt. "For how long? Forever? Because that's how long she's going to be in danger, right? I can be more useful, closer to her. But I'll do what you say, for now."

"Thank you. This must be difficult. But you being close to our girl is too risky…"

"Yeah, yeah, I get it. Being with me is signing up for a life of crap and pain. Whatever." Kicking at the gravel sending it into orbit.

"I never said that."

"You didn't have to," I say, and we both fall silent.

"Still don't get why you even bothered to give me my memories? If you want her to be normal…she would have had that with me."

"Alex, don't. We've been through this."

"I know. Just hoping for a different answer." I shrug.

"Are you coming?" Elle is back, refusing to look at me. *Snotty cow.*

"I'll be right with you." Persia nods.

"Hurry, Summer's about to climb." She leaves, anger written all over her stupid, perfect face. Even I look average next to Elle. There's a sudden tightness in my gut. Probably anxiety over the girl I love falling from a massive height.

"Your mate doesn't like me much, does she?"

"She doesn't know you enough to have an opinion."

"That will change."

Persia narrows her alien like purple eyes; "I'll see you later. And, Alex?"

"Yeah?"

"Don't do anything stupid."

"Me? Stupid? Never. Like what?"

"Like show yourself."

"You have a very weak opinion of me, Persia." I laugh.

"I *do* know you." She smiles and leaves.

Peeking around the front of the cabin, there's a clear view of Summer and that Luke guy. They're almost half-way up. He's helping her. I bet he just loves this. He'd better keep those giant man hands to himself.

She's panicking after losing her footing and dangling off the harness, yelping. Looking across to the angels; they're not doing anything…why aren't they sodding doing anything? Summer's in trouble, that's all that matters. Not thinking, running out into the open, blowing my cover. Elle hisses something at me and I'm frozen mid-stride. My whole body's stuck on pause. I can't even blink. The only thing moving is my rapid heartbeat and shallow breath.

"Watch Summer," Elle tells Persia. "I'll deal with him this time."

Dropping like a sack of crap when Elle waves her hand, flinging me hard against the cabin. *Bloody angels and their powers…bloody control freaks…if she we're human…*

A pair of expensive heels stand at my chin. My eyes follow her body up to the pissed off expression. Guess I got under her skin then.

"What do you think you're doing?"

"Is she okay?" I ask. "Is Summer okay?" Feeling dazed and staggering to stand.

"Of course she is."

Peeking around her, seeing that Luke guy's come to the bloody rescue again and his fat hands are all over my girl. *Lucky bastard…dead bastard!*

"As you can see, she's in good hands."

"You're just loving this." I stare her down or try to.

"You didn't seriously think we'd let Summer fall, did you? She's harnessed and very safe. We checked the equipment ourselves."

"And what if she had…what if 'gorilla hands' hadn't caught her, or someone had tampered with—"

"Then we would have frozen time and caught her…don't ever forget who we are."

"Like I ever could." Now she's doing a damn fine job of getting under my skin. *Points to her.*

"What were you thinking running out like that? What could you have possibly done to help?"

"Be in her life?" Swallowing hard. This Elle chick has a point…and I'm angry at our situation. Angry with that Luke guy for being where I should rightfully be…angry at the world. Wanting to punch something but go against every impulse and clench all frustration inward. I won't give this smug cow the satisfaction of seeing me lose it. I'm not broken yet. The angels already think I'm a risk. So, for now, I'll toe their invisible line. For now, I'll try to behave.

"You are only still here because Persia wishes it."

"And why is that? Eh? Because Persia knows that I'm the real deal…that if needed I'll do what you shouldn't…I'll kill for her."

"Because Persia believes in soul mates and needs to witness true love for herself. It has to exist for her, so she can finally ascend and become an archangel." Elle rolls her eyes, and I'm not sure if it's at me or at the entire stupidity of it all.

"And you don't believe? You're an angel who doesn't get love? How would that even work?"

"I never said that. My job is to protect 'The Light' at any cost. To keep it safe."

"Safe from me? And don't ever call her an 'it' again," I growl. "Summer's the safest when she's with me." I spit, and Elle chuckles. Now my knuckles strike out, hitting the wall. *Ouch. Fuck that hurt.* "Don't laugh at me!"

"Or what, Alex? Please, you're just a human. What could you ever do?"

"I can't beat you, but don't forget who holds all the cards," *slight bluff,* "I can plant a kiss on your precious 'Light' at any moment and she'd be mine again." I grin. *Point to me.*

"You wouldn't dare!" Elle closes in, so that our noses are almost touching, but I stand firm.

"Wouldn't I?"

"Don't cross me, Alex."

"Don't cross me. You don't get it, Summer is more than an object, a doorway…she's everything."

"She's a doorway to Heaven who must be protected from everything." Elle narrows her eyes. "Even you."

"Now you just sound like a bloody manual. Come on, you must want her to be happy?"

Elle steps back and points over to the rock wall. "And she is, look."

Straining to see, my girl has made it to the top. They're laughing, cheering for each other.

"If you love her, you'll give her a real chance at this…a life without the burden of who, what she really is." Elle looks almost saddened, staring at me for some sort of answer: an answer that I simply can't give. Not now…maybe not ever.

"And if you understood human emotions, you'd know that what you're asking for is wrong." Voice dry, like a broken whisper.

"For you."

"And for her." Walking away, putting some much-needed distance between us.

"Alex!"

I stop, half turning in her direction.

"Don't cross me."

"Why? Won't I like you when you're angry?" I force a laugh.

"You really won't."

"Think Persia may have something to say about that." Shrugging, trying hard to look unruffled.

"Not if she doesn't know." She smirks and strides away. I hope to God that we haven't got another 'Coral situation' on our hands. One rogue angel is careless, two is gonna be a huge problem.

* * * *

I'm more than a little pissed off taking my nightly position under Summer's window. Those angels are starting to really screw with my head. Why give me the power of choice, when they can't decide themselves whether to keep me around? Is it a simple case of keep your friends close and your enemies even closer? I even started to trust Persia after saving me from being an instrument of the Krons. But now, even she can't make a move without checking with her snotty sidekick first. I'm shattered; haven't slept for a couple of days. I'm extra-agitated and sluggish. Sliding down the wall into a crouching position, squeezing my eyes closed in a crappy attempt to refresh them.

Laughter makes my lids flutter open and I'm not sure if I dozed off for a minute. There's a group of students walking away from campus. Two of the girls are supermodel tall, it's them. I jump up ready to follow. Silently, falling in step far behind. Spotting Summer at the front of the pack. Of course, 'he' is there, with an arm draped across her shoulders. *Mine.* Every muscle I have clenches in resentment. Excited for the day when I can finally shit all over this guy's parade.

Summer stops and looks back. I sidestep behind a tree. She senses me…I know it.

"What is it?" I hear Luke ask.

"I…I thought I heard something back there," she tells him. I want to jump out and shout—me! But resist of course, for now. The time for revelations will come. I have to time everything perfectly. The moment we kiss has to be special, uninterrupted.

They exit the grounds. I dash across the car park and jump on Shelly. Sitting for ten minutes waiting for them to board a bus. Ten minutes of watching her laughing, being young and burden-free, like she should be. Guilt rises from my gut to my chest. Can I really decide what's best for someone? This version of Summer isn't even real, right?

Trailing the bus, keeping my cap low over my face. They get off outside a row of bars and dodgy clubs. I park my wheels down an alley close by. There's a guy having a piss. He looks at me dazed, smashed out of his brains, I'd bet.

"Don't piss near this bike," I growl. He staggers away and back into some pub. Exiting the alley way, there's my girl queuing for a club called 'Reflections.' Looks cheap and seedy but what would I know? Stepping across the street, concealing myself in a shop doorway, there's a clear view from here. She's dressed differently, she looks hot as hell, but not quite like the girl I know. It's like she's trying hard to be something she's not. With me, she could always be just Summer, my English rose. It's cool though, I'll take her whatever she looks like. The short dress is sexy, but then considering our situation, sexy can be dangerous. Gulping, gazing over her half-dressed body. What I'd like to do with it…if we were ever allowed. God, I'm such a pervert. Needing to shake these feelings off and concentrate on keeping her safe. It's late summer but still, she should be wearing a coat. Okay, now I just sound like a dad. They giggle their way past the muscled bouncers and disappear into the club.

Crossing the road to join the queue. The heavy bass thumps out from the crap music inside. Not my scene, but I'll go in for her. I'll do anything for her. Anything but leave…

"Sorry, mate. Not tonight." A stereotypical meathead puts his huge hand on my shoulder.

"What? Why not?" I seethe. He doesn't scare me in the slightest, if he only knew what I'm capable of…

"No, mate. Not dressed like that."

"Really?" Staring down at my ripped jeans and biker jacket, which have both seen better days. "Look, mate, can you let it slide this one time? My girlfriend's in there," I plead.

"You heard." Another, even larger bouncer steps forward. *Two may be challenging... don't want to draw attention to myself.* "Not tonight."

"Fine." I sneer. "Whatever." I walk away or let them think that, before running to the club's exit round the back. It looks unused and covered in garbage and patches of old and fresh vomit. *Lovely.* You didn't think I'd just give up, did you? I try the door handle, which of course is locked. There's a little window leading into a kitchen area that I could squeeze through. Without a second thought, I line my arm up, turn my face away and shove an elbow hard into the glass. Waiting a few moments to be sure no one heard, but the smashing must have been drowned out by the unbearably happy music. Going in headfirst, sliding ungracefully through, my arm catches on a shard of glass. Grimacing as it punctures through my jacket. I'll patch the wound up later. For now, needing eyes on my girl. What were the angels thinking coming to a filthy dump like this? Following various small corridors before finally hitting the main room of the club. It's crowded and full of leering drunks. Any one of these tools could be one of *them* — a Kron coward, or worse, my twin. If he's anything like me at all, he'll be here. Scanning the crowd, catching a glimpse of a hot, pretty blonde moving to the beat…Summer. Where did she learn to dance like that? My body tingles in all the wrong places and then the tingles turn to ice on spotting something in the far corner. I see myself across the room, no, not me… 'Him'. Liam is here and from the way he's staring at Summer, there's no choice but to get to her first.

14: Summer

"God, I can't believe we just did that!" I laugh.

"Me neither." Liv flops onto the bed and then bounces back up when her phone rings.

"Who is it?" I mouth.

"Pip," mouthing back.

Smiling tightly, I head for the bathroom for no reason at all. Let's face it, as hard as I try to get on with Pip, we'll never be best buddies. For one, she thinks I'm after Luke and you don't have to be the brain of Britain to know that she's told Liv as much. And two, we're just so different. I hear Liv ending the call, so I pull the toilet chain for effect.

"Everything okay?" Stepping back in, trying hard to appear nonchalant.

"We're all going out tonight, clubbing." She grins.

"We are?"

"Yep. Pip's got half price vouchers for this awesome club in town." Liv begins frantically texting. After a few seconds the beeps flood back in reply.

"Well?"

"Well, the gang's all in."

"Even Persia and Elle?" Frowning, things like this sort of seem beneath them.

"Yep."

"I'm kind of tired after climbing that massive rock." Sighing, knowing the excuse isn't going to get me out of this. And why don't I want to go? Not a clue apart from the unexplained anxiety building inside me.

"So, let's celebrate that then." Grabbing my elbow. "Please...for me?"

"Oh God, don't do 'the face.'" Laughing at the desperate attempt at hopeful pouting.

"So, you're in?"

"Looks like it."

"And after your…accident the other week, it'll be good to let your hair down."

"True." Trying hard to get on the 'enthusiasm train,' but something in the way she said 'accident,' feels off.

"I'm starved. Gonna order pizza. Pip will be over soon." Liv dials without even asking what toppings I want. And that's another thing, I can't remember my favourite pizza…so any will do. So far, I'm leaning towards Hawaiian. Rummaging through the wardrobe, Liv joins me. Nothing stands out between the summer dresses and casual gear.

"What shall I wear?" Biting down on my lip.

Liv slides all the clothes across the wardrobe rail. "Hmm, it's looking a bit bleak in here. I'll go back to my dorm and bring some stuff over." Grabbing her bag, "Stop worrying. I'll be back in ten." She slams the door. Looking down at my thin body and small bust in comparison to her slightly fuller shape, doubting anything she brings will fit.

Pizza arrives and with it, Liv and Pippa. Both looking amazing in their skimpy little outfits. Pip, as usual, has gone for a more blatant sexy look with her cleavage popping out to say hello. Liv looks bohemian and cool. Long brown curls bounce effortlessly around her face, Luke might be pleasantly shocked when he sees her.

"Right." Liv shoots up after I've finished a second slice of pizza. "Look through this stuff and see if there's anything you like."

"Okay." Digging through the massive holdall, she's brought half her wardrobe at least. A lot of the clothes are just not me…too tight or too bright. "This might work," I say, pulling out a midnight blue simple mini dress, which looks just long enough to be comfortable in.

"Go put it on then." Pip speaks through a mouthful of pepperoni.

Changing in the bathroom, I feel quite good in it, surprisingly. Stepping back into the room; the girls are busy touching up their make up in the mirror.

"Well?" Pulling at the bottom of the dress, knowing it won't go down any further.

"Give us a twirl." Liv laughs.

I twirl. "Well?"

"You look hot." Liv nods.

"Yeah…she looks good." Pip sighs in the mirror, not even looking at me.

"Now your face."

"I don't usually wear much."

"Just trust me." She grins.

Closing my eyes, she applies eye shadow and blush and two coats of mascara. Then rifles through my limited make up bag for a lipstick. "Natural Rose," she reads, "this all you got?"

"Yep."

"Here." Pip slings a lipstick to Liv. "Use mine."

"Thanks." She takes the top off, revealing a scarlet red.

"Um…I'm not sure that'll suit me."

"What? Is there something wrong with my taste?" Pip glares at my reflection in the mirror. "Or you think I have some sort of mutant lip disease?"

"No, I'm just really pale…" *God, it's just lipstick!*

Liv grabs my chin, "Hold still." Coating my lips. "See how gorgeous you look?" She steps back from the mirror.

"Oh," I say.

"Oh good, or oh bad?" Liv leans over me, both of us staring at our reflections.

"Oh...it'll take a bit of getting used to, but it's cool. Thanks, Liv...thank you both." I wonder why she's helping when she could easily let me look like an old sack...if she really does believe I'm after Luke. Guess she's just kind. If only Luke could see her, like really 'see' her. I like his attention, what sane girl wouldn't? He's cute, athletic, funny... *I need to so stop over thinking this.*

"You're not seriously wearing those old Converse, are you?" Pip stares at my feet in mock horror.

"Yes. I want to still be me." *Whoever that is.* "Besides, I'm a size four, you two are at least fives?"

"Yes." Pip sighs, "We have normal-sized feet." Staring at mine. "God, they are small. If my feet were that small..."

"You'd topple over, because of your massive boobs?" Liv giggles, and I can't help but join her.

"My boobs are rather spectacular." She smiles, a real smile, and for a second it feels like we're actually bonding.

"Come on." Liv checks the time. "Said we'd meet the others outside. You ready, Sum?"

"Suppose." Biting hard on my lip again. This is normal for girls our age, going out having fun...so why are there a million butterflies dive-bombing my stomach?

"Let's roll, ladies." Pip teeters to the door in ridiculously high heels. *Bet she can't dance in them.* Smiling at the image of her doing an impression of a constipated penguin. "Liv, you look great. Luke's gonna lose it when he sees you."

"We're just friends." Liv's face flushes purple like her dress.

"Yeah, right...you hearing this, Summer?" Pip laughs, shutting the door behind us.

"If she says they're friends, we should believe it." I shrug.

"Thank you, Summer." Liv looks all shades of awkward.

We laugh and fool around, making our way across campus to catch the bus into town. I notice the disappointment on Liv's face when Luke rubs her head affectionately before raising a flirty brow at me. *Again, awkward!* The summer nights are drawing in, but it's not quite cold enough to ruin this outfit with a jacket.

"Wow, Sum, you look…" Persia shakes her head, lost for words.

"You look great," Elle intervenes. Next to them, I look passable.

"Thanks, the girls helped."

"Well they did a rockin' job." Luke eyes me in such a way that I almost feel naked.

"Thanks." Cringing. "Liv looks awesome too, right?"

"Of course! All my girls look great." He chuckles." I'm the luckiest dude on campus. Got hot women all around me…" I roll my eyes with dramatic contempt.

"Maybe you should get more guy friends?" Liv jokes.

"What? And share all of you?" Rubbing his chin thoughtfully. "Nah." Sliding his arm across Liv's shoulder and then mine as we near the campus gates. Flinching, I hear a noise and stop walking, dragging the other two back a step.

"What is it?" Luke asks.

"Thought I heard something." Turning back, eyes narrowed into the trees around us.

Persia and Elle look like two meerkats, listening out for predators. We all keep perfectly still. A warm tingle pulsates over my skin.

"Well whatever it was, it's long gone." Elle begins to walk. I look to Persia.

"Probably an owl, or squirrel." She shrugs.

Looking back, feeling a little silly, Luke pulls me forward.

"Make sure someone holds Summer's hand when we cross the road." Pip laughs. I force a half-smile.

* * * *

The queue for the club is long. The place itself looks over-glitzy and tacky with its logo 'Reflections' lit up with hundreds of tiny blue lights, most of which are out, making it read 'Relctons.' We take our places at the back and wait. Now wishing I'd brought a jacket, standing around is giving me goosebumps. I notice a girl no older than ten, standing in a passageway between two pubs. She smiles at me, I turn to tell the others, but the girl just sort of vanishes. *Weird.* I don't mention it as the queue moves forward, convincing myself it's just my imagination playing tricks, again. Shaking off a disturbing, cold shiver, I swap places with Liv and talk to Elle, whilst she talks/flirts with Luke. Without looking back, I feel Luke's eyes on me. I'm not even sure if I even like him that way…even if I did, it wouldn't be worth hurting a friend over. Liv should just man up and say how she feels…then the heat would be off me. If Luke knew how she felt, then surely, he'd back off? There's something unsaid between us. But I'm not sure it should ever be spoken…

The bouncers let us by without a second look. Before we even enter, the music pounds against my ears. Inside is just as seedy and dated as the outside.

"You want a drink?" Luke shouts over the noise. *Guess any kind of conversation is out then.*

"Get me what you're having!" He raises an eyebrow in amusement.

After what seems like forever, he returns with a tray of drinks. All the girls take a shot, leaving two pints of lager. *Great.*

"Really?" I shout in his ear.

"You said get what I'm drinking." He laughs. I take the glass and sip it. I'm gonna be so bloated…

"I love this song!" Liv yelps, pulling me onto the packed dance floor. I spill some of the pint trying to pass it to Luke.

Self-conscious at first but try to relax into the music. Pip is already gaining male attention from all around us. As the night goes on and the drinks flow, my inhibitions lessen, and it feels so incredibly good. Even Elle and Persia join us to dance. I feel alive, even more so than I did climbing today. I'm happy…free. Not wanting this night to end. I could dance forever…block it all out forever.

"I want to dance with you." A large guy with dark, empty eyes stares down at me. I shiver. It's like he just appeared out of nowhere. Leaning down; his breath hits my cheek. He looks familiar. Woozy with the alcohol and ambience, I try and stand still.

"She's with me." Luke pulls me close and I'm giggling like a schoolgirl. Suddenly Elle and Persia are either side of us and they look stupidly tall, maybe it's because I'm hunched over Luke's arms…

"Ah, come on you guys…the guy just wants to dance." Giggling, locking eyes with the guy, it feels like I'm falling down a very dark hole…like Alice in Wonderland on a bad trip.

"I said," the guy shouts over the din, "I want to dance with her!" His voice pulls me out of my stupor like an icy plunger. Gasping for air, Luke's grip tightens, as I try to fight the familiar anxiety that's snaking its way up my spine. Liv and Pip have stopped dancing and join us. Small pockets of people have noticed the heated situation.

"Just one dance." The guy's no longer asking, he steps closer. His eyes look so strange…and that face…where have I seen it before?

"She said no." Elle steps in front of me, joined by Persia, obscuring my view. I can't see the guy anymore but the cold chill across my skin tells me he's still near.

A random guy to our left strikes out at Luke. Luke lets go of my waist, whirls me behind him and punches back. Fights break out everywhere. Panicking, my breathing's rapid. I need to sober up fast. The scene's like one huge brawl on some old western movie. Even Pip and Liv are pushing people away.

"Let's get out of here!" Liv shouts over the bustle. My eyes are trying hard to stay focused on my friends, if they make a run for it, I'll do my best to stay with them. "Move!" Liv hollers. My brain and body don't seem to be in sync. I'm rooted to the spot. "Wake up!" Grabbing both arms, shaking me. *Yep, that works.*

Taking a huge breath, and instead of escaping; I head into the thick of it. Needing to get to my friends who are under attack from all sides. What's wrong with everyone? Before reaching Persia, a large arm appears around my middle, dragging me backwards.

"Get off!" Screaming, trying hard to glue both feet to the floor.

"I've got her!" A deep voice bellows over the top of my head.

"Go!" Elle shouts. *What? What's happening? Who's got me? What the hell's Elle thinking?*

"Let go!" I'm raised up off the floor and carried out through the jumbled brawlers. Trying to turn to see his face, but from this angle, a cap covers most of his features. Sobering up fast, trying to keep all wits about me…am I being kidnapped? *Shit! And they're all too busy to notice…shit, shit, shit!*

"Help!" No one notices me flaying about, manhandled out of the doors. "Help!" A palm covers my mouth and I know I'm in trouble. Pulling me down a back corridor away from my friends, away from anyone. He barges into a small cloakroom, kicking the door shut behind us.

"Let me go," Whimpering against the palm. Dragged through a full coat rail, coming to a stop when we hit the far corner. "Please?"

"Sshh!" Pulling me tighter into his chest. His heartbeat pounds against my back. We stand like this for some time, both panting from the craziness outside.

"Please!"

"Stop it!" he scolds. Biting down hard into his skin, he curses and retracts his hand. "Crap! That bleeding hurt!" Growling into my ear as his other arm tightens around my middle. My skin tingles with heat where the breath hits my neck. I'm oddly calm, considering I have no idea what this guy wants with me.

"Will you let go of me now?" I whisper. "I promise not to run."

"No, not yet."

"I haven't screamed again, have I? At least tell me what's going on?" His grip loosens slightly. I draw up my foot, stamping down hard on his.

"That could've hurt." He dares to laugh. I wish I'd worn heels now. "Okay I'll let go. But you try anything else and I'll not be pleased." Removing his arm. I spin to face him.

"You won't get away from me…you never do." The last part he whispers.

"What did you say?" Taking a step back closer to the rack of coats. Planning to dive through them and get to the door.

"Never mind. Stop trying to plot yourself out of here." Shaking his head like I'm being naughty.

"My friends will find us and then you'll be in trouble." Glaring at him, inching closer to the coats that are standing in the way of freedom.

"Look. Chill out. If I wanted to hurt you, I would have. I'm banking on your friends coming for you."

"You are?" Now I'm beyond confused. "Hang on." Stepping forward, which may be utterly stupid, but need to see this guy's eyes.

"What?"

"Take the cap off."

"Why?" Crossing his arms.

"I want to see you."

"Believe me, you don't."

I do something crazy, yet brilliant. Grabbing the cap, I fling it into the coats. He's looking down, trying to hide his face.

"Why won't you look at me? I mean, after scaring the life out of me the least you could do is look at me. Or are you a coward? Is that it?" He looks up, scowling. Guess I hit a nerve. "You?" I gasp, knowing that face. We've met before…I'm almost sure of it.

"Me?"

"I remember you…" The guy from the bar who made me cry…It's so him!

"What do you remember?" He pushes away from the wall, we're inches apart. His eyes are wide; beautiful emerald green eyes staring down at me. Like they're begging for forgiveness. My stomach flips like crazy and I'm finding it hard to swallow. What the hell's my problem? This is a hostage situation…but looking up into those eyes…it really doesn't feel like I'm in any danger…*Snap out of it!* My inner voice is screaming hysterically. I inch away. "You're the guy from the bar, Persia's 'friend,' right?"

"Oh, yeah." A flicker of disappointment crosses his expression.

"So why not save her?"

"Who?"

"Persia."

"She doesn't need saving."

"Oh, and I do? What a load of macho crap." A rush of sudden heat hits my temples. "So, are you here for her but saw me, the pathetic girl who needs saving?"

"Something like that." He moves around me, grabs the cap and places it back hiding those telling green eyes. And now he's blocking the way out of this tiny room.

"So, you and Persia?"

"Nothing like that." He laughs.

"What's so funny?" My temples are still pulsating with heat or adrenaline, who knows? He shrugs, inflaming my anger even more. "You were a total jerk to me!" Pointing a finger right in his face. "I mean, you weren't attracted to me, I get it. You embarrassed me in front of the entire bar."

"If you only knew…"

"Knew what? Who the hell are you?" His arm reaches out but retracts so fast that I'm not sure if it even happened. "And what's with asking to dance out there and being all weird about it...and come to think of it, how'd you get around the back of me so fast? What are you, some sort of a creepy magician?" As my brain starts to kick the alcohol out, nothing is making sense at all. "Then you manhandle me in here…what the hell's going on?"

"Okay, you deserve answers…there's a guy that looks like me but isn't…more like my evil twin. He asked you to dance."

"You're kidding, right?"

"No. Wish I was."

"What's so bad about him?"

"Look, I can't protect you every second…I try…you need to help yourself."

"And what does that mean?"

"Okay, stop drinking."

"What?" Spluttering an unattractive laugh. "Who do you think you are?"

"You need to be aware at all times. See what happened tonight? He almost got to you. If you ever see him, you get the hell away, okay?"

"He, this twin of yours? And what does he want with me?" I'm starting to think this guy has some sort of a personality disorder.

"Look, you can thank me later, for now we've got to get you back to campus."

"No way."

"What?" Taking the cap off, raking his fingers through his scruffy black hair, which feels weirdly familiar. "You're so bleeding stubborn. You drive me insane!"

"You're talking like you know me…how can you? Did we know each other before?" Starting to freak out, feet wanting to make a run for it, but curiosity keeps me rooted. "And I'm not going anywhere until my friends are safe." I cross my arms.

He walks forward until our toes are touching. Looking down at me, his eyes sparkle with amusement. And when he flashes a wide grin, his whole face lights up and my stomach rolls over. "It's too dangerous for you to go back in there."

"It's too dangerous to stay in here," I whisper, unable to look away from those enchanting eyes.

"I like a little danger." His face comes closer to mine before he steps back, like I'm some sort of hideous sea creature.

"So, you go." Trying to hide the humiliation. "Get the others out. Why am I so special? Why does this twin of yours want me?" Annoyingly, he ignores these questions. "You'd better give me something or next time, I will dance with him!" Yes, I'm being childish but after being forced into a cupboard and told a lot of nonsense, I deserve something, right?

"You bloody won't!" Something about the way he cares makes me dance a little inside. "Let's just say, you were never in an accident with a cyclist..."

"What? What do you mean? What happened to me?" I feel sick.

"Look, I'm not supposed to say anything."

"Who says? Why can't you? Think I'm gonna throw up." Stumbling through the coats and he keeps stride with me. Hurling my guts up in the corner, he pulls my hair away from my face. The hottest guy I've ever laid eyes on has just watched me vomit. *Classy, Summer, real classy.*

"Here." He passes me a scarf from the coat rail to wipe away the sick.

"God, I'm so sorry you had to see that." He chuckles, and the anger flares up again. "No, no I'm not. Actually, I wish I'd thrown up all over you!"

Holding his hands up. "Okay. I totally deserve that."

"Why are you still here? Thought you were gonna help my friends?" Pushing his upper arm, yet he doesn't move a muscle. The guy's solid. My skin tingles at the contact. *I haven't taken my hand away...I should take my hand away...*

His eyes close for a few seconds, like my touch is unbearable. I remove my hand.

"Right." His eyes flick open. "If you promise to stay here, I'll go back and help your mates."

"Promise. Why are you suddenly being nice? And why has Armageddon broken out in a back-alley club?" Swallowing down the old taste of pizza.

"I'm still a total bastard if that helps?" He leans over and whispers, "Don't ever forget that."

My knees go weak, like you read in romance novels, weak. His stubble brushes against my cheekbone, I think about kissing him. What's come over me? Is this the real me coming out? Or is this the last of the drink thinking? Maybe pints and I aren't a good mix after all.

Opening the door, he checks that the coast is clear. "Just stay here. You promise?" I nod. He shuts the door behind him leaving me alone. My heart is thumping into my mouth. The noise outside seems to be dying down and I wonder what's keeping them all so long…maybe they've left and are looking for me…

The door opens, and an arm slides the coats to one side. *That was quick.* A familiar voice, a familiar face…but not the one I was hoping for.

"Stay away from me! Where are my friends?" I back up and hit the wall.

"Sshh now, Summer." Black eyes staring back with a coldness that makes me shudder. "I've come for that dance." He hisses. "Now if you come quietly, I promise not to kill your little friends." His sullen, empty eyes narrow onto mine.

Grabbing my arm, sharp nails bite into my skin. We exit. Quickly, I glance back down the corridor, not making a sound in case he goes back for Persia and the others.

"And if you're looking for my rather stupid twin to come riding in to save the day…I'm afraid he's otherwise engaged." Shoving me forward out of the exit into the back alley. Four more men are waiting. Tape is slapped over my mouth and I'm plunged into darkness when a sack is placed over my head. Terrified, trying not to sob too loudly. I'm thrown into the trunk, and as the bonnet slams down overhead, I get a strong feeling that this is the end but have no idea why.

15: Alex

For the next few hours I keep my eyes trained on my twin and my girl. Will he make a move? Needing to stay focused and alert. I'm so damn tired. The repetitive beats and pulsating lights are keeping me awake but adding to the anxiety. Pulling the cap low over my eyes, I lean against the wall closest to the DJ box, closest to Summer. He's leaning against the opposite wall. Does he know I'm here? Does he sense me? Is this all just to mess with my head? Wandering around the edge of the dance floor, his soulless eyes never leaving Summer. So yeah, guess you could say I'm wound up pretty tight…points to him.

She looks like she belongs here, seems happy. Shouldn't I let her belong? Even if the threats are taken care of, can I walk away and never look back? I already know the answer. Maybe I'm not that strong. Maybe if I were a decent guy, I'd be on Shelly riding far away… guess I'm just a selfish arsehole…

I need to focus, snap out of these all-consuming thoughts. Ordering a large coke, downing it, hoping it will keep me alert. Not taking my eyes off him until turning to place the glass back on the bar. Turning back, he's vanished. *Shit!* Frantic, pushing through the crowds, heartbeat now keeping time with the pumping electric beats. I spot him making his way through the crowd. Not once looking away from the target, my girl. Pushing through the throng of gyrating bodies'… he looks to be much closer than me. This is my fault. This is all on me.

"Move!" A woman's voice inside my head, orders. *Persia?* Obeying, running into what seems to be a sudden fight outbreak. What the hell? People all around me, who

were oblivious and ignorant moments ago, are now punching out. Pushing on, elbowing and lashing out at anything that tries to stop me. Are they all under some crazy spell? Or is it much worse…are they all Krons, demon kind?

Persia gives me a quick nod before rising off the floor, forcing some of the attackers back. Seeing my chance, I grab Summer from behind.

"I've got her!" I yell across to Elle, who's throwing grown men across the room without touching them.

"Go!" She doesn't have to say it twice. I drag Summer out through the brawl, out to safety. She's feisty, kicking, thrashing against me, screaming. Just holding her again, makes my skin hum. Making herself heavy by dragging both feet along the floor. Lifting her easily, she screams out, I clamp a hand over that beautiful mouth. Feeling those soft lips against my skin, my mind tries to play happy memories that will have to wait. I'm feeling like a giant shit right now. This isn't how I wanted us to meet again. We exit the main room of the club, pulling Summer toward the back exit, but it's locked. Spying a cloakroom to the left, shoulder-barging it open. I could've kept on running with her, but if we ran now, we'd be running forever, always looking back, never being free of this cursed life. I've never been a quitter; I'll stay and fight for what's mine.

"Let me go!" Screaming against my palm. Dragging her backward through the coat rail until my back hits the wall the other side. Hate to admit it, but through lack of sleep, battling with my feisty girl has left me a little breathless. Pulling her into my chest, we both try to get our breaths back. Dipping low to smell that beautiful, sweet, familiar scent, wanting to kiss that soft neck so badly. She smells so good, she always does. The pattern of our breaths begins to steady, as we stand in silence, alone. Wanting this moment for so long, but now it's here, I have no idea what to do. All sense and reason seem to fly out the window whenever she's near. In my imagination, Summer wasn't frightened of me, she was kissing me, and I was more than willing. I need to stop thinking like this and put her needs first.

The fighting in the club has quietened down.

"Please?" she mumbles against my hand.

I tell her to stop which is rewarded with a clamp down of teeth into my skin. Tearing the hand away, cursing, she's drawn blood and I'm sort of proud that she's fighting. I need her to fight…just not with me. Tightening my arm around her, she gives me a pathetic promise that she won't run. Yeah right, I know this girl better than anyone, better than she knows herself.

A sudden heaviness streaks across my foot as she stamps down on it. Surprised, I let go. Luckily, she chose to wear trainers, which don't have much impact on heavy army boots. I can't help but laugh at the feistiness. God, I've missed her. Spinning to face me, if looks could kill… Even with her face as red as it is right now, she's still as sexy as hell. My laughter seems to aggravate her more…will I ever learn?

"You won't get away from me…you never do." *Shit, why did I say that?* My tired brain is not communicating with my mouth.

"What did you say?" Staring at me wide-eyed, edging to the coat rail, plotting a way out. There's no hope of that.

"Never mind."

"My friends will come and then you'll be in trouble."

"Look, chill okay? If I wanted to hurt you, I would've. I'm banking on your friends coming for you." Shrugging, pulling the cap down lower.

"Take that cap off," she orders, inching closer to me.

"Why?" Folding my arms, readying my defence.

"I need to see you."

"Believe me, you don't." *Hurry the hell up angels!* Trying to back up, I've run out of wall. Quicker than I can blink, the cap is flying across the room and she's looking pretty damn pleased with herself. *Point to her.*

Focusing on the floor, trying to keep hidden. If she looks into my eyes, she might see that this is killing me.

"Look at me. Or are you a coward?" I'm no effing coward. I may be a lot of things but that ain't one. Annoyed, looking up, our eyes meet. The blood from my feet feels like it's rushing up to my brain. Needing to get out of here before doing something I really shouldn't. "I know you."

She remembers! "You do?" My heart beats double time. I step forward as does she, until we're close enough to touch. Clenching every muscle, trying to restrain myself.

"You're the guy from the bar that night." She narrows those gorgeous amber eyes.

Of course, she doesn't remember us...just some piece of shit who was a jerk. I've stopped listening. Upon tuning back in she's ranting on about me and Persia being a 'thing.' *What?* I retrieve the cap and slip it back on, a bit late now, but I can play this part better if she cannot read my eyes. This girl, memory or not, has a talent for reading me like no one else ever could.

"I mean, you're not attracted to me, I get it. You made me feel crappy in front of the entire bar!"

"If you only knew." *I'm walking a thin line. Those bloody angels better get here before I cave and spill my guts or shut her up by putting my bloody tongue in her mouth.*

"Knew what?" she whispers.

Reaching out, needing to touch her, stopping myself before this goes too far. I can't afford to drop myself even further into the deep shit that is my life. More importantly, if I kiss her, she may hate me for it. This is beyond messed up right now.

She has questions of course, questions that I'm not supposed to answer. Where the hell would I even start? Oh yeah, by the way, Summer, we are in love and you're a gateway to Heaven. We can never be intimate in case you heat up and explode, and there's a race of demonic creatures trying to take you away from me…yeah, I should stay mute.

"So, what's with asking me to dance back there and then being behind me all of a sudden? What are you, some sort of creepy magician?"

There's no choice but to explain about my twin. Only divulging a bit, in hopes she'll start protecting herself. The angels' keeping her out of the loop is wrong. I'll let them answer the rest of her questions, but she needs to know of the dangers at least. Now I've crossed a line, screw it. Right now, it's talk to Summer or kiss her. Asking that she stops drinking makes her laugh. Wanting to shake her, make her understand how important it is to keeps all wits about her. Opening up about my twin just brings more questions.

"And what does this twin want with me?" she demands, which I ignore, fuelling her fire deeper.

"You're so effing stubborn." I sigh. "You drive me insane!"

"You're talking like you know me. How can you? Did we know each other before?" She bites her lip and it takes every ounce of strength not to throw her against the wall and show her how we know each other. I suggest we get back to campus, but she refuses to budge. It's so tempting to throw her over my shoulder and make her…but that would bring us unwanted attention. Plus, don't want to frighten her.

"And I'm not going anywhere until my friends are safe."

Walking forward until we're toe to toe, unable to hold back a grin for my cute, but stubborn girl.

"It's too dangerous for you to go back in there," I say, hoping she'll back down.

Instead firing off more questions about my twin, why she's so special to get his attention...

"You'd better give me something or next time I will dance with him!"

"You bloody won't!" Snarling, seeing nothing but red. Yep, that hit a nerve...another point to her. She deserves something and before engaging my brain, I say, "Let's just say, you were never in an accident with a cyclist." *Shit! Nice one idiot! What the hell's my problem? Those angels will be ultra pissed with me now...*

"What?" Her voice is high, "What do you mean? What happened then?"

I tell her I'm not supposed to say, and she turns pale, like milk-bottle pale. She runs through the coats and I follow, but instead of aiming for the door, throws her guts up in the corner. Wanting to say, 'I told you so,' about the drinking, but instead hold her hair away from her face. Guess this is real love, as the sight doesn't repel me, although the thought of kissing her isn't as appealing...

I grab a scarf from the rail, and she wipes her face and apologises, which is funny in itself, when I've sort of kidnapped her. Unable to hide my amusement, which brings that fetching red colour back to her cheeks. Those golden eyes blaze with anger. I stop chuckling.

"Why are you still here?" Nostrils flaring. "Thought you were gonna help my friends?" Pushing my arm. I close my eyes tightly, willing her to take her hand away. The smallest touch sends my pulse racing into all the wrong places. Thankfully, she removes the hand. When my eyes open, the anger is replaced by a look of bewilderment. She's right, I should go check on the others, but want to stay here indefinitely. Hidden in this tiny room, where nothing can touch us, and no evil truths can get in. I make her promise to stay here and to be honest she looks too frightened to leave. She asks why I'm being nice now and I say to still think of me as a total bastard.

Leaning close I say, "Don't ever forget that." It's just easier to stay away this way. I tell her to stay put and I'm gone.

Trying to shake the feeling of dread as I rush into the club. The fighting is over and most of the people have been herded out onto the street. There's still a few dazed and injured sprawled about the dance floor, questioning each other about what had just happened.

"Where's Summer?" Elle steps in my way.

"She's safe. I'm not a complete idiot." I huff. She raises a questioning brow. "What needs doing here?"

"It's a bit late to help now." She scoffs. "The hard part is over."

"Make your bloody mind up. You told me to get Summer out. That's my priority!" *I'd never back away from a fight!*

"And mine."

"Can't split myself in two!" I mutter some choice curse words.

"Check on her friends whilst Persia and I wipe everyone's memories of tonight." *Bossy cow.*

Walking over to two girls, the one called Liv nods at me, still in shock.

"Can you stand?" Putting both hands out, I pull her to stand. There's a few bruises to her arms and a scratch to the cheek. "Looks like you've been in a proper bitch fight." I smile. Liv attempts one back. Turning my attention to the busty blonde girl… Pip? She's sitting knees curled under her chin, sort of rocking with a wide-eyed expression.

"Are you alright?" Grabbing an elbow and pulling her up. The girl bursts into tears, and pushes two huge boobs into my chest, holding on for dear life. I take a step back, but the girl just grips tighter. I need to get back to Summer. "Are you hurt?"

"Please don't leave me." Sobbing against my shoulder.

"It's going to be okay." Carefully pushing away, trying not to be a complete insensitive arse.

"No, it won't! I'm traumatised. Please stay." Clamping herself to me again. I look around for help, but the angels are busy doing whatever angels do after a massive brawl, probably brought on by witchcraft. Suddenly, I think of Kit…no, she wouldn't…would she?

"Look, love." Peeling the girl off me. "You're strong, you'll be fine." I smile, trying to escape her clutches.

"But…but…" Grabbing my hand. "I'm scared."

"Persia!" I hiss across the room. "Look after this one. Got to get back to Summer."

"But?" The little Texan protests and Persia arrives. Pip releases my hand with a frown.

"We'll all go," Persia insists. Elle and the others, including the surfer limpet, join us; pity he didn't get his pretty face mangled. But weirdly, I'm sort of glad he was here. I lead them out to the little cloakroom and fling open the door.

"She's in here."

Elle steps in, looking over the coat rail. "She's not here." Silver eyes widen with horror that must match my own.

"Search the place!" Persia orders and everyone scampers back into the club. Summer isn't here. I feel it. Cold panic runs over my skin as I head out of the back exit into the night. A car screeches, speeding around the corner…my girl's been taken.

16: Summer

I think about death a lot lately. Cramped inside the boot of this car, I've thought of nothing else. We've been travelling for about half an hour. My limbs are non-responsive and useless. Feeling woozy, trying hard to breathe inside the sack covering my head.

Death is a strange thing but losing all memories, and my identity…it feels like I was sort of dead before, or that I've just been born. I'm about to die, with no idea why. I'm hoping it's quick and that they, whoever 'they' are, show some compassion. When I go…will there be somewhere to go to? Or will it just be blackness and I'll be nothing again, just gone? If so, what was the point? Terrified, pulse throbbing, and my mouth's so dry, it hurts to swallow. Who are these men? Why have they come after me? Did I anger them in some way before my memories went? It's hard to imagine the girl that I am now, the one I'm reinventing, doing anything to cause attention from such 'people.' Was I a bad person before? Feeling claustrophobic, gasping hard against the sack.

And what's with the whole twin thing? One looks at me like he wants to hurt me, the other looks at me like he wants to... And then there's the huge question concerning the so-called bike accident. The green-eyed twin suggested it never happened…that my friends are lying. Can't believe that. I won't. Yet, memories are patchy with so many blanks to fill…I can't stop thinking about that guy…the cute one, not the evil one. Maybe it's a coping mechanism, to focus on anything but my impending death…

Then there's the fight at the club…it was like everyone had a switch flipped and just went crazy. I'm cold and half naked in Liv's little dress. Wishing now I'd opted for jeans and a big sweatshirt. Wishing that guy hadn't left me alone earlier and that I hadn't been such a brat. Hindsight must be a wonderful thing…

Listening, there are no other cars behind us. We haven't passed one in ages. Where the hell are we going? Laughter from the kidnappers' echoes around the small space. A tear drips across my cheek and over my nose. There's no family to pay a ransom. They may torture me or do stuff that I can't even think about. Stretching Liv's dress over my knees, this is the second time tonight I've felt like puking.

My breath catches in my throat as the car comes to a sudden stop. *I can't breathe.* Heavy footsteps make their way to the rear end of the vehicle. Gasping, gulping for air when the bonnet cranks open and night's cold arms wrap themselves around me.

"Please," I whimper, against the tape covering my mouth.

"Please? Did you hear that, boys? The lady has manners." Their laughter angers me. Sweating, skin vibrating with heat. Grubby fat hands grab at me, I thrash against them like a wild animal. I won't go down without a fight.

"Ooouchh!" one man yelps. "She's bleeding boiling!"

I am?

"The bitch burnt me fingers!"

I have? What the hell's happening to me?

"Put your gloves on," a low voice orders, which I recognise as the evil twin from the club. "I told you this might happen."

Latex smacks against wrists. I'm lifted out of the trunk. It feels good to stand. Roughly, the sack is pulled away. Eyes blurring before focusing on the man in front of me. His irises are black, you could mistake them for holes and fall right through them. Before second-guessing myself, I step forward, head-butting his smug face. But my legs are wobbly from the drive. Bet my face hurts more than his.

"Ooh, aren't you a feisty one?" Grinning, rubbing his chin. "I like that in a woman…a bit of fire…guess you have that in spades." He winks, pulling the tape from my mouth and I spit at him. The small fire within now fuelled by confusion and terror. Dripping with sweat, feeling like I could erupt any moment. Am I ill with some sort of disease? Is that the reason they're trying to get rid of me? Am I contagious? A danger to others?

Two men grip an arm each, both wearing protective gloves. Trying to wriggle from their grasp but only exhausting myself further with the inhuman inferno building inside. Needing to stop and cool down before I damage myself.

"Take her to chill out," Black Eyes orders.

"You won't get away with this!" I scream.

"Think I will."

"People will come looking. The police will be—"

"Babe, may I call you babe?" He doesn't wait for an answer. "Babe..." His lips are close to my ear, but unlike his twin earlier, it doesn't send tingles, but shudders. "I'm above the law. You and your angel friends can't stop what's meant to be."

What? What's he talking about? The guys clearly lost it! Are they all on drugs? Is this a gang thing? They must have me confused with someone else.

"Please," I plead, "you have the wrong girl!"

"Do I?" Black Eyes, laughs.

We walk to a large, derelict factory in the middle of nowhere, and through a storage area. Judging by the large rusty hooks hanging from the ceiling, it was once a meat plant or abattoir of some sort. Sniffing, regretting it instantly, as my nostrils fill with the putrid smell of mouldy old carcasses.

"You and those bleeding angel freaks have had their day in charge."

"What?"

"They didn't tell you. Why am I not surprised? Throw her in the icer until she chills." I'm hurled into a narrow walk-in freezer. The door screeches as it's bolted from behind.

My fists bash against it. "Let me out! You have the wrong girl!" Yelling until I'm blue, cold and frosty in the face. Peering through the tiny window, my captors disappear down a long, dark corridor. I slide down the door onto my bottom. Yep, this dress was a big mistake. How long are they planning on leaving me here? Or is this it? No torture, no ransom, just death by fridge?

Time seems non-existent, but I've sat here long enough for all toes to go numb. What was he talking about…angels? Is he on something? He sounded unstable. Is this some sort of warlord gang? Where do I fit in?

Wrapping both arms around my knees, I rest my chin on them. Hours pass, wishing for that odd heat to come to life from deep inside me. Maybe that was a fluke, a one-time thing? Maybe I'm some sort of witch? Pointing a finger at the door, I demand it to open. Of course, nothing happens, and I'd feel pretty stupid if anyone were here to see it. I'm no witch…maybe an angel? He kept mentioning angels. This place is getting to me. I'm delirious and thinking like a paranormal novel, and I've never liked those. This is real life. This is my life.

It's getting too cold in here to stay awake, but I'm frightened that I won't wake up. Brain and eyelids are in constant battle. *What a pathetic way to die.* Eyelids win, I can't fight anymore.

He's looking down at me with such passion in those deep emerald eyes. Placing his lips over mine, we kiss tenderly. Feeling warm in his arms, happy and secure. Feelings such as these are no longer alien. Something in the pit of my stomach indicates that this is wrong. But I don't care. All I want is him, all I see, is him.

"I will always find you." He whispers, placing light kisses up my neck and around my ear. Moaning with bliss, I should feel ashamed, but don't. This person's a part of me. He's my home. More kisses trail along my collarbone, and I freeze.

"We mustn't." I say, surprising myself.

"You want me to stop?" he asks, with an uplifted brow.

Stuttering to answer, not knowing what's holding me back. All thoughts are scrambled.

"Sum, do you want us to stop?"

"I...I..."

"You...you?" He mocks.

"Please don't...I..."

"You what, babe? You're either a total prick tease or a bloody virgin who's so far out of her depth she may just drown."

A breath catches inside my throat upon looking up at him. Horrified, his emerald eyes sink into themselves like sand disappearing down an hourglass. Two black holes appear where light had just been. He grabs both arms, tight; I feel them bruising. Laughing like a pantomime villain and his face, like his eyes, crumbles and falls away. Blinking, telling myself this is a dream, but I'm not waking up. His body floats away into the breeze like dust swimming on wind.

A girl stands in his place. Her entire body glows golden with an iridescent radiance. I reach out to her. Red curls bounce around a beautiful face. I'm freezing again. Waking up, but don't want to leave. She looks so sad, so alone.

"What's happening? Where are we?" Shouting, panicking she'll disappear. Teeth chattering in a double time rhythm.

"I'm going to leave you a gift." She smiles.

"A gift?"

"Be ready for it." Dissolving, taking her warmth away. The old gypsy woman is gripping me, and it hurts like hell.

"You!" I whisper. "What do you want from me?"

"He is coming for you."

"Yes, you keep saying that…" The wrinkled face bubbles and the skin peels off its bones. The smell of singed flesh makes me gag.

Gasping for air, eyes opening remembering my predicament. Not knowing if I'm safer awake or asleep, both options scare the life out of me. My skin has a pale blue tinge to it. All limbs seem to be rusted into a cradled sitting position.

I startle when the heavy freezer door opens.

"Time to go, babe." The black-eyed twin grins down.

He's coming for you. Churns inside. If this is my last hour alive, I wish that I'd lived more…tried more things and known my parents, my past. And more than anything, wishing I'd known what love feels like, just once, I'm not greedy.

"Get her out, will you, boys?"

Two men from earlier duck under the doorway, grabbing my arms.

"Ouch!" I'm yanked upwards to stand, scared but thankful to be getting out. We march down a long corridor. The lights above short out, flickering off and on at will. The urge to scream builds inside. The urge to beg plays a close second. Guess this is the walk of death and if it is, what was the point of living? What was the point of making it out of the fire just to die like this?

Holding on to a misguided sense of hope as two more lackeys drag another prisoner towards us. The woman looks up and our eyes meet. She's older and seems broken. Wanting to reassure her. But there's nothing to say that could distinguish the hopelessness in those swollen green eyes. This person looks familiar somehow, which makes no sense at all. Turning a little, trying to get a last glimpse before she's gone from sight. *What did they do to her? Will they do the same to me?*

"Eyes forward." The creep on the left snaps. *What kind of place is this? Have I fallen prey to a kidnapping ring?*

We enter a large room with more flickering lights. At best I'll come out of this with just an awful headache…at worst, I don't come out of this. Needing to remain calm and listen to everything. This must be a mistake. After all, what could they want with a mediocre literature student?

"Take a seat." Black Eyes orders and I'm shoved down into a chair. The two men tie my hands and feet together, like I could even attempt an escape? Maybe I could kick one of them in the groin, but it would be pointless. It seems to be some sort of workroom with lots of dull silver machinery and those nasty hooks are in here too, hanging above me. Gulping, imagining myself dangling from one like a carcass, which is not a calming thought.

"Do you like the place?" Dead Eyes asks, cocking his head to one side.

"Not really," whispering, voice hoarse from the earlier screaming fit.

"Would you like a drink?" he asks. *Yeah, like I'm gonna fall for the old poison in the water classic!* "It's perfectly safe. We don't intend on killing you, just yet." He smirks, taking a sip from the glass and handing it to me.

"My hands are tied." *Jerk.*

"Open up then." I do, I'm too thirsty to be proud. Taking a few gulps before he pulls it away. "See, I'm not a monster."

"Then what are you?" I snarl.

"Babe, it's best you don't know…not yet anyway. You two may go." He waves the men away, and now it's just the two of us. I'm trying hard not to freak out.

"Do you believe in God?" He bends down, and our eyes meet. "A higher purpose? Angels?"

"Err, haven't really thought about it."

"Well I have…a lot." He stands up and I breathe a little easier. "Think about it, babe…all that power…over everything, complete control. Must be cool, right?"

I shrug. *What a complete nut job. What's any of this got to do with me?*

"You're wondering why you're here?" Placing both palms on my bare knees, I squirm, trying hard to keep a look of indifference.

"Don't touch me."

"Oh, babe." Pushing his hands up towards my thighs. I kick out with bound feet. He stops just inches from my 'area' and grins. "Isn't that what you want? Your deepest desire…to be with him, the guy with this face?"

"I…I?" I'm confused. Why not just do what he plans to instead of all these mind games?

"If you kissed these lips, you could pretend they're his."

"No idea what you're talking about." Pulse beating erratically, skin tingling with a building heat. "Stay away from me!"

"You getting all hot between the legs for me?" His laugh is like a hissing snake, which suits him. Wanting to slap hard right across his smarmy face. Lowering himself, shoving his mouth hard over mine. My lips clamp together when he tries to force his slimy tongue in. The taste is bitter, I can't even think of a similar taste.

"Shit!" He pulls away holding his mouth. "You singed my lips! You frigid bitch." Okay, there's something very wrong with me... What am I? "You've gone very pale, babe." Dabbing the water from the drink around his burnt lips.

"I'm not your babe. Why am I here?"

"You're asking the wrong questions."

"Why am I so important to you? What am I?" Knowing I'm different, I feel it. Shaking, hoping that he doesn't answer. There's something wrong with me. I feel it deep down, like a whisper always muttering somewhere inside.

"What makes you think you're not some random girl and I'm not just a crazy psycho who likes hanging people from meat hooks?"

"So, is that what you do to us?" Now I'm cold, goosebumps break out everywhere.

"Depends on my mood." He walks in slow circles around the chair. "You see, you are the key to everything. You, like me, we are very special. Together we will change life as we know it. Let me explain...you, my sexy prick tease, are a gateway to Heaven."

"What?" *Seriously, what?*

"You, my dear Summer, are just a product of your lying angelic friends."

"You're crazy! Let me out of here!" I demand, not wanting to hear anymore.

"Come on. You know you're different, right? The hot flushes…the huge laughable memory loss. Do you see them? Do they all reach for you…the dead?"

"I? What? Dead?" Afraid of what he's saying but needing to hear it. *Hold it together! Hold it together! Dead people…Gateway… People appearing and vanishing…*

"If what you're saying is true," I stutter, "what are you going to do with me?"

"Let's just say, babes, if you do believe in angels, Persia and that snotty Elle chick… start praying."

"Persia and Elle? You're lying!"

"Think about it. Two girls looking like they do…and what's with their eyes? You've honestly never questioned it?"

"I thought they wore contacts…"

"And your eyes? Gold? Are they contacts too?" Shaking his head. I feel foolish, betrayed. "Guess every time you came close to the truth; they'd just wipe your mind. That's what I'd do anyway."

"You're lying…" About to puke but swallow it back.

"And then there's the whole 'is she dangerous' issue…your abnormal temperature that reaches new heights when your emotions go nuts. That's one reason to keep you two apart, you know, in case you get it on with brother dearest and light up like a candle, taking the world with you. They, your 'friends' are protecting you, but they're also afraid of you."

"If they are angels then they'd be here, saving me."

"Ah, they would, but I have very evil friends with links to very dark spells. You're off the grid here."

Crap! "I don't believe this! You're lying!" But he's right; everything he's saying feels right.

"Yes, you do. And like I said, if you believe in them, you'd better get on your knees and start praying."

17: Alex

A swarm of colours dance before my eyes. My lungs seem to overfill with air, like a balloon, and then like a balloon they expel, deflating. The more I try to breathe, the tighter my chest becomes. Unsteady, reaching out for anything to support myself. My hand connects with a wall and my feet crash hard onto what feels like a floor.

"Why the hell did you zap us here?" I ask, looking around Summer's room.

"She's not here." Persia appears from the bathroom.

"No shit!" Raking both hands through my hair to keep myself from strangling the pair. "I could've gone after them! Why would you 'poof' us back here? And next time, could you at least warn me, that was not a fun ride."

"He has a point." Persia looks to Elle. "Why did you bring us here?"

"They would be long gone before we could do anything. We need to regroup; we need a plan." Elle gives me the mother of evils.

"So, Pip, Liv and Luke?" Persia asks, and I'm glad I'm not the only clueless one here.

"Are safe back in their rooms." Elle nods. "Minds wiped of most of the evening."

"But Summer's not! What the hell kind of plan is that? Why didn't you just poof us to where they took her?" I pace.

"Because, something or someone is blocking us, something very powerful. We can't sense Summer anymore." Persia places a hand on my shoulder to stop me pacing. "We will find her." I brush it away.

"And how do you propose we do that, eh? We have sod all to go on. You should've let me follow them."

"And you would have got yourself killed." Elle huffs.

"So? What do you care?"

"Of course we care, Alex." Persia sighs. "You are a part of Summer, whether she is aware of that or not. You are soul mates. To care for her is to care for what she wants…"

"And when she's dead…when they kill her, what's the good in saving me? At least if she had any memories, she would've stood a fighting chance. Maybe been more cautious…and what's with going out tonight, putting everyone at risk?"

"We wanted Summer to have a full life, Alex." Persia can't look at me.

"She can't have a full life without me! Without knowing her true self…that's a false life." Pacing again, "God knows what they're doing to her. If he so much as touches her, I'll fucking kill him! She'll be scared shitless…if you'd have come clean and let me tell her—"

"You are here because Persia wishes it," Elle booms, and I shut up. "You and Summer are some sort of freak happening, that no one can explain, or will admit to. So, for now we ask that you do what we say until the time comes when, if, she is ready to take on her true self."

"And who will decide that?"

"We hope Summer will." Persia glances my way and I want to trust her, not Elle, but her.

"Well, let's hope she gets the chance to choose…if my delightful twin hasn't got to the Krons and sacrificed her already…"

"Tonight, is not a full moon. The next is in three days." Elle talks to Persia like I'm not even here. *She can pretend all she wants. I'm here and I'll always find my girl, made a promise to.*

"What if he's not waiting for the Krons, what if the intension is to be the Light himself? What if he just kills Summer to hurt me?" Walking to the door, Elle blocks the way.

"Where are you going?"

"Searching the streets is better than this."

"No. I told you to stay put until we come up with a plan."

"What if you contact your sister?" Persia asks. "Kit?"

"Haven't seen here for a while…don't even think she'd respond. What if she's in on this? Maybe Kit's the power that's blocking you. Maybe I can persuade her to drop the blocking spell…she will for me." Cringing wondering what will be expected in return.

"No, this sister could lead you into a trap." Elle points a finger in my face.

"What do you care?" Squaring up to her. The door handle turns behind us. I gasp when Summer walks in. Looking cold and dirty. Dress torn, and her blonde hair is matted with mud.

"Hi," is all she says. My heartbeat is almost leaping from my chest. Frozen to the spot, not knowing if I can go to her.

"Thank God you're alright!" Persia throws her arms around Summer. Our gazes meet, and my skin tingles. Unable to look away, wanting to take her far away from all this and cradle her forever. Safe from Krons, witches…guys named Liam and Luke…

"Where have you been?" Elle demands.

"I thought he'd taken you." I move closer, but she steps behind Persia. Of course, this version of Summer doesn't remember the real me, just some guy who trapped her in a cloakroom. *Well that's about to change…*

"It's okay," Persia says, "Alex is helping us."

"What happened?" Elle asks again.

"I don't know…I woke up in a ditch at the side of a motorway and hitched a lift back here." *Seeming way too calm; maybe it's the shock…*

"That is strange." Elle paces the small room.

"Thank God you're safe." Persia takes another hug, which is fine but as soon the chance arises, I'm kissing her. The time is right, and I can't protect her, not like this.

"Can we have a few minutes alone?" Summer nods my way and my stomach does a huge flip of excitement. I'm gonna kiss the crap out of those lips…

"Okay…we'll be just outside this door." Elle's silver eyes narrow on mine like she knows what I'm thinking. Finally, we're alone, standing too far apart, neither of us speaking.

"Look," she says, breaking the silence, "I know who you are, and want to thank you for looking out for me."

"You know me?" Stepping forward. She holds a hand up signalling me to stop.

"What's wrong?"

"You are."

"What?"

"Please, just listen."

"Go on." I nod.

"I'm not interested in who…what I used to be. I don't want to go back to that life, not now, not ever." The light seems to have vanished from those gorgeous amber eyes.

"Is this a joke? Who told you about this? What did that prick do to you?" Approaching but she grabs the door handle.

"I'll let the angels back in."

"Don't," I say, "I'm listening."

"I don't want to remember you, us. As I understand it, we were in a dark, cursed love." Summer looks at the floor.

"Look at me." I demand. If she's about to stamp all over my heart she could at least look me in the eyes. Slowly, looking up meeting my gaze. "We were in love, are, in love…to me it was never a curse."

"I'm told that I'm special, some sort of key to Heaven?"

"A gateway."

"Yes, and if kissing you brings that all back, then we can never be together. I don't want to spend the rest of this life miserable, always chasing what we can never have."

"We were never miserable. We had each other and that was enough." Panicking, sensing her slipping away, from us. "For me, anyway."

"Was it? Not really. I'm just getting used to this version of me. I'm happy and when you leave this room, the angels will wipe all memories of you." She turns the handle, I reach above her head, slamming the door shut. We're face to face I should just lean in and do it.

"Don't," she whispers, our mouths inches apart. It takes every bit of strength there is to tear myself away.

"Don't wipe me away." I think about begging, but I've never seen her quite so cold, so removed from any real feelings.

"I'm sorry, Alex."

"Don't do this." Grabbing an elbow ready to just do it; she couldn't do a thing to stop me…

"If you do love me, you won't force this." Turning away.

Knowing she could despise me forever…I remove my hand from the door.

"I do…and won't ever force you." Sighing, fighting tears I won't show. "Maybe I'll get them to wipe my mind too." I say the words, but don't believe them.

"You should. I'm moving on, maybe we both should."

"I'll go then…" Wanting her to stop me but does the opposite and moves away from the door. Those tears are pushing now. I walk out, without looking back. The angels shout after me as I pass in a state of shock. I exit the building and run until hitting an empty park. Letting out a guttural wail, shouting, emptying out all despair and anger. And I cry. I'm not ashamed to say it. Crying is a rarity; haven't cried since killing my first deer. I waited till Lennox fell asleep. Before that, I fell from a tree when I was about five and broke an arm. I cried, sobbed, and was ordered to 'man up.' The tears now are for the girl I've loved over and over and lost. Summer's the reason for everything that's happened in this crappy life and now everything's pointless.

The rage comes, a crazy energy that has me kicking the crap out of a couple of trees and a bench. A litterbin finds the end of my boot as it hurtles through the air. Can't remember ever being this angry, this frustrated. Armies of demons have ruled my life, stolen any scrap of childhood, but rejection from the one person I love most in this bitter world is unbearable.

After a while, calmer, devoid and tired of emotion, I head back to the usual spot under Summer's window. I have issues with letting go, and before taking off, I need to know my girl is safe. Even though her mind will be wiped by now and will never think of us again, I will think about her every day, nothing but her. I'll never give up hope. Sweet memories may be the one thing keeping me from going back to being that monster I was. So, for now, I'll be a shadow, a watcher in the dark, until it becomes too hard to watch anymore.

* * * *

Feet shuffling nearby brings me out of the indulgent moping. I see Summer, scurrying over to the main building. I must have dozed off as the sun's up. Too tired to notice which moments are dream and which are reality. That nightmare last night was real enough. She wants me gone, yet still, here I am following, stalking. It's six in the morning…is she meeting someone? A guy? Bet it's that tosser Luke…I may break his pretty face yet. It won't help, but I'll feel so much better.

Quietly, entering the foyer, following as she passes the lecture hall and heads into a girl's toilet. This is weird. Why not just use her own bathroom? I wait for ages for her to emerge. The door swings open, *finally!* Ducking behind a snack machine to watch, but the feisty blonde Texan comes out instead. Something's off. Waiting for the clip-clopping of Pip's heels to disappear, before walking over to the toilets. I push the door open.

"Err, hello?" Sounding like a total creeper. "Is anyone in here?" There's no response. I check all the stalls; nope, no one's here. Summer was here; my tracking skills aren't that off. Opening the small window at the end of the room, I look outside. Would someone even fit through this? There's no sign of life outside and why on earth go out this way anyway? Unless she has something to hide? Did she come here to meet Pip? Did they argue? Pip was in a rush to get away. So, what were they doing here so early? Unless…unless…Oh shit! Think…I know…and if I'm right, my girl's still very much in danger.

18: Summer

I'm manhandled into a large, long room filled with cages. It smells like rotting meat. I wonder if livestock would be kept here or if the cages are a new addition to keep people in? For now, relieved I'm still alive and unhurt, well physically anyway. The larger of the two meatheads unlocks the nearest cage, pushes my head down and throws me inside, scrambling to the back of the cage. He clips the padlock in place.

"Please…"

"Shut your stupid mouth." The fatter man whistles when they exit. Crawling to the front of the cage, my face leans against the wire. All the other cages seem to be empty. *I am so screwed.*

"Hello?" a weak voice calls from a cage at the opposite end of the room. "Is someone there?"

"Yes! Yes, I'm here! Are you alright?" I ask, praying that this isn't another trick of the imagination or a spirit coming to pass through me, I can't even begin to get my head around that yet. I can just make out half of a face; it's the older woman from before.

"Who are you? Are you real?"

"Sshh! Quiet. They're always nearby, listening." The woman whispers just loud enough to hear. "Of course I'm real, wish I wasn't here though."

"Who are they?" Copying her tone, "What do they want from us?"

"I don't know why you're here. But my sons are somehow connected to all this…guess I'm insurance."

"Did they hurt you?"

"They've starved me and kept me locked up for what seems like forever…but I'm okay."

"Is there any chance of your sons rescuing you?"

"The leader, the one with the lifeless eyes…he *is* my son."

"Oh." *Oh shit!* "And he's doing this to his own mother?" *What hope is there?* "What about your other son?" I ask, connecting the dots. Thinking of him brings a sense of distorted hope.

"It's a long story."

"Looks like we have time." Sighing, straining my neck to see this new ally.

"Well, it's all still a shock. I'm hoping to wake up and this just be some horrid nightmare. It started almost twenty years ago. I gave birth to twin boys. Ethan was strong and healthy; Liam was sickly and needed extra care. I only popped out for a few moments to visit Liam in the special care unit, when I returned Ethan, my beautiful little boy, was gone."

"Oh God…I'm so sorry." This poor woman, I can't even begin to imagine that kind of pain.

"I never got over it and Liam, the one who brought you here, has become a bitter, twisted and very sick individual. He's the bad twin, the kind you read about in horror stories…and it's all my fault." She sobs.

"No! This is not on you. This is all Liam. He made these choices."

"He's evil and as a mother I should never say that about one of my own, but he's not the child I gave birth to. I tried, despite everything, to love him. Seeing what he's capable of…the pure hate in his eyes, don't know if I can ever forgive him."

"You're only human." Trying to say something that's not completely inane but fail. "What about your other son?"

"Yes, Ethan." Her voice is full of pride. "He found me, just a few months ago, but so did they…he has some sort of task to perform and that's why they took me. He doesn't call himself Ethan anymore he goes by Alex. They look very alike, apart from their eyes. Alex has my green eyes…"

"We've met briefly." A sense of calm flutters like tiny butterflies inside, at the memory of Alex pressed up against me. I should have stayed with him. Doubt I'd have ended up here.

"He's the one I lost, but it seems I've lost them both now."

If it were possible to reach across and hold her hand I would. "Please, you mustn't blame yourself. This Alex came back, right? So, he obviously holds no grudges. He's a good person…you'd be proud of him." *Yes, I haven't spent a lot of time with him, but feel right about this.*

"Thank you," she whispers. "Liam hates me, but I think deep down, he hates himself more."

"That's not the impression I got."

"It's the only explanation…for all the bad he's doing."

"Sshhh, someone's coming." We both scramble to the back of our cages and wait. Heavy feet march into the room, and I pray that it's not time to die.

"Hello girl." A thin, sinewy, old guy takes off his hat and stares down at me.

"Who are you?" Voice shaking.

"I'm Lennox, the real boss here."

"What do you intend on doing with us?"

"You and I have done this dance so many times now."

"We have? I don't—"

"Don't remember?" He grins a crooked grin. "Why would you, child, when your so-called friends do nothing but lie to you?"

"You don't know my friends!" Straightening as high as the low-bearing cage allows, stooping over with my forehead pressed against the bars.

"They couldn't even be bothered to tell you your true purpose."

"So, I am some gateway?" *Say no… say no!*

"Yes, you are. You should feel humbled to be sacrificed for such a huge honour. You and I will soon change the entire planet. Isn't that amazing?"

"I don't want to be a part of any of this. I just want to go home."

"You don't have a home, unless you count Heaven, and I will try hard to send you back there."

"Why is she here?" Nodding further down the cages. "Why hurt a helpless woman? She can't harm you…or is she a gateway too?"

Laughter followed by a patronising shake of his head, grates on every nerve.

"No, she's here to make sure her son did his job in bringing you to us. But it seems his feelings for you have swayed him again, so he hasn't much time left to come and attempt to save you both. Still, it will be interesting to make the fool watch. If the poor boy ruled with his head and not his heart, then mother dearest would be tucked up safely in bed right now. If he had kissed you, you at least would have known what you're capable of. The boy's either stupid or selfless, I can't decide which."

"What?"

"Never mind. Two nights from now, we will drain your light and rule everything and everyone."

"You're crazy."

"Yes, I am." Walking away, he chuckles. *I really don't like him.*

"Are you okay?" The woman's nose is back at the farthest cage door.

"For now."

"What was all that about?"

"That man and your son believe that I'm some special light, a gateway to Heaven. And by draining me they can take the power and, if I'm right, rule the world with it. Something about your son, the good one and a kiss…nothing makes sense."

"I'm Ruth by the way."

"Summer. Unless we come up with a plan and soon, looks like we're in deep trouble."

"Does anyone know you're missing?"

"Yes, but I don't think they'll find me. We seem to be in the middle of nowhere." *Maybe it's time to start praying.*

"Hopefully the police are searching for me, but it's been a long time…they should have found this place by now."

"We'll get through this together." Needing her to stay positive, even if I'm not.

"Okay."

"Okay."

"Summer?"

"Yes?"

"I'm glad you're here…that didn't sound right, I just meant…"

"It's okay, I'm glad you're here too." I smile. Then there's just silence. After a while, I think she's fallen asleep. Sitting back against the cage to rest a cheek on my knees. Thoughts rage. *If they drain me, will I go to Heaven? What happened to my life before all this? Are they looking for me? Will he come for me?*

* * * *

There are no windows here, but it feels late. I'm too frightened to sleep, preferring to be awake if they come back. There are too many unanswered questions. My mind keeps focusing on Alex. How can they look so similar but be so very different? And this 'kiss' business...if we kiss, I'm guessing I'll get all the answers. Whose stupid idea was that? Mine? The angels? Why didn't he just do it when he had me in that cloakroom? He could've, would I have stopped it? Do I want that old life back or would it be easier to just forget? Am I real, human? God, I need to get out of here, away from these people. Both of us must get out. If Elle and Persia are in fact angels, then why aren't they here fighting for me? These thoughts are interrupted by the door creaking open. Torchlight invades my face. *Crap. They've come for me.* They continue walking to the last cage...*shit...Ruth!* They drag her out kicking and screaming.

"Leave her alone!" Yelling against the bars.

"Save yourself," She calls out passing my cage.

I try to say something comforting, that I won't leave her, but my mouth just hangs open.

"Take me instead!" The door closes behind them. I can still hear her putting up a pointless fight. Will I ever see Ruth again? I'm frightened for her, for me. A feeling like molten lava rushes over my skin. Repeatedly, I bang on the cage door. The wire changes from rusty silver to red as it begins to melt. *Am I doing this?* Liam enters with the two men from earlier, his empty eyes widen as he too witnesses the freakish scene. The door is melting at my touch. What the hell am I?

"Take this one back to the icer!" There's a touch of fear in his voice.

The door is unlocked. Rubber gloved hands grab my arms, yanking me out.

"You, little girl, need to chill out." His eyes narrow on my lips and I step back.

"Don't worry. I'm not going to kiss you, not after last time. Do I look stupid?"

I decide it's best not answer.

"And we wouldn't want you falling for the wrong brother now, would we? Although I got the looks and the brains…"

His henchmen laugh, indulging his twisted ego.

"What've you done with Ruth?" I demand, skin still singing with heat.

"She's just having a few mug shots done to send on to brother dearest."

"Why?"

"Because he'll come for her, for you."

"You have me. Let the poor woman go and be with her real son." Sweating profusely, actually wanting to go in that big freezer.

"Ouch, that almost hurt my feelings, Summer." He pouts. "I'll kill all three of you pathetic losers and be done with this. Can't be worrying that your love limpet will turn up trying to scupper our plans of world domination."

"You sound like a bad movie."

"And you look like you're about to combust." He winks. "Tell you what, as I'm in a great mood, when Alex, Ethan or whatever the hell he's calling himself these days gets here, I'll let you have your kiss."

"Why?"

"So you can die knowing how real love feels and that you've lost it again, forever."

"You sick bastard!"

"And you, little gateway, are as good as dead. I'm going to enjoy cracking you open; bet you taste so good."

"You sicko!" Feeling like I'm going to pass out from my own body heat.

"So feisty! I like it. Take Summer to cool down before she erupts."

I'm thankful to be thrown into the icer. It felt like my insides were melting; still, I seem to be going back to a normal 'me' temperature. Don't know what I'm capable of, but it seems to be brought on by emotions.

My skin is back to its milky-white tone and now I'm freezing. The tears come; I sob myself into a tired mess.

"Wake up. It's time for your gift." A tall beautiful figure stands over me. A face haunted by sadness. Bright red curls bounce on an invisible wind as she holds out her hand.

"Summer, you must wake up."

"I am awake," I say.

"No! You're in trouble!"

My eyes open. The door to the ice prison is ajar. *Is this my gift?* Walking my palms up the wall to lift myself, every single bone is tired and stiff. Leaning over, pushing the door a little, I stick my head out. Stepping out, there seems to be no one about…which doesn't add up. *If I'm this all-important light thingy, then why is nobody on guard?* From here I can see the exit, which is also open. *Is this some sort of sick game and they'll be waiting on the other side to jump me?*

"Move," a woman's voice whispers in my mind.

Tiptoeing across the dank space. Pushing the door, there are open fields waiting to greet me. Running, I don't look back. It must be early morning as the sun is starting to rise.

My feet carry me through the fields of wheat, arms pushing their long stems away. Some catch my legs and I'm itchy but too scared to stop. There's a back road ahead, bringing instant relief, even though they may have realised I've escaped by now, I can try to keep to the trees and follow the road without detection. Goosebumps prickle across the back of my neck as if someone's watching. Guilty feelings rise remembering Ruth's desperate face. I stop, wanting to go back for her. *What could I do? If I get caught, then we both die... I should go back...*

That voice is back inside my mind, "Move!" she yells, and I do, like a coward, leaving Ruth behind. If I can get back to the others, if they really are angels, then surely, they can help? Alex's sad eyes flash in my thoughts...the kiss that never happened goads me as I venture forward. *Do I want it? Do we belong together?* My heart races and I'm not sure it's from the running or imagining different kissing scenarios. I need to get back from the middle of nowhere probably hours from campus. But I'm determined; whatever happens after this, our first job is to save Ruth.

19: Alex

"Kit? Where the hell are you? Call me back." I've lost count of how many times I've hit redial this past hour. Kit's playing a large part in this; it reeks of her.

Kit's the reason for the blocking spell and if I'm right, she's playing a very dangerous game. She's more powerful than ever now. I should've gone straight to Persia with these suspicions hours ago but want to be one hundred percent sure. I've checked and re-checked Summer's room knowing it's empty.

After more hours of searching the entire campus, the quest finally comes to an end. On entering the canteen for the fifteenth time this morning, there's Liv sitting with that Luke Prick and Pip, who has her back to me. They're drinking coffee and laughing, how 'nice.' On approach, I notice Pip's black satchel hanging across the back of the chair and in big white letters the design reads, 'I'm up and dressed. I'm a student. What more do you want?' Gasping, stopping in my tracks. *How bleeding thick am I? It's the same bag from that night with Andie in the library! Same bag...same girl? She looks different...but...I've been so blinded by getting Summer back, that I didn't see what was right in front of me! If I'm right, then my Summer, the real Summer is still out there somewhere, like I suspected.* This can't be a mere coincidence; my gut tells me it's the same bag, same girl. I'm the stalker who's been out friggin stalked!

Liv stops chatting upon catching my eye, there's no choice but to do this now. This bitch is going down.

"Hey guys." I put on a warm smile.

"Oh, hi." They answer, all with a look of shock on their faces. I wonder what they know or have the angels already wiped their minds, well Luke and Liv's, doubt Pip's is wipeable.

"Hey, Pip isn't it?" Leaning over her chair; her face reddens instantly.

"Err, yes."

"Can we talk?" Grinning widely, "In private?"

"Of course." And the girl is up out of the chair. *Always desperate for my attention.* By the way she's looking at me; like I'm the winning lotto numbers, I know I'm right about this.

"Err, Pip?" Luke doesn't look happy and he too is now standing. *This dick doesn't know when to quit.* "It's that dude from the bar, he was cruel to Summer…"

"Yes, and I'm sure I'll be safe." Pip chuckles.

So, they only remember me from that night? No memories from the club or the incident at the cinema. I'm pleased, the less people that know the truth the better.

"I promise she'll be back before you've finished your drink." Winking at Liv who fiddles with her mug. "She's totally safe."

"Okay, but if she's not back in ten minutes, I'll come looking." Luke crosses his arms over his muscle vest chest, and I bite down hard, not to laugh.

Pip weaves in and out of the tables and I follow right behind. We leave the noisy canteen. On my way in, I noticed a small storage cupboard and gesture that way. Opening the door, waiting for her to step inside, which she does. Looking to check if anyone notices, the students are too busy in their own ignorant, indulgent worlds to care.

"Step into my office. Thought we could be a bit more private here." I seem to be spending a lot of time in closets lately, thinking back to that club cloakroom with Summer, sighing at the memory of our closeness. *Should've listened to my instincts and just kissed her right there and then…bloody angels and their half-hearted plans…*

"So?" Pip asks.

"So…"

"So, what's this about?"

"You may like this." Closing the door behind us before leaning into her personal space. This is way too easy. What kind of girl goes into a closet with a stranger? Guess 'Pip' and I aren't strangers though; we go way back…I just need to prove it.

"Like what? Is something wrong?"

"Why would you think that?" Stepping in closer, teasing even more.

"Well, you never noticed me before…"

"Before?"

"Err, yes, the night you were mean to my friend."

"Oh yeah, then. Well I'm noticing you now, aren't I? And I don't think you can call that girl your friend, do you?" Glaring down at the busty blonde.

"W-what?"

"You and me, we have a connection, don't pretend you don't feel it." Speaking against her ear, she whimpers. "I want to get to know you, the real you."

"I'd like that."

"Bet you would." My lips skim her ear before pulling away. She gasps. "First though, just have to make a quick call. You don't mind, right?"

"Course not." Twisting pieces of hair between her fingers.

"Bear with me." Pulling my phone from my jeans pocket and hit redial on Kit's number. Now I wait, not taking my eyes off the fake blonde, fake tits, fake everything girl.

Seconds later, her bag starts ringing. There's panic in those cold eyes as she looks from me to it.

"Aren't you gonna answer that?" I ask, still with the phone against my ear.

"I'll get it later." She's inching around me trying to get to the door. I grab the bag, ripping it from her shoulder. "Let me…great bag by the way, I've seen one just like it recently…"

"What are you doing? Give it back!"

Pulling her phone out, checking the screen already knowing my name would be flashing up. Showing her both phones, I raise a brow.

"Busted," I say as she stumbles back into a stepladder.

"It's not what you think."

"It's not?"

"No…I found that phone." Scratching her palm and I wait for head to cock to the left, which it always does when she's lying.

"Your lies are deafening, Kit."

"What? I'm Pip. You're nuts. Let me out!"

"Who's Alex then if not me? Hang on…" Answering her phone and talk to myself in it then respond to myself on mine. "Hi."

"Hi." I smirk. "Is that Alex?"

"Alex, how the hell are you?" I swap phones.

"It's been so long…yes, it's me." I carry on, Pip or rather Kit, becomes pale.

"Why yes, Alex, yes it has…" My little skit fails to amuse, and she grabs for the door. Throwing Kit's phone at the door, it smashes above her head and she flinches away. "Shall we just end this now?"

"So, you know…how did you find out?"

"Aww come on, you didn't really think I wouldn't. And you can drop the phoney Texan accent now…but don't change back into you. I may hurt you if I see that lying face."

"You hate me that much? You can't even look at your own sister?" Her eyes fill up.

"Where is she, Kit?" Ramming her back against the stepladder. "Where is she?"

"She's gone, accept it."

"No…you're lying. If Summer were gone, I'd know it, feel it. You'd better tell me or…" Placing a hand around her throat, I start squeezing.

"You'll kill me?" she chokes. "Then you'll never find her."

Letting go, no longer that monster that she helped to create, and she's right, I do need her. "Why, Kit? Why would you do this?"

"Because I love you." She sobs, and I feel nothing but pity. Thinking of yesterday when I thought Summer didn't want me, that was worse than any pain. Kit must feel this way every day, which sucks. I only ever saw her as a sister…now I don't know if I can even see her as that. My loving sister disguised herself as the girl I love and tried to destroy me. It almost worked too.

"If you love me at all, then please, just tell me, lift the spell and let the angels help before it's too late. I can't live with that kind of pain…please don't make me."

"Tomorrow, Lennox and Liam will drain Summer and take over this world. Decades from now you, me, your girl, won't even matter, none of this will," she whispers.

"I'm sorry, okay? Is that what you wanna hear? I'm sorry I can't love you like that, but you're the one that took my love for you as a brother away." Raking both hands through my hair in sheer frustration. "You hurt me just as much as I hurt you."

She's silent for a while. "Kiss me and I'll lift the spell."

"You're bloody joking?" Pip stands before me, but the accent has gone, and I hear Kit.

"Kiss me the way you kiss her, and I'll free you, and break the shielding spell on their location."

"You're serious?" The thought sickens me.

"One time offer, little brother."

Before processing my actions, we're kissing angry and hard. Trying to blank out any thoughts or feelings, hoping I don't puke. Surprisingly, she pulls away first.

"Now tell me!" Wiping the taste of old gum from my lips, trying not to gag at the wrongness of it all.

"No."

"What?"

"You don't kiss *her* like that. I need to feel it." Pip's image changes to Summer in the click of her fingers. The sight makes me tremble. *Shit, she really is all singing and dancing with power.* "Does this help?"

"I still know it's you."

"Then close your eyes and think of her, nothing but her…"

I do and feel a breath on my cheek. Warm lips are on mine and I move to a new rhythm. Scrunching my eyes, concentrating on the real Summer, the last time we kissed, and how happy we were. Her tongue explores mine as my arms wrap around her. It's just me and my girl locked away in our secret farmhouse. Reopening my eyes, the kiss has ended. Kit stands before me as herself, the dread haired big sister…who I've sort of missed.

"I understand now. If you love her half as much as that kiss showed…I could never compete with that. I'm so sorry, Alex."

"So am I." Avoiding eye contact, feeling dirty. Kit's family, but I can't see us ever being that again.

"The spell is lifted. Your angels will soon find her."

"Thank you." Touching her arm but it's brief and uncomfortable.

"I am sorry, brother."

"I know…it'll just take time."

"I'll see you around." She smiles and vanishes.

"See you," I whisper, believing I'll never see my big sister again.

20: Summer

Warm, sticky blood squelches in-between my toes and the cool, early dawn screams at my chattering teeth and bones. Wanting to give up, taking another disappointing look up and down yet another empty road, biting back the tears that I can't afford to cry. In the last few hours, there hasn't been one single car. Sitting down on a grassy verge, just for a few minutes to rest. I'm far enough from the road not to be spotted; close enough if a good Samaritan happens to drive by. Now I've finally let myself rest; the tears come. I'm not just sobbing, no I'm talking all out girly, woe is me, wailing.

Let's face it; so far, life sucks beyond sucking. Whichever version of me I choose, both options aren't looking very welcoming. I could stay as this me, the 'no memory' girl, but with a possible normal future where my angelic friends wipe my mind every time evil comes to show its nasty face. And that is simply not an option. Pisses me off. Or I could revert to the real me by kissing a guy I don't know, which on reflection wouldn't be such an awful thing, because God, he's hot. And there's an undeniable connection between us, I know him, deep down even feel him. So yeah, I'd be myself again and finally get some happiness, but we'd always be hunted, always running from what we are. Whatever future I pick, one way or another it's bound to suck. I'm a 'thing.' Am I even human? *I'm a joke!* Spluttering an angry laugh as more tears spurt from swollen, tired eyes.

Standing in the distance, a woman rocks a baby. Relief washes over me, at last, someone may help. Wiping the tears to get a better look, but you've guessed it, they too are nowhere to be seen. I think I see ghosts; spirits making their way toward me. Which I guess would make some sort of sense if I were indeed a gateway to Heaven.

"Oh, thank God." An engine rumbles in the distance. I spring up feeling elated. The old camper van draws nearer, so I jump up and down waving both arms. Slowing down, it stops just metres away. A kind-faced, white-haired, old timer rolls the window down and sticks his head out.

"What you doing all the way out here, girly? You need a ride somewhere? I'm heading into town."

I don't even ask which town. "Yes, please."

He opens the door and steps out. "Get in."

"Are you real?"

"Sure am, girly." The guy looks confused before offering his hand. "Flesh and old bones see…"

Before I've put one foot in front of the other, a pure white flash of light erupts from nowhere, blinding me. Shielding my eyes, straining to see. Hoping the kind old guy isn't hurt. The light dulls to a warm glow and as my vision adjusts, there are two tall figures silhouetted against it. Blinking, recognising Persia and Elle. They look almost alien-like, like beings not of this world. They tower over me with a faint golden aura that I've never seen before, not this version of me anyway…

"Persia, Elle…thank God!" Running to them.

"No!" Persia booms, stopping me dead.

"Get away, demon!" Elle lifts up both hands, and without touching him, forces the old fella back against the van.

"What are you doing?" I shriek.

"Stay back, Summer, this isn't what you think. He isn't." Elle eyes the poor man, who looks like he's about to have an embarrassing accident in his slacks.

"He's trying to help me!"

Persia's hands are on me, and somehow, she's standing at my side. Elle turns briefly, and I realise that she's hovering just above the ground. *Holy crap!*

"Please, I meant no harm…" The old man chokes against Elle's invisible hold.

"Show your face old man, your real face."

"Elle? What are you doing?" Trying to break out of Persia's tight grip, getting nowhere fast.

"Summer." Persia looks down, "Do you trust me?"

Now there's a stumper. "I think so…I…most of the time…" *Black Eyes was right …these guys are angels! Holy crap! Angels! They must be good then, right?* Looking wounded for a second before smiling, a smile that's so full of love and compassion that yes, I do *want* to trust her.

"Believe your eyes." Waving her hand over my face before stepping back. Gasping, when the old man's face changes into a face of someone not so kind…Lennox. He grins that disgusting yellow grin and disappears as in poof, gone!

"What the F- where did he go?" Stuttering, as my brain tries and fails to make sense of all this.

"It's okay, it'll all be okay." Persia pulls me in for another hug. "We'll take you back to your room and look after you."

"Look after me?" Trying hard to push her away, but the girl is made of stone or something. "Like by wiping my mind again?"

"Summer, you don't understand." Elle intervenes.

"Oh, I think I do, and I'm not going anywhere until you both swear to tell me everything." I'm shouting. It feels refreshing to be angry, after all they deserve it, right? They did this, didn't trust me enough to be honest, and made me this 'Light,' this shell. "And don't you dare try and lie your way out of this! I know what you are, what you've done to me and…Alex."

"Calm down, Sum." Persia seems sad, but they can't treat me like a puppet anymore.

"No. I bloody won't!" Skin aching with heat.

A hand grips my shoulder, spinning me round. Elle smiles softly, "Sleep." She whispers, arms catch me when I fall.

* * * *

"Ruth!" Bolting upright in the bed. I'm washed and in clean pyjamas. *Was it all some bizarre, lucid dream?* Persia stares from the corner, like a guard watching a prisoner.

"Hey, are you alright?" She glides over to the bed, perching at the end.

"Think so. What did you do to me?"

"We calmed you, helped you to rest."

"How long was I out?"

"Not long actually…you were restless."

"How'd you find me?"

"Alex figured out you were not you…it's a long story."

"You didn't wipe my memories?"

"So, you know…"

"Yes, I know. That creep Liam told me."

"It was for the best, we thought…I'm so sorry, Summer." Reaching for my hand, but I wince back.

"Where's Elle?" I ask, changing the subject. I'm still angry and don't want to get overheated again.

"She's around."

"Outside the door you mean?" She nods. "So, am I *your* prisoner now?"

"Don't be silly, of course not. We just wanted the chance to talk to you properly. Who is Ruth?"

"What?"

"You screamed that name a moment ago."

"Oh, God." Jumping out of bed, Persia stands too, *like I'd even planned on running.* "I promised I'd go back for her, that we'd both get out. I promised!"

"Okay, start over." Persia frowns.

"Ruth was taken too, weeks ago. I thought she might be like me, a Light, but she's just a poor mother looking for her sons, Alex and Liam, you know all about them, right?" Which is more a statement than a question. Narrowing my eyes, checking for the smallest hint of remorse, but Persia doesn't falter. "As far as I can gather, the plan was for Alex to bring me in exchange for his mother, but he didn't, because he and I are…well you know…"

"I see."

"I see? Is that all you've got to say? You are angels…go do your angel thing and rescue the poor woman."

"There's a force keeping us from seeing that location, but we'll do everything we can, I promise. First, we need to have a real talk."

"So, I'm this thing? A gateway to Heaven?"

"Maybe we should sit."

"I don't bloody want to sit! Is it true demons could use me to take over the world?"

"Yes, but we'll never let that happen." Persia puts a hand on my shoulder, which I shrug off.

"And all memories, stuff with this Alex guy, you've taken away?"

"We thought it was best for you…for him."

"I decide what's best for me from now on. Don't you dare wipe my mind ever again. You have to promise, promise that you won't!"

"Okay." She sighs. "Promise."

Elle enters and leans against my door.

"Hello to you too." Snarling in her direction.

"See, she's fine." Elle ignores me, talking over my head to Persia.

"I am here you know!" Storming into the bathroom, cleaning my teeth angrily, making my gums bleed. A knock at the door stops the crazy brushing. I can make out a male voice mumbling in the corridor. Almost forgetting to breathe, trying to listen in. *Is it him? Is it Alex? Has he come to wake me up? Does he know about his mum?* Straightening my hair with my fingers, before rushing out to see what's happening. Peeking through the door, my heart sinks seeing Luke talking with Persia and Elle. He wants a chat. I could use a friendly face right now.

"Summer's not feeling well today, come again tomorrow." Elle lies. *Not very angelic of her...*

"You said that earlier...can't you at least ask her? Pip said Summer needed to speak to me..."

Pip did? I haven't seen Pip... I step into the corridor.

"Hi, Summer." Luke beams.

"It's okay, you can let him in. I know where you both are if I feel 'unwell' again." Sighing, waving him in. "Sorry about the pjs." Feeling myself blushing at the pink pigs that cover my nightwear.

"I like 'em." He too is a silly pink colour.

Slamming the door behind him, shutting out their lying faces. "I'm so glad to see you." I flop onto the bed.

"Yeah?"

"Course. I've been through hell. Could do with a friend."

"What do you mean?" Sitting beside me.

"Guess you don't remember either. You think I've been poorly?"

"Haven't you?"

"When's the last time you saw me?"

"You're being weird." He tucks a loose strand of hair behind my ear and it feels like he shouldn't.

"Humour me."

"Okay, you went home ill from the nightclub two nights ago, we put you in a taxi. You wouldn't let us come with you. You said to stay with Liv…remember?" Looking at me like I'm on heavy medication. "So, you're better now?" Placing his hand over mine.

"What did you want to see me about…something to do with Pip, wasn't it? Are they coming later?"

"Pip sort of told me your little secret." Luke stares into my eyes. I gasp. "Yeah, told me how you've been talking about me…she said that you're in to me?" We stare at our overlapping hands.

"I don't know what to say…" *Why would Pip say that? Why would she want to hurt Liv?*

"Shit, Summer, you must know how I feel about you?"

"Err…"

"I was hoping...I've been hoping that our friendship would become more…a lot more. You feel it too, right? Or am I making a complete tool of myself?" He grimaces.

"Oh, Luke." Pulling my hand out from under his, unable to look at him. "Any girl would be lucky to be with you…"

"Don't think I like where this is going."

"We have to think of the group."

"They'll understand…"

"No…Liv won't."

"Liv?"

"You must know how she feels about you?" Turning to face him. "You're not that stupid."

"I know Liv has feelings for me, but they're not like the ones I have for you."

"To her they are. She's also a good friend…you look shocked?"

"I am…Pip assured me you felt the same way…I wouldn't have made a move otherwise." He gets up, and I join him.

"She would've known this would destroy Liv, all our friendships…what's she playing at?"

Luke shrugs. "Please, just give us a chance…one chance?"

"There are things about me that you don't know…"

"Then tell me, tell me everything. Is there someone else?"

"There might be... I'm not sure of anything anymore." I sigh. He reaches for me, grabs my arm, pulling me close.

"One kiss. And if you still feel nothing I'll walk away, and we'll be friends again as if nothing happened."

"I don't think we should."

"Just try?" Warm hands are in my hair and rough lips are on mine before there's time to protest. We're kissing. He's putting everything into it, but I feel nothing. There's no spark. Shouldn't there be a spark? *This is wrong.* Emerald eyes flash in my mind, and I pull away. Luke stares at me, still with one hand in my hair and I see it in his eyes, he knows we don't fit. We can never fit, not when my heart and soul belong to somebody else. And whether I accept it or not, he is haunting me. I can't shake the guy from my mind and don't want to.

I jump a little when the door flies open and it's him, Alex. My heartbeat echoes against my breathless chest. He looks wild almost, like he's about to strangle Luke. I'm drawn to him, wanting to be nearer, drunk on him…Luke drops his hand and steps away.

"Well now, isn't this cosy?" Alex snarls.

"It's not what it looks like," I say.

"Summer, are you okay? I've been so worried…" Alex steps closer.

"Sum? Who is this douche?" Luke crosses his arms over his chest. "First, he's all over Pip, then he spoils our moment…it's like the dude's stalking us."

"Luke, we didn't have a moment." Cringing as soon as the words come out. He looks at me open-mouthed before storming out.

"Everything okay?" Persia sticks her head around the door.

"Give us a moment, will you?" I snap. She closes the door leaving just Alex and me and I'm terrified and thrilled all at once.

"So…" He chews his lip.

"So…" Peeking through the hair that's fallen in my eyes.

"This is awkward… what do you know about me?"

"Most of it…I think." My face heats. He walks to me, uncrossing his arms. "Nice pjs." He smiles. "So, you know we're supposed to be…together?"

I nod, feeling giddy this close, hot and giddy. The effect he has over me is bordering on ridiculous.

"Summer, I need you to trust me."

"I don't know you…"

"You know me better than anyone…you just have to wake up."

"I'm scared," I whisper.

"Me too." Raking a palm through his hair, and something about that feels familiar. "A part of me will always be waiting for you."

"You shouldn't have to. I'm selfish to want you to." Focusing on his boots, he pulls my chin up gently. Our eyes meet, my entire being turns to mush and my limbs want to crumple in on themselves. I hunger for his touch.

"Be selfish, be anything, just be with me."

The hottest guy I've ever laid eyes on is asking me to be his... what? "I need time to get my head together...time to say goodbye." Swallowing hard.

"Goodbye?" Letting go of my chin. "To who?" He frowns.

"I'm not sure..." And I'm not. Whichever life I choose, there'll be people I'll have to leave behind.

"I'll wait for your answer. I'll be at the campus gates at midnight

tomorrow. If we survive the full moon tonight, I'll be waiting. If you don't want me, us, then I'll leave, and you'll never have to see me again."

"The full moon?"

"Yes tonight. That's when they, the Krons, want to drain your light and put it into my not-so-friendly twin. I will be close by, protecting you."

"Oh." I'm not sure I'm ready for this.

"I won't let that happen...if for some reason I don't survive, or you don't come tomorrow night, and God, I hope you do, I need you to promise me something."

"What?"

"Don't ever look back. Live your life and never be sorry." The words take my breath away. His beautiful eyes are so sad.

"This is too much...I don't know..."

"You're freaked out."

"Freaked out doesn't even cover it." I chuckle because if I don't laugh, I may just melt into a gibbering wreck.

"God, I love your laugh." We're dangerously close, our chests almost touching.

"You do? So…" Clearing my throat, staring at the floor to hide my blush, "so there's a kiss, and I'll remember all of it…all of us?" Daring to glance up, his eyes sparkle with mischief, my breath catches.

"If that's what you want?"

"Isn't it what you want?" Without realizing, pulling my fringe over my cheek to hide the scar. Feeling naked in his presence, like he sees me, the parts that I can't.

"Summer." Grabbing my chin, forcing me to look up. "I want it more than anything. You never have to hide yourself from me." Wrapping my fringe back around my ear. His fingertips touch my cheek and I melt a little. "This is the first time you've been given the choice so choose wisely."

"What?"

"I don't want you to resent me for it. I won't force myself on you."

"I wouldn't resent you."

"You may. You won't just remember us; every horrible thing from your past will flood back into your head. This way, you could live a carefree life."

"With a bit of memory wiping here and there." I turn away, but he grabs my elbow spinning me back. He smells so good, musky and rugged, I could drink him in forever. Feeling a little dizzy, a good stomach-flipping dizzy. I lean into him, pushing my chin up to his neck. I think he's going to do it, kiss me…

"I kiss you only when you ask me to." He sighs heavily, like it hurts.

"Uhu," I mumble.

"You're making this so difficult…God, I want you…" Squeezing his eyes tight and when he opens them, he seems more composed.

"We're always finding each other, right?"

"I will always find you…"

"I'm right here." One hand reaches for him, but he steps away. "I don't get you!" I'm freakishly hot. Frowning, he takes a large step back. *Am I about to breathe fire? Wait, can I do that?*

"Summer, listen, you should think about this." The buzzing of a phone snaps me back to reality, like a bucket of ice to the face.

"One sec." He pulls it from his jacket pocket. His eyes widen. "Shit."

"What is it?"

Showing me the screen there's a picture of a beaten woman who I recognise instantly.

"Ruth."

"You know her? How?" His expression has changed into something dark, something distant.

I go over what happened when I was taken, and that I have no clue where we were held. Describing as much as I can recall, telling Alex over and over that I'm sorry.

"I just ran in any direction. I can't remember getting to the road…"

"Did that sick shit hurt you? Did he touch you?" He growls.

"I'm okay." I can't bring myself to reveal the details of how his twin kissed me…touched me. Shuddering at the memory, how I'd like that wiped from my head forever…

"You did the right thing. And don't worry…Lennox has been very helpful and sent me an address. Promise me you'll stay here?"

I nod. He kisses the top of my head leaving his lips there for a few seconds.

"I have to find her." He opens the door, turning to me. "If I make it through this tonight, I'll be waiting at the gates…tomorrow, midnight. You get a whole day to decide…maybe even pack." He smiles, and I feel nauseous. A cold feeling in my gut tells me I'll never see that beautiful, lazy smile again.

"Wait! It's too dangerous! What if it's a trap?" I call after him, but he's gone. Persia and Elle are no longer in the corridor, which is weird when they're supposed to be protecting me tonight of all nights. I hope that they're helping in some other way. Maybe they've gone after Ruth…

A few hours pass, and night is here once again. Helpless and frustrated, I've no idea what's going on. I go to the window, check my phone then return to the window again. The moon is out, full, dangerous and beautiful. Will this be the last moon I ever see? Will he be the last thought I have? I've heard nothing. Where are the angels? What's happening to Alex right now? No news is good news, right? Here I'm just a sitting duck. I must leave now if they're coming for me…

I text Persia. CAN'T SIT HERE WAITING. OFF TO FIND ALEX. HOPE YOU GET THIS SOON. WHERE ARE YOU??

I wait a few minutes. The phone stays silent.

"Sod this!" Putting on a jumper and sturdiest boots, grabbing my phone, a snack bar and a bottle of water, I venture out of the building onto the campus car lot. Feeling a new sense of freedom without the angels breathing down my neck…bet they never saw this coming! I promised I'd save Ruth. All this is because people are trying to keep me safe, but I have to stand up for myself. If Alex dies because of me, how will I live with that? Getting captured is the one chance at finding them, but the plan after that? I'll have to improvise.

"Okay, you want me…come and get me!" I cry out into the night.

"Well, there's no need to shout." Pip smiles, grabbing me hard. "My master will be so pleased."

"Pip?"

"Pip? Pip who?" She laughs. "God, Summer, you really are dumb."

21: Summer

Stunned into silence as busty blonde Pip morphs into a slightly stockier girl with purple dreads and smaller boobs. She's right, I've been dumb, beyond dumb. Didn't think this through at all. Staring at this stranger, it sort of makes sense now why Pip and I always clashed. But I'd never have guessed in a million years that she was some sort of shape-shifting witch, playing for team evil. I've been stupid, numbed from everything because of what I am, a threat to the world. Maybe if my memories were intact, I would've known to stay away from this girl. Thinking about the angels wiping my mind, God knows how many times, like I don't matter, makes me angry. It would be easier to just hate them, but I can't.

"Wow, the look on your face is priceless." The Texan drawl has gone. Her voice is much lower than before. *Shit. What do I do now? Where are the bloody angels when you need them? No, this is what I wanted, to be taken back to that factory. If the angels aren't here, they'd better be with Alex. Nothing else makes sense.* "Cat got your tongue?" She laughs.

"I…" Yes, I think it has. Life's gone from hard to crazy town in seconds, what with angels…and now witches? Needing to stall the girl and try to find a way out of this. If she can morph into other people, what else can she do? Maybe I can get her on side and get the factories' address…without putting an evil spell on me.

"You, you what?"

"I thought we had a connection, a small one yes, but we were sort of friends…" Yeah, totally grasping.

"You're so funny! Let's get real, shall we? You never liked me, and I've always hated you."

"Why?"

"You're so stupid. You're the reason Alex and I aren't together."

"What?"

The witch morphs into his image.

"What the hell are you?" Stumbling then regaining balance, before backing away.

"Not to be too cliché, your worst nightmare." Laughing, the girly chuckle doesn't match the hard exterior. Thankfully she changes back into the girl with dreads.

"If those angels of yours would just leave your tiny brain alone, you'd remember me. Bet it's all just mush in there now." Nodding at my head. "I'm Kit, Alex's... sister."

"His sister? That's kinda sick." I blurt. Her eyes narrow like she's about to turn me into dog food. "So...so you're one of those Kron people?" I say, hoping not to end up in some sort of slug stew.

"Points to 'The Light.' They made a winner when they plaster-casted you." Kit sneers. Admittedly, I'm scared. Are others coming? Will it hurt when they drain me? Will it be quick? Will I see Alex again? Tears sting, but she won't see me cry.

"You'll never have him," I say. "He'll never forgive you for this."

"Oh, but when you're dead, I'll tell the story of how I tried to save you."

"He'll never believe that."

"Time heals wounds...and I have plenty of time... I can always wipe you from his mind again." Kit winks, and I clench a fist wanting to punch that tiny nose. I don't know how to fight, but this cow deserves a good smacking; powers or not. Intense heat rushes down my arms into every fingertip, heat that must be released before my insides start to boil. Before making a move, her hand flies up, and even though she hasn't touched me, I'm lifted high into the air before landing hard on my backside. *Ouch!*

"Aww, you gonna cry to mummy? Oh yeah, you're a freak and never had a mum…" She nears, smacking her fist into her palm and smiling like it's the best day ever. I roll onto my knees and stand. Lower back aching from hitting the floor. Pulling her hand back, slapping hard across my cheek…now the tears come. A fist flies at me, astonishing myself, grabbing it a few inches short of my nose. Kit's eyes widen—she looks as shocked as I am. Heat continues to rise. Tearing her hand from my grasp, she screams. The witch's hand is smoking. It smells of singed flesh. *I did that. Is this self-preservation? Something the Angels built into me?*

Chanting, focussing on the damaged hand and before I can blink, the hand is normal again.

"What the hell are you?" I gasp. The plan to be taken by this *thing* is changing quickly.

"What am I? What the hell are you?"

"Look, I know you're supposed to take me to your people, so they can…drain me." Gulping. "But please, isn't there a tiny bit of humanity in you? The part that loves Alex?"

A palm collides with my nose and I taste blood. *Holy crap that hurt! Guess I hit a nerve.*

"Alex is mine. Do you hear?" Turning a funny purple colour like her dreads.

"You're crazy!" Wiping the blood away with my sleeve.

"When you die tonight, he will mourn you. But guess who'll be there to pick up the pieces…"

"Stay away from him." My heartbeat is vibrating into my throat. It's not just the adrenaline making me shake or the fact that I may die tonight, but the thought of Alex being with *this thing* or anyone else really, makes my body heat in ways that could take out a small country.

"You're threatening me? Ha! Now that's bloody priceless! You don't even know how to love. He's wasted on you. He was right there for the taking…and you didn't take him."

"I…" She's right, I didn't. God, I'm so stupid.

"You won't have the chance now. You'll be dead before you kiss him. Did you know he kissed me yesterday?" Kit's eyes flicker with excitement. I'm hot, like volcano hot. Trying hard to slow my breathing and cool down. Picturing this cow and Alex doing stuff that he should be doing with me, I feel rage.

"You're lying!" Hands pushing forward, a bolt of fire releases from each fingertip. Screaming, aiming all frustration at the scheming, twisted witch. Power surges through my body, I feel invincible and like it.

"Stop!" she cries. I stop, and instantly my temperature cools. A sick feeling hits the pit of my stomach over what I've done. Kit's on fire, throwing herself on the ground, rolling around, trying to put out the flames. I'm frozen as the fire eats away at her clothing; even her dreads are burning. Maybe I'm not what they think I am, maybe I am capable of burning the world to ashes. My hands are trembling. Maybe I am an abomination. Staring down at the screaming girl, horrified, I run, aiming for nowhere in particular, just away from here.

Slowing down a short while later, trying to get my breathing back to a normal rate. Night has crept up like a stealthy traitor. No one has followed me, except for the full moon, which has always chased me…watching, waiting.

I'm in a field in the middle of nowhere, lost. I could keep running and never look back. After all, the angels will find me sooner or later…but I can't keep hiding from what I am. I'm tired and want to stop running and dare I even think it...live. I'd never forgive myself if I don't at least try to help Ruth and Alex. God, just the thought of him in danger makes me ache with despair, anger or something in between. Knowing what must be done, they cannot die, not for me. Memories or not, what Alex says is the truth, I feel it deep down inside. He's a big part of my past, and must live, even if it's without me.

Turning my watch to the moonlight, I can just make out it's around ten p.m. That leaves me two hours to find them, two hours before the ritual is no longer valid. If I wait until a minute after, will they kill them anyway? Hopefully, we'll all make it out alive. Hope is all there is left. Where are the angels?

My mind flicks back to that girl I burnt alive…guilt sits on my chest like an iron fist. I could have saved her, or at least tried. Will he hate me when he finds out? Will I be able to look into those amazing eyes and admit to killing his sister? Yes, the girl was warped and twisted beyond the realms of crazy, but still, I had no right. Will there be a punishment after I die? *I'm a killer. I deserve to be punished.*

The welcome engine of a car forces me onward. Standing in the middle of the road waving both arms about like I'm having some sort of fit. *Help is here! It's not too late!* The car comes to a halt inches away, and by a fantastic stroke of luck, it's a police car. The lady officer I vaguely remember from the hospital steps out of the vehicle.

"Well now, what are you doing out here all alone?" Shining a torch in my face and I shield my eyes.

"Officer Penny? Do you remember me? A few weeks ago, there was a bike accident …" (*yeah right, figure Persia altered her memory too*). "Summer?"

"Of course, hello again, twice in a month, you sure like getting into scrapes." Switching off the torch.

"Please, I need your help."

"Get in and tell me on the way." Opening the passenger door and I slide in. We drive, and I tell her about the woman I'd been kidnapped with. Officer Penny glances at me, I'm not sure if she's frowning at me or with me. I tell her about the old meat factory, and she thinks she knows the place. I leave out all the paranormal stuff on purpose.

"Please, you have to take me there."

"I should call for back up, but I'll check out the situation myself first."

"You don't believe me?"

"Never said that. Don't want to get twenty cops out here if the building is empty…"

Guess she has a point. But that place is far from empty. I also know we're heading into a trap. I'm not that naive. But I have to hope we can save them somehow or the angels will intervene. *Where the hell are they?*

The next twenty minutes are spent in silence. Scratching my arms as an odd new coping mechanism. Officer Penny stares straight ahead keeping focus on the winding, narrow roads. Am I putting this woman at risk too? Surely, she has a gun, a taser? I'd like to stick a taser right up Liam's backside that would give a bit of life to those unnaturally dead eyes.

Turning onto a lane, spotting an old building at the end of it. It's the factory; I'd know it anywhere. My pulse quickens sensing he's near. Goosebumps erupt on goosebumps picturing Alex beaten, or worse.

"That's the place," I whisper.

"You're sure?" Penny slows and parks.

"Afraid so." Every instinct yells to run. Even if we get inside what can a police officer and a teenager do against pure evil? Liam could snap our necks in a second. And even if Penny does have a gun, she'll be dead before she can draw it.

"You okay?" No! I want to scream, far from it! But don't, instead I take a deep breath, and nod. "Okay then, let's do this. Stay behind me at all times." She gets out and comes around to the passenger side, opening the door. I reach for her hand but it's hard to grasp, it feels greasy, almost slimy. *What the?* Roughly, I'm hauled out.

"That hurt." Gasping, Penny's features dissolve inwards, leaving something black and demented in their place. Trying to pull my hand from its now leathery skin, but it's no use whatever this thing is, it's too strong. I'm yanked down into the dirt.

"Now look what we have here. How lucky can one be?"

Slowly, my eyes follow up his body and I gasp seeing Lennox, the old leader that had me caged like an animal. My mouth forms an O shape to scream but no sound comes out. My brain's spiralling into a frenzied panic and yet, what did I expect would happen? I came here knowing I'd be caught.

"Where is the policewoman?" I stutter.

"She's fine. Promise." He hisses.

"I don't believe anything you say."

Lennox walks around the back of the car and pats the boot. "Hopefully she's still sleeping and when she wakes up, all this will be a distant memory."

"You coward! Let her out!" Stumbling to my knees, trying to stand before he can push me down again.

"I could kill her now or are you going to behave?" His eyes narrow, and a cold shiver runs up my spine and over my skin.

I just stare at him.

"Good girl."

Dusting myself down, he gestures towards the door. "Come, let's go inside. There's someone in there that you'll want to see."

"If you've hurt Alex or his mother..." I stop, knowing it's just an empty threat. Even if I heat up and burn the place down, I'd risk killing them both. So, I'm pretty much out of options, sighing, knowing what must be done. I have to give myself to them willingly in exchange, but if they drain me won't the world be in danger? Should I just try saving these two lives, putting all hope in the angels to save the rest? Is saving two lives but risking millions selfish? Would I still do it if it weren't Alex? Yes, I think so. It feels right…and if it's wrong, and God I pray it's not, something or someone will stop the demons…won't they? There can't just be two angels, what about all the ones in Heaven? "If I promise not to heat up, will you promise to let them go?"

"I don't see why not. They're not much use to us anymore. Not now I have you and Liam."

"Summer!" Hearing the beautiful sound of Persia's voice, relief floods like a tidal wave. *They're here! Everything's going to be fine.*

They run forward, both face planting into what has to be an invisible barrier of some sort.

"No!" I scream, trying to wriggle from Lennox's grasp. There's sheer panic on their faces as they claw at the force separating us.

"I'm good, right?" Lennox shrugs, dragging me inside. The smell of old meat wafts under my nose. If Persia and Elle are being kept out, I'm totally, utterly all types of screwed. *I'm going to die!* Liam and a tall redhead are waiting for us.

"You…" Staring hard at the redhead.

"Yes?" Looking a little worried. Why would she be?

"You look familiar…" But can't seem to recall why, which me being me isn't a complete shocker.

"You're mistaken." Her gaze drops to the floor. Pushing her way between them both, is a girl I do recognise. Kit, Pip, or whatever the witch calls herself, stands twirling her dreads. Not a burn mark on her that I can see.

"You? How?"

"I'm full of surprises." She winks and blows out a big blue gum bubble.

"Take me to Alex." Demanding, trying to keep the fear from showing.

"Yes, Your Highness." Liam smiles. It's hard to believe he and Alex are related, two people couldn't be more different. He leads the way with Kit. Lennox and the quiet redhead fall in step behind. We walk down the long corridor, the lights above flicker like my erratic heartbeat. Stopping at the last door, Liam steps in.

"Oh, brother, we have a surprise for you!"

I'm pushed into the room; my breath catches upon seeing Alex. "Oh God." Tears threaten to spill. Alex's mouth hangs open.

"God has left the building, child." Lennox forces me to kneel in front of Alex's cage. "But don't worry, you'll soon be with your God."

Wanting to scream flames seeing what they've done to him. Now I'm a new kind of terrified.

22: Alex

"Why have you come? Do you have a death wish?" The tall redhead frowns.

"You! I remember you…what you did. Coral, right? The angel who betrayed us all by dating 'daddy dearest'? How's that working out for ya?"

She lifts me up by the shoulders. *Shit this girl is strong!* I'm tossed into a wall. My back smacks into the bricks. Skin tears along ribs upon sliding down the harsh surface. I'm lifted and pushed behind a large dumpster, which reeks of rotting flesh. A bloody arm hanging over the side, I breathe through my mouth before gagging.

"Why are you here?" Crossing her arms like Lennox had done so many times before when he'd been displeased with me.

"Why are you?" I snap. "Is this what you wanted?" Gesturing to the dumpster; presumably full of bodies. "You hate being an angel that much that you've become a murderer?"

"No…I didn't…it doesn't matter. Why have you come?" She looks confused.

"Why do you think? I mean, you're in on the whole kidnapping an innocent woman and beating her to within an inch of life…of course I'd come. You must've known I would?" *What's she playing at? Is this all part of some elaborate game?*

"Look, there's no time to explain. Let's just say I've made a huge mistake…I've seen Lennox's true face," whispering, looking about anxiously.

"You're fucking kidding." Crossing my arms, the punch line has to be coming soon. Sighing, Coral looks at the floor.

"You're not joking?" *Holy crap, this may be the help we needed! Should I trust her?*

"No. I've done things…I don't want any more people hurt, especially not Summer."

"You should've thought about that first. That was your job, your one bloody job!" Trying to push past, but the girl is made of iron.

"You need to leave. This is a set-up; thought you'd know that."

"Of course, I fucking know that! I'm not an idiot!"

"Keep your voice down."

"I must get my mother out of here." Nerves are jumbling out of control. "That's all that matters…"

"Yes, right now it does. But think, what happens when Summer comes to trade her life for yours?"

"She won't."

"Sure about that?"

"She's not…she doesn't have those memories. We never kissed. Summer doesn't care enough to endanger herself for the likes of me." God, I hope I'm right and the angels have taken her somewhere far away. "She won't come." Saying the words hurts like a hot poker to the heart.

"She may not remember you but feels the connection you two have. Summer will come, you know our girl better than anyone to know that she's already searching for you."

Shit, she's right. My girl is nothing if not stubborn, selfless.

"So, what do you suggest? Runaway tail between my legs and hope that your evil boyfriend and my 'oh so crazy' twin show mercy and let my mother go? Come on, even you aren't that naive." Sidestepping her to get away from the stench of the dumpster.

"He's not my…never mind. Don't you get it? You're already fulfilling the prophecy by leading Summer here." *She's wrong surely? Summer won't come, not for me…* "I could just snap my fingers and zap you miles away." The angel steps toward me.

"You do that and my mother dies…so will you, believe me." Don't care what powers she has or who she's screwing. I'll kill the scheming cow.

"Really?" Coral smirks. My fists clench wanting to plunge into every part of that traitorous face.

"Really!"

"Well now, I can almost see what our Summer sees in you…finally."

"My Summer, she has no ties with you anymore." The angel flinches. Guess that one hurt. *Point to me.* "If you can zap me away, then you can zap Ruth out of here."

"I can't. There's a strong power here. Even stronger than me."

"Does that power have dreads?"

"Look, you have to trust me…"

"Ha! Funny that!"

"Will you keep your voice down?" she hisses.

"So, let's get this straight. I leave like a bloody coward and hope that *you* will save my mother? Think I'll take my chances, but thanks."

"Then you are stupid. You're going to get her killed."

"I intend to trade places."

"Not your mother...Summer." My heart jumps to my throat as two beady eyes appear over Coral's shoulder. *Lennox. Just brilliant. Well it's too late to leg it now anyway. Sure, I can outrun him, not his powers though or a whole clan of slimy demons.* The guy's so quiet when he moves, it's disturbing.

"Here you are, Coral my love. And you've brought a gift." He grins. Coral gasps and mouths the word 'run'. But it's far too late for that. "How delightful to see you again, son." He smiles a crooked smile.

Clenching my teeth, wanting to knock those little gravestones to the back of his throat and out the other side. Balling both fists, but Coral shakes her head. Annoyingly, she's right. She may be a lying piece of shit, but I need to calm down in order to save Ruth. "Let's take you to see your mummy. After all, that's why you're here." Stepping away from the dumpster, straightening up as I pass Lennox, trying to show that I'm not defeated...not yet. He looks so much smaller now, and I'll take that as a little win.

Forced into the building, ten large men join us, and I'm frog-marched down a corridor as lights flicker overhead. The place smells worse than the rotting dumpster. My stomach tightens, and nostrils burn. We stop at a large hanger type room, which holds lots of little cages. Animal cages? It honks of death. Every instinct is to fight, but there are too many of them, I wouldn't get very far, or save her...

"So, where is she? Where's my mother?" There's an unnatural shake to my voice as I try to keep calm. They can't know I'm scared. If all goes to plan, I die...I'm more scared for Ruth...for Summer...okay, I'm not too fond of dying, not now there are so many reasons to want to live. "So, you're not going to let me see her? Just stick me in a cage? How very cliché of you." Bravado is my weapon of choice; it's all I have to hide the growing anxiety. Where the hell are those angels? Always breathing down my neck when I don't want them...bleeding typical.

"Of course not, brother." My less attractive twin steps out from the far corner. "She's right here, come say hello, have tea with us." He points at the cage furthest away. I barge past Lennox and push through his lackeys. Running to the end of the room, to see Ruth crouched at the back of a cage, hugging both knees to her chest. Looking so much thinner, older than our first meeting. She's badly beaten yet looks up and smiles. Tears stain her features as she crawls to the door. Reaching a hand through, I grab it. It's so cold and frail. She holds on so tightly...I don't ever want to let go. Tears well in the corners of my eyes. Figured she'd be hurt, but nothing could ever prepare someone for seeing such an inhuman act. These 'people' will pay for this.

"Mum..." The word escapes and it feels painful to say it possibly for the first and last time.

"Is it really you Eth...Alex?"

"Yes. I'm gonna get you out of here. Can you walk?"

"You shouldn't have come. That's what they wanted."

"I don't care...as long as you're safe."

"Oh, son, my beautiful son." She weeps.

"Well isn't this cosy." Liam almost spits.

"Shut your mouth you evil boy," Ruth orders. Guess I get my fire from her. "You're not my son...not anymore."

"Oh, but, Mummy...don't you love your little soldier?" he mocks.

"I did love you and I'll always love the idea of you, not this thing...this barbarian that you've become." Ruth breaks down. Inside I feel a sense of warmth, yes warmth, that I'm not seen as a monster anymore. That in this woman's eyes, I'm the son she loves and never stopped loving...that maybe I'm finally worth it.

"Leave her alone." I snarl. Liam shrugs, leaning against the cage. "Never speak to her again." He laughs, shaking his head.

"I'm so sorry, Alex." Ruth cries.

"Never be sorry…ever, okay? I'll be alright, promise."
Yeah, so that's a lie, but it's a kind lie. "They just want me,
they'll let you go now." Looking to Lennox. "Right? You
don't need her now."

"Oh, let the pathetic woman go." Lennox sighs. A Kron
man walks forward with a bunch of keys, unlocking the
padlock on the cage, and pulls it open. Taking a hand, I guide
her out slowly. After a while she's able to straighten up; God
knows how long she's been cramped in that tiny space.

"Alex." Ruth reaches a shaky palm to my cheek and
wipes away a runaway tear. I turn away, so the others can't
see my weakness.

"Alex, I love you…" Before I can reply, she's yanked
away by two burly men and thrown through the doors.

"No! Wait!"

The Kron men block the way.

"Alex! Alex!" Shouting until her voice becomes distant,
and I'm alone. My head screams out in pain upon hitting the
floor hard. There's laughter…then nothing.

* * * *

"Wakey, wakey, Al."

Everything's a blur. My brain feels like it's being
squeezed, and my body's heavy and sore. And now I
remember…*crap!*

"Are you alive, brother?"

Willing my eyes to open, just making out someone in
front of me.

"Come on, Al, don't overplay it."

"You!" Regaining focus.

"Me."

"Where is she? Where's our mother? I swear, if you've
hurt her—"

"You're funny when you're helpless." The look-alike grins and if I weren't tied to a chair, I'd rip his throat out. I need to keep a clear head, suss out the situation.

"Where's your gang?"

"Thought we could spend some quality time together, get to know each other. You know, before you die," Liam shrugs, and I can't tell if he's actually serious.

"What's the point?" I sneer. One of us will die tonight and judging by the lack of angelic back up, all bets are on me. *Where's that Coral chick when you need her? Guess it was all just part of some screwed-up act…*

"Seriously, I'd love to hear all about the life you've had. The life you stole from me." He spins a chair backwards and plonks himself right in my eye line.

"You're kidding?" Wincing as a shooting pain erupts in my head from being pounded on earlier.

"Nope. You want an aspirin?"

"Like I'd take anything from you," I mutter. There's a knife in my boot…could I reach it?

"Don't think you're getting out of here. Those pesky angel friends won't be rushing in to save the day either. We've sent an army of demons after them…should keep them busy for a while. And they'll never get through our barrier spell. You're here to be traded or die. And you'll never reach that knife in your boot."

Damn this guy's good. Bet he keeps a weapon on him too. As far as things in common, that's about all I can guess, apart from our obvious looks of course. I pray that those angels are strong enough, but if they're not…*crap*. I have to keep this prick talking. I must believe they will come, and Summer won't.

"Oh, you still believe that The Light will come for me?" chuckling smugly, which sends another pain around my head. *What did they hit me with, a fucking chair?*

"She'll come for you." His empty eyes narrow on mine.

"No, she won't. Fact is, we never kissed. Summer remembers nothing. She won't sacrifice herself for a guy who's pretty much a stranger. She's not stupid." Raising both brows. *Point to me.*

"Oh, but if that were true...I'd be inclined to kill you right now." He grins. *Am I that ugly when I smile?*

"Do it then."

"What?"

"Do it. Kill me and let's end this. Then I won't have to look at your sallow, pale face any longer." We sit in silence; he looks confused for a moment.

"Ruth," he says.

"What?" My voice is much higher than intended.

"Ruth, she'll be the reason the girl will come. If not for you, for her." Liam smiles knowing he's got me. *Point to you, arsehole.*

"You're wrong. Summer won't risk herself for one life, the angels won't allow it."

"It will happen. See Kit here?" As if on cue, my creepy so-called sister enters from behind. "Kit sees your girl's already coming. And Lennox has gone to make sure that she doesn't get lost. As for the angels, I'm guessing they're already on a one-way trip back to Heaven." *Crap! Crap! Crap! Ten Points to him.* "It's a few hours till midnight. We wouldn't want little Summer to miss her own death now, would we?"

"You're all sick!" Trying to get up, but I'm strapped down tight.

"Alex." Kit crouches before me.

"What? What do you want?" I can't bring myself to look at her.

"I'll ask one more time. Join us. Let us wipe your memory once more? Be with me…be on the winning side." Now I'm looking at her.

"You're fucking nuts! And you lied! You never removed the cloaking spell on this place, did you?"

"I'm trying to help you."

"You're trying to help yourself. You make me sick! Get away from me! I don't ever want you near me again!" My entire body is shaking ready to rip someone apart. Kit scurries out of the room and at last, I think she's got the message.

"Well now, that was a little harsh. Maybe I'll have a go on your sister after I've taken your girl." He leans down and whispers against my ear, "Your heart."

"You stay away from both of them!" Head-butting his chin. He tumbles back, rubbing it, but it didn't have quite the impact needed.

"Oh, so feisty, brother. What do you think it'll feel like? All that goodness, that light pouring into me. Can you even imagine? And I get to taste your girl from the inside…lick her clean out…does she taste like butter and whipped cream?"

"You are going to die a very slow death," I warn through clenched teeth. "Don't ever talk about her again!"

"Maybe I'll let you kiss your love just before her light goes out…or maybe I'll let you kiss me, see if you can still taste her on these wet lips." Running his tongue over both lips.

"Don't fucking touch her! You hear!" Straining against the ties, trying to reach my boot, my knife.

"Looking for this, brother?" Liam holds the knife, my last hope, before dropping it and letting it clatter to the ground. "Pathetic."

Four large thugs enter, and I feel light-headed. "Make him look all pretty for his lady friend, boys." Liam exits, hissing with laughter all the way down the corridor.

"Get on with it then." Gulping, looking to each man in turn. The waiting is unbearable. "When I get free, and I will… you all know what I'm capable of." Yep, bravado is all I've got now. The first punch is a shock, but the rest feel dull against my skin as I block them out and try to keep the image of Summer alive. I could take any pain if she was far away from here…safe. But she's not. Kit's visions never lie. She's getting closer. I feel it.

23: *Summer*

Our eyes meet, and for the first time I see him, like really *see* him. Beaten and bloody, makes me want to hurt whoever, whatever did this to him. Kiss or no kiss, I know trading my life for his is the right decision. This guy loves me, and I want to be worthy of loving. Unable to look away, his gaze scares me more than the thought of dying, because now I believe everything he's said is true. Just got to take a deep breath and jump.

"You came." He looks tired, sad.

"Of course, couldn't let Ruth die...you die..." Trying hard to hold the tears back. He needs me to be strong.

"You should've run. They'll kill us both now." He seems mad with me. No, worse—disappointed.

"I didn't have a choice."

"You did, but you picked me? I'm not worth it." Closing his eyes and wincing.

"What've they done to you?"

"It doesn't matter. I can take any pain...but not the pain of losing you..." His eyes flutter open, watery and defeated.

"I'll be fine," I say, but I'm miles away from fine.

"Wish that were true." My heart hurts seeing him almost broken, verging on giving up.

"I'm sorry, Summer."

"So am I." Kneeling at the front of the cage. We have an audience, Liam and his clan, but I want this last bit of privacy with Alex. It may be the last time we're together.

"I wanted to protect you from all this...but my feelings for you have put you in danger, again. And now—"

"Now, at least I get to see you and say goodbye." The insistent tears give me away.

"What?"

"I'm trading myself for you."

"You're bloody not!" Scrambling to the front of the cage, putting his palm up to the door. Putting my palm to his so we're almost touching. "If you die, I die."

"He's right!" Liam chimes over us. "You're both going to die."

"I thought…" Turning to him, realising that no bargain had been struck and even if it had, he wouldn't stick to it.

"You two are just the cutest." He laughs, they all laugh.

"God…Alex, I thought…I'm sorry. I didn't think this through at all." Now the tears flow freely.

"Don't cry," he whispers. Yearning to melt this doorway between us and kiss him before it's too late. To feel his lips on mine just once, to know how love really feels before we…

"At least we'll go together." Trying to smile to hide my utter terror.

"How very touching." Liam pulls me up by the elbows and away from Alex.

"Get your dirty hands off her!" Alex bangs on the cage door.

"Oh, brother, I've had more than my hands on her." Liam chuckles. Alex's eyes widen.

"Summer, didn't you tell him about our kiss?"

"No!" I try to wriggle from his grasp. "It was disgusting! You're disgusting!"

"I'm gonna knock your fucking head off, you low life piece of shit!" Alex pounds against the cage door.

"Stop, Alex. Save your strength." I beg but feel his anger.

"For what?" Liam cocks his head. "He's going to die anyway. I'm just not sure which will be more fun…him watching you die or you, him? Hmmm?" He pretends to think for a few seconds. "I've decided he can watch whilst your light drains out."

"You sick bastard…you're just like him, just like Lennox," Alex growls.

"Thanks. Yes, our father does have some strong qualities. Take them both and get them ready. We have little time before the moon goes down."

Watching helplessly as two large men drag Alex out of the tiny cage. Struggling to stand between them. He's a mess. They've gone all out on him…because of me.

"I'm okay." He lies, but I'll play along. Seeing him this way brings out a powerful urge to burn the entire building down, just to save him…hold him… Trying to resist the urge of fire burning through every vein, not knowing what I'm capable of. I could kill us both.

"Where's Ruth?" I ask. We're both dragged out into the corridor with the flickering lights.

"They let her go." Alex groans from behind.

"Thank God, one of us got out."

We're back in the room with those meat hooks hanging above our heads. I imagine us both dangling from them, blood dripping down our dead bodies. All hope of a future together has gone. All hope for a future for the world has gone. I'm the one who has condemned everyone because I'm loved and want to be loved, want to be normal. Guess I'm just as selfish as these kidnappers…

"Time to die folks," Liam says with such glee I'd have no guilt burning him alive.

"Good to see you both again." Lennox steps from the shadows. Followed by Kit and that familiar redhead. Kit is chanting some sort of spell.

"What's she doing?" Alex asks.

"She, my dear boy is the trump card in all this. As long as she chants, the barrier keeping your angel friends out, will hold." Lennox raises a smug eyebrow.

"You haven't even got a ritual stone, have you?" Alex goads. "Good luck draining her."

"Oh, my poor, poor, Alex. So brave you are, and yet so incredibly stupid." Lennox sighs.

"What are you talking about?" I dare to ask, struggling against the two large men holding my arms.

"Your beloved here hasn't done his homework." Lennox touches my cheek and I cower away. "You see, little Light, we don't need the stone, not now we have something even better."

"Just tell us." Alex sounds worn out, like it takes every bit of energy just to speak.

"Ta-dah!" Lennox gestures toward the tall redhead, standing in the corner.

"I don't understand." Staring at the girl who appears a bit apprehensive. And it's still bugging me where I know her from.

"Let me enlighten you. Coral here is an angel."

I gasp. *No, that can't be! What the hell is an angel doing helping demons? This makes no sense...*

"So?" Alex coughs. He doesn't look at all surprised.

"So, here's the good part. Coral can stand in as a conduit, transferring The Light's power through her body and into Liam's, making a new gateway to Heaven. My gateway!" Lennox grins so wide that I think the skin may tear under his ears.

"I'm sorry, Summer...I didn't think.," the angel whispers.

"Do I know you?"

"Quiet!" Lennox barks and the redhead shuts up instantly.

"What did you do to her?" I ask.

"Nothing that she didn't want at first." He winks. I'm repulsed.

"And now?" Alex strains his head to look at Coral.

"Now Coral does as I please or they'll be one less angel in the world."

"This is a joke, right?" Alex glances at me with real terror in his eyes. Then it hits me. *I'm actually about to die!* I begin to shake uncontrollably. My limbs are getting heavy and I'm falling. Hands grab on tighter before I crash to the ground. Hyperventilating; it's not just a far-off thought anymore. Death. I'm about to die right here, right now. Alex knows it. I know it. I've been so frightened of dying after that fire that I've been too afraid to live. And now it's too late. I'll never get to experience the love he feels…never get to grow old. Never tell him how much I wanted that kiss…

"Bring her!" Lennox commands. I'm pushed forward. "Wait!" Lennox grins. "Tell you what, little girl, you can kiss your true love as a parting gift."

"What?" I gasp.

"Here." He places me in front of Alex.

"What are you doing?" Alex demands.

"I'm being kind. You want this so badly, taste her, see if she was worth your efforts, your betrayal." Held inches from his face, his ragged breath hits my cheek. He looks at my lips like it burns his heart to do so. "Go on then, boy! Have at it." Lennox laughs.

"No."

"No?" Lennox looks offended.

"You can," I whisper. "If you want to say goodbye…"

"No." Putting his mouth to my ear so the others can't hear. "I won't make the pain worse for you. It's maybe for the best that you never knew us…"

"No. Don't say that." Sobbing, our faces touch.

"I'll always be waiting." He sighs.

"That's enough! Bring her!" Lennox wails. My cheek feels cold when it's ripped away from his.

"Nooooo!" Alex yells, and time slows. I'm pushed toward the angel who keeps her gaze on the floor, unable to even look at me. I'm put into shackles bolted into the ground, chained by the wrists and ankles. "Don't do this!" Alex pleads. We lock eyes and I can see just how deeply he loves me. My heart plummets into my guts. Wanting to free him from this curse, the curse of me.

"I'm so sorry," I mouth. A lone tear rolls over his cheek. His suffering is too much. "Please?" I beg. "Please spare him. He's no use to you now. Please…don't make him watch."

"Oh, but where's the fun in that? He's going to die right after you anyway. I'm going to slit his throat. So, you crazy kids won't be apart for long. See?" Lennox smiles. "I can be a good person." Sweating profusely, knowing it's a sign that I'm about to heat up big time. "Don't even think about it, my dear." He squints his beady black eyes. "If you light up, then so does Ruth and your police lady friend, and let's not forget your student buddies…Liv and Luke, wasn't it?" *Shit! Shit! Shit!* "I want you to remember, as we're draining you, that because you acted on your human instincts trying to save the lives of a few, you will go to your end knowing that you've cost the lives of millions." Lennox laughs.

"No!"

"Yes! I really hope our Alex was worth it!"

"Let's do this." Liam steps forward, taking Coral's hand.

"Get away from her!" Alex splutters.

"Yeah, funny that, brother, but no." Liam sighs. Coral takes my hand so that she's in the middle and we are all linked. She still refuses to make eye contact.

"Do it now!" Lennox screeches. "We don't have long left!"

There's a scream so shrill that it hurts. The scream erupts inside and takes over my entire being until it vibrates out of the tiny pours of my skin. I'm convulsing like a rabid dog. It's happening. Any moment my screams will stop and when the silence comes…I will be gone.

"Keep it coming!" Liam shouts with a blissed-out tone that echoes round my head drowning out every thought. "I feel it! The power…it's amazing!"

It's the weirdest sensation having the light practically ripped out of me. Coral's entire body is shaking as my light pours into her, through her into Liam. I've done it. I've betrayed the world. Alex is calling my name somewhere, maybe miles from here. Can't hold on any longer. So close to death now, I can taste it, bitter and raw. I'm scared of never knowing love, him. And for that selfish reason, maybe I deserve to die.

24: Alex

They're killing her! I've never felt so useless, so weak after my beating. Shouting her name over and over. Never prayed before but I'm about to start. Helpless to act as the pure glowing light leaves Summer's body and connects with Coral's. Not even caring that it'll be my turn next. If she dies, then what's the point?

"Move." Coral's voice whispers inside my head. Suddenly, I'm very awake. Feeling rejuvenated, stronger than ever, and ready to kick some evil butt. Did she do this? Did the angel fix me? Deciding it doesn't matter, all that matters is saving Summer before they take all of her. She folds to her knees. "Move." Coral hisses.

Moving so fast that even I can't quite believe it. Breaking from the capturers by head-butting one guy and giving the other a swift, hard elbow to the throat. They drop away, leaving me open, with a chance to save Summer, and the world.

"Stop him!" Lennox commands.

Glancing at Kit, a part of me still hoping that she'll stop chanting and help. But that's just foolish. Don't know why it hurts so much, but it does, she does.

Flying at Liam, we hit the ground hard, ripping his hand from Coral's, stopping the transformation. Looking back briefly, Coral has caught Summer. Can't tell if she's alive. I lay over Liam, repositioning myself into a kneeling position. Punching his stupid face over and over until he's spitting blood and my knuckles hurt. If she's dead…God help all of them.

"Enough!" Lennox shouts. Standing, leaving my twin whimpering in a ball. Furious, I swivel toward him. He eyes me with contempt, and the little boy inside me cowers, but I won't show it. He won't get the satisfaction of knowing he almost broke me. Summer coughs in Coral's arms. Relief warms me. She's alive, and even if I die, I'll go knowing she'll go on. Summer's light will never fade. "You've made the last mistake you'll ever make, my boy." Lennox scowls.

"I'm not your boy." Hoping my pretence will hide the fact I'm crapping myself. Now it's here, I don't want to die. I'm scared I'll never find her again. Maybe she'll be the gateway I'll pass through, if I'm even allowed upstairs after everything I've done? We never got our kiss...never got to see if she could love me again.

"Goodbye, son." Lennox raises a hand, and I brace for impact. A flash of white-hot electricity blinds me. Summer screams. I fall backward as someone dives, knocking me out of harm's way. It takes a moment to compute what's just happened, as the reality of Kit lies on top of me. Sitting up, rolling her onto my thighs. In the distance there's explosions, like doors being blown off the building. Persia and Elle appear. Lennox has vanished along with my slimy twin. Coral pushes Summer toward Persia and poofs herself away.

"Alex?" Summer's eyes flicker open, her glance strays onto Kit. "Is she?" I look down at Kit, the girl that just saved my life, her entire stomach is a gaping, bleeding hole where the lightning blast struck.

"It should've been me. Oh God, Kit!" Pulling her up, cradling her like she did me when I was a scared kid. "Kit? Kit!"

"It's okay, little brother." Her voice is hoarse, and I strain to hear the words. Leaning closer to hear. "It's going to be okay."

"Yes, we're together now. Me and you against the world." Staring hard, blinking back the tears.

"We are? You and me?"

"Yes." Stroking her cheek.

"Do you remember when we were kids and you burnt a hole in Lennox's tent?"

"I remember. You dared me to do it. Said it was my initiation into the cool gang."

"You already was the coolest kid in the whole camp." Her hand finds mine and squeezes.

"Never as cool as my big sis."

"You got into such trouble. I'm sorry."

"Don't be. It was worth it to see you laughing so much."

"Don't cry." She smiles.

Rubbing an escaped tear away. "I don't cry, remember?"

She chokes on a laugh. "I'm so sorry for all the hateful things I've said. All the things I can never take back. My voice breaks.

"Do you forgive me?" She winces.

"Of course."

"Thank…you…" A subtle smile appears just as her head lops to one side. Her hand falls out of mine.

"Kit? Kit? No. Don't do this to me!" I shake her.

She's gone and a massive part of me goes with her. Hugging the body for the longest time. Everyone is quiet. Unable to fight the grief any longer. Laying my dead sister on the ground, I stand on wobbly feet.

"Summer, are you okay?" I go over to check. She's being held up in Persia's arms.

"I think so." Looking at me like she wants to hold me. I can't, won't be able to control the tears. She can't see me like this. I was always the strong one, right? A shaky hand reaches for my cheek. Fingertips tremble on my skin. Sighing, the touch so comforting and needed, and yet I pull back. This isn't fair. She's the one who needs support. This isn't about me, never was. Needing space so I can return stronger, clearer headed and ready to fight for her.

"I need to go." I turn away.

"Yes, of course. We'll take care of her." Persia reassures me and I'm not sure if she means Summer or my dead sister. Running out of the room and from the building until I can no longer see it. Now the tears come, the anger, the feeling of pure rage. Yelling all grief into the darkness, falling to my knees in defeat. Kit's dead. Everything I touch turns to crap. I've risked everything, everyone for love. If Summer has any sense, she'll get as far away from me as possible. But tomorrow at midnight, I'll still wait for her. I'll always be waiting.

25: Summer

"I'll go after him." Slowly rising to my feet, still feeling weak.

"No." Elle steps in the way.

"Why not?"

"Alex needs space, time to grieve."

"Elle's right." Persia places a hand on my shoulder. "Give it time."

"But he looked so…" *Broken.*

"He wouldn't want you seeing him that way." Persia places a hand across my forehead, checking my temperature.

"Am I okay?" I dare to ask.

"You'll be fine. You just need some rest."

"Am I…Am I still...?"

"Yes, you're still The Light. The procedure was stopped before they could transfer it." Persia nods. I'm a little gutted but try to hide it. No, I never wanted evil to have the power, just wanted for me not to.

"So, has that Liam got some of it…my light?"

"No, thankfully, you don't appear to be any different." Persia looks into my eyes.

"I think, I'm not certain, but that redhead stepped in somehow…I think she helped me."

"How so?" Elle frowns.

"I know it sounds farfetched, this whole thing is, but one minute it felt like all the strength was being pulled out of me and then it felt like it was pouring back in. Do you think it's possible? Do you think that angel helped me?"

"I pray that you're right. If you are, then Coral is not completely lost to us. She can still be saved." Persia raises both brows at Elle.

"Yes, if Coral helped, there is still hope for her."

"What do we do with the body?" I ask. The word 'body' makes me shudder, looking down at Kit's glazed expression and glancing at the horrific wound. "Guess in her own way, she really did love him."

"I'll take care of it," Elle says, unfazed by the sight. Guess she's used to being around death.

"And I'll take Summer back to her room to rest." Persia takes my hand.

"But Alex?"

"He will return to you when he is ready." Squeezing my hand.

"Now close your eyes."

"I don't want to."

"Trust me."

I close them.

"You can look now." I do and we're back in my dorm room. It's about one a.m. and I'm suddenly very sleepy.

"Get some rest. I'll be back in a few hours."

"Where were you guys earlier? You left."

"We followed Alex to save him and his mother. There was a protection spell on your room so nothing could get in. We never thought you'd leave by yourself. I'm sorry. Try to rest now."

"Don't leave."

"I'm never far away. Now sleep."

"Yes, Mum." I yawn. She rolls her eyes and then 'poof' she's gone.

Laying down, head buzzing with all that's happened, but I'll have to process it all later…much later…

Sounds of a waterfall tickle my ears. Arms wrap around me, pulling me into a naked chest. I look down. I'm wearing a little blue bikini. Feeling vulnerable but safe at the same time. My skin hums against his and it feels fantastic.

"I can't do this." Backing up tighter into him, away from the ledge, which hangs over the huge lake.

"But we're here now, all undressed and everything." He laughs against my ear and that does dangerous things to my lady parts.

"You are so naughty."

"We jump, or I'll have to take advantage of you, right here under this waterfall… nobody can see us," he whispers. Oh God! I think I want him to!

"But we can't…you know that." My entire body heats up.

"If you get all hot, the water will cool you down." He strokes a finger along my neck. Oh wow! Turning around, those gorgeous green eyes flicker with excitement…lust. My knees start to tremble… this is so wrong…

"These boxers may just accidently on purpose fall right off." He grins.

"Stop it!" Slapping his chest, he grabs my wrist. Pulling me in forcefully, kissing me, and the kiss is so deep and devouring. I fear that it will unravel me.

"Stop." Breathless, I pull away.

"Okay." He scratches his stubble. "But only if you jump."

"You're a nightmare." Looking back over the ledge. It must be at least forty feet down?

"I won't let anything happen to you. I've done this a million times, it's totally safe."

"I know, but…."

"You told me that you want to live, that you feel like a bird trapped in a cage?"

"I did, I do…but…"

"Then let's open that cage, shall we?" Wriggling his brows, challenging me. He offers his hand and I take it. We walk to the very edge of the rock.

"Together?"

"Together." I nod, shaking from head to toe.

"You got this," he smiles, "after three. One...two.... three."

Awakened to a hand stroking my hair. Panicking, I shoot up.

"It's okay, it's just me."

"Elle? What you doing here? Where's Persia?"

"It's after five in the afternoon. You've slept the whole day away." She smiles.

"There's something really familiar about you sitting by my bedside...."

"I was at your side after the fire. I healed you."

"You did?" I'm sort of shocked. Elle was the one who cared for me?

"What were you just doing?" I ask.

"Healing you."

"Did I need healing?"

"You just needed a pick-me-up...a strength boost. Yesterday zapped all your energy, I was just putting it back."

"So, I'm still The Light then?"

"Yes."

"Oh." I hoped otherwise. It's wrong to wish it away, but I just want to be normal. "Is everyone okay? Ruth? That policewoman? Have you heard from Alex?"

"Everyone has been taken care of. We haven't seen Alex. Give him some time. He's always around somewhere. I will leave you now."

"Is Persia coming?"

"She's running an errand. Get dressed, eat, you look awful."

"What errand?" I ask, and she's vanished. Really hate it when they do that. I mean, I don't get any cool superpowers, just the crap that comes with this gig. Burning stuff when I get angry is not a proper power.

I take a long shower. I eat a little and try to read. But mostly reflect on things. But all thoughts just go right back to Alex. Will he still be waiting for me at midnight? Will I go? Wanting to more than anything but scared of what that brings. To be with him is to remember all of it, the good, the bad and the damn right painful...will I get to carry on with this life? Will I want to? Does being here, playing at being a college girl put my friends in danger? Must I leave them to keep them safe? Are my needs just selfish? We haven't even kissed, but God I've thought about it, a lot! He's insanely hot. And now knowing him a little more, I feel like I could love him...I want to try. Every urge within craves for him. Think I'm falling for the guy. When he looks at me, there's a fire inside that isn't harmful, it warms...he warms me. Does he still want me? My head hurts with questions. I've wasted the day away trying to decide. My stomach is weak with anticipation. Alex has put the ball in my court but I'm not ready to play.

Startled by a heavy thumping at the door. Have those *things* come back to finish the job? Is it him? *Has he lost all patience?* Glancing at the clock. It's eleven forty-five.

"Hello?" Putting my ear to the door.

"Summer, it's Liv. Let me in."

Disappointed, pulling the door open, she storms right in.

"Hey…what's up? You want to sit?" Not taking my eyes off the clock.

"I'll stand, thank you."

"What's wrong?" Placing a hand on her forearm: she pulls away.

"What's wrong?" She huffs. "What did you do to him?"

"Him?" I frown. There's too much going on right now to be playing guessing games.

"Luke. What did you say? He's pretty upset."

I'd forgotten about our awkward moment, what with you know, evil demons trying to drain me and stuff.

"What did he say I said?"

"Don't play dumb. He didn't say anything, didn't have to. I know the guy better than anyone. He's hardly said a word all day."

"And this is my fault because?"

"Because when I mentioned you, he tensed up." She flops down onto the bed. "So?"

"So…I…Well he did come here…we talked." And I still feel like a total cow about it.

"About?"

"This is awkward." Scratching at my neck, knowing it's bright red.

"Go on."

"Well… he's somehow developed feelings for me. I promise I never intentionally led him on." *God, I hate confrontation. What time is it? I can't think straight.*

"And?" Liv's voice barely a whisper.

"And I told Luke that I, we couldn't do that to you. And that I'm falling for someone else." The sound of the clock ticking louder with every second, counting down to a huge life changing decision.

"To me? Don't know what you mean?"

"Come off it. You're in love with Luke. Just admit it." I shrug, distracted.

"Is it that obvious?"

"To everyone else." Sitting beside her.

"Anyway, who's this guy that you've fallen for, eh?" She nudges me in the side, and I move away a little so she can't do it again. "Spill!"

"Okay, but don't freak out, run…or be afraid of me…"

"Summer, you're scaring me." Her eyes widen and I almost back out. But I need a friend, and if she doesn't accept me for who, what I am, then I guess she's not one.

"Okay, here goes…"

I tell her everything, in a shortened version of course, from being The Light of Heaven, demons, and angels, Pip being Kit or vice versa, to almost being drained last night. Then I get to the whole crazy love story part. How Alex was supposed to kill me and how he's probably waiting for me right now. Then we kiss, so I can fully remember our love and my past.

When I'm done, I dare to look up. Liv hasn't spoken in a long time. Confusion is etched on her face. I've overwhelmed her.

"Please… say something…anything."

"So…so, Pip was this witch, Kit all along? The entire time playing us just to get to you?"

"Yes, sorry."

"And now she's…dead?" Her eyes well with tears.

"I'm sorry, Liv." Putting my hand over hers, relieved when she doesn't pull away.

She splutters, "I don't even know why I'm upset."

"Because in spite of everything, you liked her."

"Guess so…and you? Are you human?"

"Yes."

"But you're also this amazing Light that helps people and stuff?"

"Yes."

"How do you even cope? It's too much to process…I'm trying."

"I know, and you're taking it loads better than expected. Thank you."

"You're still just Summer…to me anyway. I mean, all the other stuff will take a while for me to like, understand."

"You don't know how happy I am to hear that." Squeezing her hand. "Can I ask, that night at the cinema, when I supposedly ran into a cyclist…what do you remember?"

"Exactly that. It's all fuzzy."

"Thought so. You guys had your memories altered."

"What?"

"Persia and Elle, you know being angels, they can do that."

"Well that's shitty."

"They only did it to protect you."

"Angels, eh? That explains a lot. I'm gonna wake up any minute, right?" She raises her brows.

"I keep telling myself the same thing."

"So, this Alex guy, do you love him?"

"I could…I think so…there's so much more to him than what you see."

"But he's gorgeous, which helps."

"Yes." I laugh, "he is. But when he looks at me like I'm the most important person in the universe…wow, I could never get bored of that. And he's strong and thoughtful and sort of annoying, kind and deep…."

"Swoon much?" She chuckles. "This guy will be awaiting your decision at midnight?"

"Yeah." I look at the clock, "Crap!" It's eleven fifty-six.

"So, what are you doing still talking to me?" She pushes my arm.

"I don't know if I deserve to be loved."

"You're joking, right? Look at you! You're thoughtful, caring and beautiful inside and out. He'd be crazy to let you go."

"So, we're still friends?"

"Of course, stupid!"

"Luke will wake up one day and really 'see' you."

"And maybe I'll still be around." She grins. "Here!" Tossing my trainers at my feet. "Get a move on, you only have a few minutes, hurry!"

Trying to tie the laces, but I'm shaking so much that Liv has to help. I'm up and heading for the door. *Am I really doing this?*

"Liv... Thank you."

"Bloody go, will you!"

Practically flying down the stairs, exiting the building, running out into the night. Heading for the gates, I spot him in the distance. I hear the tormenting revving of an engine. He looks back, but I don't think he sees me. My pace is slowing but I must get there…stop him. Trying to shout his name, but it just comes out as a weak cough. The bike is moving away. Arriving at the gate, out of breath, he gets further and further away. I follow, running down the road because in my heart of hearts I'm praying that he'll turn around. Deep down knowing that I've blown it. I've lost him all over again.

26: Alex

"So, you told her midnight? It's eleven fifty-five...you think she'll come?" Andie asks on the end of the line.

"God, I hope so."

"Well she'd better get a bloody move on."

"No shit." Checking my watch again, squinting hard against the dull night sky.

"She's cutting it fine."

"I know!"

"Chill, will ya? It's not my fault."

"Sorry, Blue...It's just..."

"I know, it's fine. So, the plan is Summer turns up, you guys kiss and boom! It all comes back?"

"I guess." My gut tightens.

"Will I remember too?"

"Maybe." Chewing hard on the side of my mouth. "Andie, I'm gonna go now. Just wanted to say thanks, you know for being there...if you don't hear from me for a while, then you know she didn't come. Don't worry about me, okay?"

"She will. And, Alex?"

"Yeah?"

"I'm so sorry about your sister."

"Thanks...me too. Later, Blue."

"Later."

I hang up. Thankful that if nothing else at least I still have Andie. It's eleven fifty-eight. My breath deflates like an old balloon. She should be here by now. If Summer comes and I'm praying she does, we'll be together for real. It seems like an unattainable wish. I'll finally get to show, tell her how I feel, and she'll remember me, us, all of it.

If she doesn't come, I'll be lost, on a path of no direction, without purpose. Will I have enough strength to ride off and stay away forever? I'm selfish and just want her, that's all, anything after that is a bonus. Couldn't save my sister but won't let that reality sink in just yet. I want to save Summer, with or without me, she must survive.

It's almost midnight. Guess I'll drive to Ruth's and stay there for a few days and then…no clue. Maybe I'll do something manual, a mechanic or something. I'm pretty good with my hands. Imagining a life alone, hurts like crap.

It's midnight. *Shit*. Should I wait a little longer? What am I thinking? Someone like me would never be good enough for her. Bet Elle's whispered nothing but nasties about me in her ear, and some of it would be true. I've done stuff in the past I'm not proud of, but I've changed. That angel never liked me. Looking back one last time, knowing the choice has been made.

"Oh well, old girl, it's just you and me." Turning Shelly's key in the ignition, putting my foot down, she roars to life. We escape into the night. My chest's tight and empty like my hearts abandoned it.

"Stop!" A tall, figure appears in the road. I squeeze hard on the brakes.

"What the bloody hell?" I skid into a grassy verge at the side of the road.

"Alex, it's me."

"Elle? What the hell you playing at? I'm going, aren't I? Just like you wanted. You don't need to try and take me out." Dismounting, unharmed, standing right up in her personal space. Not caring anymore, if this bitch wants me gone, she may as well just do it.

"I wasn't trying to harm you."

"Yeah right. What do you want? It's been a rough couple of days, so spare me the lecture."

"Stop." Smiling at me, which is strange.

"Yeah." I frown. "You already said that."

"Look." She points behind me.

Turning, I can just make out a small shadow getting closer. *Is it her? Is it Summer?* Holding my breath, until I see those beautiful amber eyes reflecting in the moonlight. Jogging toward us, blonde hair bouncing around her shoulders. She stops when our eyes finally meet. *She came! She's here!* I'm the luckiest guy alive right now. Running to meet her before she changes her mind.

Stopping a few metres away, wanting to close the gap…what if she's just came to say goodbye? I wait for her to catch her breath.

"Alex." She pants.

"You came." Stepping forward, every inch of me screaming out to touch her.

She steps closer too. "Yes. Had to be sure I wanted to remember…and that I'm good enough for you." She looks at the ground.

"You're joking, right? Why on earth would you ever think that?"

"Because of what I am…what I'm capable of…the fact that we can never…"

Taking two strides, placing both palms on her cheeks. "Look at me." She does, and my stomach does that stupid flippy thing. Tears form in her eyes and I gently thumb away any stragglers. "None of that matters. Nothing does if we're together. Do you want that? Do you want to remember?"

"If you do," she whispers.

"I'm here, aren't I?" Smiling, lowering my forehead, placing it against hers.

"I want to remember all of it... all of you."

"Yeah?" Those damn tingles are back whizzing over my skin, making me want her more than ever. Those soft lips are inches from mine, begging to be kissed.

"Summer, I need to tell you something important." Suddenly a little shaky but hold my nerve.

"What?"

"I love you. Always have, always will." There, I said it.

"Show me then. Kiss me," she whispers.

"Thought you'd never ask." Tilting her face upward, my lips cover hers. Electricity pulsates into every single part of me, parts I should mentally hose down. Pushing my tongue deeper inside her mouth to caress hers. She tastes so good, then again, she always did. Melting into my chest, whimpering. I groan. Standing in the road, we kiss for so long, not caring if a car comes our way. When we come up for air, she's crying. I step back. "Shit! I've ruined everything, haven't I?"

"What?"

"You regret it. We shouldn't have...now you hate me? I'm sorry, Summer. I'm such an idiot!" I growl, pacing, hating myself.

"No, Alex! These are happy tears." Grabbing my hand, placing it back against her cheek.

"You're happy?"

"Never been happier. I remember everything. Some of it I'm sure will hit me later." She's trembling. "I'm happy you're here and that I remember us...but there are things I cannot bring myself to think about...bad things." Moving in, holding her against my chest, she lets out a long, painful sob.

"It's okay. You're strong, you can do this."

"I   remember   all   of   it...the fire...Coral...Lennox...us...." Sniffling, drowning my shirt in tears. Waiting for her to acknowledge it all, to let go of the past. She cries in my arms for so long. After exhausting herself, she's still. "Tell me again."

"Tell you what?" I kiss the last tears away from her cheeks.

"Those three words you could never say…"

"Oh." I laugh. "I love you." Wrapping my arms around her, pulling her closer.

"I remember," she whispers against my ear. Grabbing her face, we kiss until we're breathless.

"What now?" Pulling herself out of the embrace.

"Where did Elle go? Oh well." I shrug. "Let's get Shelly."

"Not sure if I can compete with Shelly." She chuckles.

"It's okay, I'll put in a good word for you."

"You love that bike."

"I love you more."

"And then we look to the future?"

"Guess we have to, as much as I want to throw you over my shoulder and lock you up forever…whatever you decide I'm cool with."

Pushing the bike back to campus we talk, laugh, and we stop a lot to make out. The old Summer is gradually resurfacing, bringing back the me that I actually like. Arriving back at Summer's room, eventually. Pinching myself over and over, because suddenly, I've got everything I've ever wanted.

27: *Summer*

We talk and kiss into the early hours, cocooned inside the duvet, and him on top of it by my side. It must be this way, safe, but still it's unbearably frustrating. We kiss like we're making up for lost time, our stolen moments, not ever wanting these giddy feelings to end. We stop occasionally to reminisce on our lost pasts and try to forecast our uncertain future.

I awake to his sleeping, beautiful features. The sun shines through the curtains, leaving a golden glow across his face, he looks almost angelic. *This guy loves me! This beautiful, amazing, strong, selfless creature loves me!* Reminding myself in case the dream shatters taking my heart with it.

"You're staring at me," he mutters, his eyes still closed. I am! Staring so hard because if I look away for even a second, I'm frightened he'll vanish.

"No, I'm not."

"Stop it." He grins and opens his pure green eyes sending my breath into a giddy panic, whenever he looks at me 'that way.'

"Or else?"

"Or else." He growls.

"Yes?"

"Or else I'll kiss you with this not so pleasant morning breath."

"I have that too." Sliding my tongue over my teeth.

"Then it's not a problem." Rolling on top of me, pinning me down with the duvet that still separates us. Covering my entire face in tiny kisses and I don't care how we both taste when he parts my lips and kisses me like it's our first time. Every inch of my body awakens as his lips trace along my collarbone and he nuzzles into my neck.

"That tickles!" I squeal as stubble collides with skin.

"You asked for it." He laughs, his fingers joining in the fun.

"Stop it!" I can't breathe for laughing.

A sudden cough from the doorway, and we freeze. Elle's watching us, looking unamused.

"Great." Alex huffs, getting up off the bed.

"I see you two didn't waste any time," Elle tuts, and I feel my cheeks flush.

"We're not kids." Alex pulls a jumper over his head and I glimpse that little sun tattoo sitting on top of his hipbone as his t-shirt rides up. *Aaahh.* Sighing blissfully, a massive goofy smile appearing on my face.

"But you do have to be careful."

"Like we'd ever forget! And talking of forgetting, you angels ever take our memories again, and you'll be more than sorry." He narrows his eyes. My heart beats double time; this side of him is so hot.

Elle doesn't argue, but looks amused, like she may burst out laughing. Thankfully, she remains quiet.

"Where's Persia?" I ask, trying to break the tension. "Don't tell me, she's on another errand?"

"She is. She'll be here soon with a surprise for you both." Elle smiles.

"I've had enough surprises...can't you just tell us?" I grumble.

"You'll like this one. Trust me."

"Trust has to be earned." Alex grunts.

"So, what happens now? Guess we have to move again, right? We can't stay?"

"No, you can't. Sorry, Summer."

"I don't want to put my friends in any more danger." Sighing, knowing very soon I'll have to say goodbye to them.

"So, where to next?" Alex asks. "And I'm coming…don't try to stop me."

"I gathered as much." Elle nods. "I've been talking to other angels and you may have already guessed that you are not the only Light?"

I nod, the world's a big place and I'm just one tiny doorway. "Yeah, I kinda figured."

"Well, other Lights are in danger too."

"And?" Alex shrugs. "Get to the point."

"Persia and I thought we could find them, help and protect them." Looking to me then to Alex.

"Well?" I ask him.

"If you're in, then so am I." He nods.

"Sounds like a plan," I say.

"You sure?" Alex takes my hand, kissing it.

"If you're coming, then I'm sure." Smiling, and in the corner of my eye, I see Elle shaking her head. Persia appears at Elle's side.

"Where've you been?" Crossing to her, we hug.

A knock at the door, makes me jump. Guess I'm still jittery after the whole demons trying kill us saga.

"Open the door." Persia releases me.

"Okay." Puzzled, I walk to the door and open it.

"Surprise!" A small blue-haired girl shouts right in my face.

"Oh my God!" Grabbing her, holding on so tight; I really thought I'd never see her again. "Andie!" I shriek with excitement as we jump up and down, still hugging each other. I step back to take her in. "I missed you so much." I say, grabbing hold again to check she's real.

"And I missed you, now that I can remember." We giggle. I notice her huge bag.

"What are you doing here?"

"Coming with you of course!"

"Really? Really, she can?" I ask the angels and they both agree.

"I'm told there are more Lights like you, so I'm here to fight the good fight." Pushing her glasses up her nose. *How I've missed that little action…*

"No way!"

"Way!" She laughs, going over to Alex to hug him too.

"Alex said that you two are friends…I'm so pleased he had you…"

"Aww, it was nothing. I'm a sucker for a sob story." She lets go of him and he winks at me, and for a second, I wish we were alone.

"Yep, just couldn't shake her." Alex rubs his knuckles across Andie's head.

"Oh please! You came to me!" She pushes his arm. "So, where to next?" Andie looks to Persia then to Elle and her mouth hangs open, the way they do in kids cartoons.

"Andie, this is Elle," I say. Elle offers her hand. Andie shakes it before rushing back to my side. Her face is bright red.

"Andie?" I whisper, "You okay?"

"Can I have a word in private?" she whispers.

"Won't be long," I say, pulling her into the little bathroom. Slamming the door behind us, she slumps against it. "Well? What's up, are you feeling alright?" I frown. "Have you changed your mind about coming…risking your life n' all? Giving up lessons is a big thing."

"Who is that?" she asks.

"Why are we whispering?"

"The tall blonde…Elle was it?"

"Yeah, Elle's one of my guardians, she took over from Coral. God, there's so much to tell you."

"She's just so…so…" Andie smiles.

"What? Wait. No way! Oh God, Andie! You like Elle? Like, like her?" I gasp.

"Shush, will you!"

"But you don't 'like' anyone…not in that way anyway." I'm doing lots of hand gesturing and shrugging.

"I know!" Pushing her glasses up, "I've never, like ever had a reaction like this to anyone ever…didn't think it was possible. This is brand new…what do I do?"

"Calm down." I laugh. "This is natural, maybe not for you or that you're crushing big time on an angel. I mean, you guys can never…"

"I guess this is good. I mean, I've never been interested in all the physical stuff. Maybe I can just bask in her presence." She sighs.

"This is so sudden, and no offence mate, it's a bit bizarre."

"Please don't tell anyone."

"Promise. Wouldn't even know where to start."

"Not even Alex?"

"I swear. Now come on before they get suspicious. Just try and act like your usual crazy self." Peeling her from the door, opening it pushing her through.

"Everything okay?" Elle looks to me, then Andie.

"Yep, right, Andie?"

"Uh-hu." She nods slowly. *God, can she be any more obvious?*

"So, when do we set off?" I ask. Alex bounds over and takes my hand.

"About an hour. Pack what you need, leave the rest," Persia orders. I look around my little sanctuary, knowing that I can't take everything. I'll just pick a few favourite clothes and books...but which ones? "So soon? Can't we have a little longer? One more day, please?" I pout.

"No."

"Okay, sorry. I didn't mean to make you cross...Is everything alright?"

Persia exhales fully, "I don't know."

"Okay, now you're freaking me out." Alex crosses his arms. "Spill."

"It's nothing. We should just leave and soon."

"Persia, I know you, you have that 'something' face." Unease sweeps over me in a thousand goosebumps.

"Tell them." Elle insists.

"Well, it may be nothing but...okay, do you remember at your last college, when you and Alex got your memories back?"

"Yes." My skin prickles just thinking of our broom cupboard kiss.

"Well at the time I told you that as your memories returned, so would mine?"

"Persia, what is it?"

"Well, not all of mine came back."

"Spit it out, would ya?" Alex starts pacing.

"Well I told you that we'd wiped our own memories of Alex because you begged us to, because you couldn't live in a world without him..."

"And?" I urge.

"And when I try to think back, I can't remember agreeing to that. It makes no sense that I'd wipe my own mind of him. Why would I, when his people were such a threat? It would leave you vulnerable and that would mean I wasn't protecting you. I would never do that…even if you begged."

"So…what are you saying?" Alex demands.

"I'm saying that whoever has the power to block an angel's mind, is much more powerful than we can imagine. Only an archangel or a greater demon could even attempt it."

"I'm confused." Andie frowns.

"She's saying that whoever blocked her mind had a reason and that we are up against something far bigger than we thought. So, we need to keep moving until we can figure it out." Elle says. "We may have to find all the Lights and their guardians, not only to help them but just to fight this thing."

"Persia, are you scared?" I ask.

"More worried."

"Could it be an archangel who took your memory?"

"It's unlikely, but I'll ask around," Elle tells Persia. "That would mean there's a traitor, one of our own…"

"Well Coral, hello?" Alex huffs.

"Coral is nowhere near strong enough," Persia says.

"Why are you only just telling us this now?" he asks.

"I kept thinking it would come back to me, and with everything we've been through lately it was never the right time. I've been compromised, I'm ashamed." Persia's eyes well, and I can't bear it.

"So, we'll keep moving, find the other Lights and figure it out as we go," I tell her.

Persia nods, but I clearly see her torment.

"Just having a piece of my memory blocked…makes me feel disgusted for taking yours so many times."

"Persia, really, it's okay. I understand. You were just trying to keep me safe." Reaching out to hug her, but she turns and leaves.

"Well that was awkward," Andie mutters.

"She'll be okay. Give her time." Elle says. "Right, you have an hour. Do what you need to do." Elle exits. Anxiety grips at my gut. I've never seen Persia so worried.

"Babe, you mind if I take a quick shower?" Alex grins down at me, and I sweep aside my worry at the thought of him naked and wet in the next room. My face flushes instantly. I realise I'm biting my lip. "Naughty girl." Breathing into my ear, laughing as he shuts the bathroom door behind him.

I need to say goodbye to Liv and Luke. I text them both, hoping more than anything that Luke's forgiven me, and he'll show. When I've stuffed in as much as the holdall will carry, Alex comes from the bathroom smelling clean and looking fresh. Staring idly, still in shock that this amazing guy has chosen me. He is my boyfriend…mine.

"Let's do this then." He smiles down, grabs my bag and kisses my forehead.

"I just need a minute alone." They all leave. I'm going to miss it here, this life, and this pretence…*Goodbye room. I'll miss you.*

We congregate in the car park. I'm so relieved to find Liv waiting with a sheepish looking Luke by her side.

"Hey." Going to Liv first for a hug. Looking over her shoulder, trying to gauge Luke's mood. To my relief he smiles. I step out of Liv's hold and hold my arms out for him. He hugs me tightly. Alex clears his throat somewhere behind and Luke lets go.

"So, you're like some heavenly big shot then?" Luke asks, his eyebrows raised.

"You told him?"

"Yeah, hope that's okay?" Liv winces.

"Of course."

"So, this isn't s wind up? Thought she was messing with me." Luke scratches his messy blond bedhead.

"Afraid not." I sigh.

"It's cool, I guess," he continues, "I have friends in very high places."

I hug him again.

"Thanks." I speak into his ear, "Sometimes the thing we're looking for is under our noses all along." Stepping back, I glance at Liv, hoping he takes the massive hint. Alex strides over to Luke and offers his hand, who looks bewildered for a second before shaking it.

"No hard feelings?" Alex asks.

"Nah, after all, who can compete with soulmates?" Luke shrugs, letting go of Alex's hand.

"No one." Alex eyes him firmly.

"Okay then." I pull Alex away before his testosterone level goes into orbit. "Guess this is it?"

Liv looks like she's about to cry. Quickly, I introduce them both to Andie before I start to cry too.

"You'll come back someday to visit, right?" Liv splutters.

"Of course."

"And you have our numbers…"

"Yes!" I hug her once more before joining Alex who's already waiting on his bike.

Persia, Elle and Andie get into Persia's car. Andie still has a look of awe when she looks up at Elle before getting in the back. I still can't quite get my head around that one…it's just so unexpected.

"We'll be right behind you," Alex tells Elle. Straddling Shelly, I place my arms around his waist.

"Well," I say, looking back at Liv and Luke one last time. "This is it…guess I'll see you soon." Unable to control the tears any longer. Goodbyes are too hard.

"Hold on, gorgeous," Alex shouts over the revving engine.

My cheek rests against his back. I don't know what's in store for us or if we can help the other Lights. Lennox and Liam are still out there somewhere ready to catch us off guard. But I have two amazing and selfless angels on my side, and who'd have thought I'd find my best friend again? And then there's this guy who'll love me no matter what. All that matters is that I'm the happiest I've ever been. We're finally allowed to be together, not completely, but this will do…for now. Pushing my cheek harder into his back to hide the biggest, girlish grin that I hope will never fade. Monsters may come for us, but we'll fight them together. We've found each other again and nothing can ever come between us…I won't let it.

Summer

So, I'm a gateway to Heaven and I guess that's okay if I have Alex. We have a murky future ahead of us, but as long as there are these amazing people in my life, I'll go down fighting.

Alex

I'd lost everything until I found her again. We know the fight isn't over and we don't know if we'll all survive. But now I have someone worth fighting for, worth dying for…worth living for.

More by Kristy Brown

<u>Kiera's Quest</u>

Awakenings

Sacrifices

Perceptions

Choices

<u>Summer Solstice</u>

Summer's End

Summer's Lost

Just Sam

Cinderfella

About the Author

Kristy Brown lives in England with her husband and two sons. She trained as an actress and has a degree in Contemporary Arts. After her first child was born, she began writing a short story whilst he took a nap. That was the beginning of the "Kiera's Quest" teen fantasy series, which is published by 'Muse It Up Publishing.' Kristy then went on to write "Summer's End," the first book in the YA Paranormal romance series, which is also published with Muse It Up Publishing. "Just Sam," is a YA/ Teen contemporary romance book set loosely in the world of tennis. Kristy is currently editing her YA modern retelling of Cinderella, "Cinderfella." She is also writing the third book in the "Summer's End" series and has many more stories in mind, yet not enough time in the day!

* * * *

Did you enjoy Summer's Lost?

*If so, please help us spread the word about
Kristy Brown and MuseItUp Publishing.
It's as easy as:*

*•Recommend the book to your family and friends
•Post a review
•Tweet and Facebook about it*

*Thank you
MuseItUp Publishing*

MuseItUp Publishing

Where Muse authors entertain readers!

https://museituppublishing.com

Follow us on Facebook:

http://www.facebook.com/MuseItUp

and on Twitter:

http://twitter.com/MusePublishing

−for exclusive excerpts of upcoming releases

−contests

−free and specials just for you

−author interviews

−and more!

Printed in Great Britain
by Amazon

84151769R00150